WHEN A ROOSTER CROWS AT NIGHT

To Trailside center.

With fond memories and
gratitude to all Korean War Veterans!

Thomas Park
徐 桂 生

WHEN A ROOSTER CROWS AT NIGHT

A Child's Experience of the Korean War

Therese Park
Author of
A Gift of the Emperor

iUniverse, Inc.
New York Lincoln Shanghai

When a Rooster Crows at Night
A Child's Experience of the Korean War

iUniverse, Inc.

For information address:
iUniverse, Inc.
2021 Pine Lake Road, Suite 100
Lincoln, NE 68512
www.iuniverse.com

ISBN: 0-595-30876-7

Printed in the United States of America

The Center for the Study of the Korean War
Graceland University
Independence, Missouri

proudly presents

When a Rooster Crows at Night

By
Therese Park

Mission Statement

To develop insights into the causes and costs
of the Koreans War, and war in general, in order to
understand and promote peace.

Goals:

• To identify, collect, preserve, display and make available archives, books, and artifacts of the Korean War.

• To acknowledge the contribution of Korean War veterans, and the war's significance in American and World history.

• To prompt scholarly and popular inquiry into the Korean War, why it was fought, and what can be learned from it.

To all who fought the Korean War

We fretted over quagmires.
We panicked, shivered, huddled in fear
But you walked us through the stormy night
Until the break of dawn...

CONTENTS

▼

Foreword

It has now been more than half a century since war broke out between North and South Korea. It has been fifty years, as well, since a cease fire ended the combat phase of that war. But the war has never ended. No peace treaty has been signed and many of the causes for the conflict remain unsettled today. Yet this war was a watershed for the people of the world, as well as for those whose lives were shattered by the outbreak of violence on their homeland.

Often, it is far easier for us to remember serious conflict and military action as a series of events separated from our boundaries and the people we are familiar with. It is somehow more to our liking to see war as an international event and in the implications of its causes and outcomes. But history, national or international, is always local history. War, like all events, takes place at a time and in a place that forever changes by what happens. And this is true of Korea and its people.

This is a book about Korea during that war, and about how the fighting altered and endangered the ordinary men and women whose lives and deaths were a major part of that war. This is a book about a young girl and her family, and about the meaning of life at a time when all of life's securities were threatened. The author is able to take us through the awareness of war, the hiding, the anti-communist movement, and eventually to a new life. This is a book about fear and about courage, and, to a large measure, about how diversity affects a family, as well as a neighbor and a nation.

Therese Park is a writer whose heart and soul has been touched by her experiences and wants to share a part of herself with her readers. She writes with the caution of the craftsman and the vivacity of a painter. She creates a three dimensional picture, action-feeling-response, that draws events and scenes on the pages as you read. Her work reflects her pride in her own nation and in its fight for freedom. She is proud as well of her affiliation with the United States and pays tribute to the Americans who fought the war and nurtured her homeland over the years to be what it is today.

The Center for the Study of the Korean War is proud to work with Therese Park on this project. It is the memory of a sensitive woman that, in many ways, is also the memory of a sensitive nation. Both are well worth experiencing.

Paul M. Edwards
Executive Director
Center for the Study of the Korean War
Independence, Missouri, USA

CHAPTER 1

▼

SURPRISE ATTACK

My rooster Sunriser died the day the North Koreans launched a surprise attack on the South in June 1950. He was slaughtered early that morning for crowing in the middle of the night and turned into a pot of soup for breakfast. As I sat before my steaming bowl, I vaguely remembered hearing a frantic cluck and flutter of wings from my bedroom, but I had never imagined that he was in danger. Had I known about it, I'd have run outside and rescued him. Instead, all I could do was pick up his bloody feathers scattered in the well area and shed a few tears.

As if Sunriser had never existed, my brothers and sisters said nothing as they ate, slurping soup, lips smacking, spoons clattering. Only my mother seemed uneasy, watching me stare at my bowl. I could feel her glance penetrating the side of my face, which I ignored. Finally she said, "Your rooster must have gone mad, Jong-ah, blowing his horn in the middle of the night."

I didn't respond.

"There was nothing I could do," she said. "You know what the neighbors might have done if we didn't get rid of him. A mad rooster brings nothing but ill-fortunes."

I secretly wished that Sunriser had never come to us. Had he stayed at Uncle Hong's spacious farm surrounded by thick cornfields, he would be still alive, chasing hens or striding proudly in the yard, boasting his colorful feathers.

It was the previous summer when Sunriser had joined our family. My mother's cousin farmed in a nearby village that had neither a train station nor a post office, and all summer long, he made weekly trips to the local market on his three-wheel motorcycle that had a trailer attached to it. Once in a while, he stopped by to see us on the way to the market, his trailer loaded with baskets of yellow corn, tomatoes, cabbages, and huge watermelons glistening with morning dew. That morning Uncle Hong was a celebrity. As soon as his three-wheeler pulled in, we gathered around him, asking, "What's that noise, Uncle Hong?" Smiling, he parked his motorcycle, walked to the trailer, and lifted a bird the size of a football with colorful, fluffy feathers.

Everyone exclaimed, "A rooster!"

"I thought you kids might want to raise him," he said, untying the straw rope around the rooster's feet.

"We do!"

"This kind is rare," he explained. "The Chinese use them mostly for cockfighting because they're Mongolian and Siberian, the toughest you can find."

The next moment everyone gasped as the rooster liberated himself from Uncle Hong's hands and rose effortlessly toward the roof, cackling.

"Rascal," Uncle Hong muttered, his eyes following the bird, his chin tilted to the sky.

The rooster landed safely on the tile roof, flapped his wings, and crowed, "Cockodecockoooo…"

Uncle Hong grabbed the broom standing in the corner and swung at the roof, but the broom didn't reach the rooster.

He flew off again, his wings wide open, and came down on the brick fence, only a few feet from his assailant. As he flapped his wings, Uncle Hong swung the broom, and the rooster dropped to the ground like a duck shot out of the sky.

Uncle Hong snatched him up, smiling. "Keep him in a box today," he ordered Eldest Brother, handing him the bird. "By tomorrow morning, he'll calm down and behave as if he's lived here all his life." Uncle Hong patted the rooster for the last time with his calloused hand and headed to the three-wheeler. "See you all soon, if it doesn't rain."

"Thank you, Uncle Hong," we chorused.

Shifting his glassy eyes, the rooster was eager to escape again, and I got nervous. "He'll get away," I warned Eldest Brother, but he didn't seem worried. He gently lowered him to the ground, and the rooster began walking toward the fence, his head lifted, inspecting his new home.

I followed him everywhere, the woodpile along the fence, the back of the house, passing the grain storage room and kitchen on the way, and the front again. I offered him food, too. When he paid no attention to a fistful of rice I had sprinkled in front of him, I chopped green lettuce and served him on a chipped ceramic plate. He still showed no interest, so I gave him sesame seed mixed with rice-cake crumbs. He only pecked at the plate briefly and walked away, clucking. Just as I was about to give up, the rooster stopped before the wooden tub collecting rainwater from the gutter above the kitchen, picked up a water bug, and swallowed it, without even blinking.

All that afternoon, I chased flies with a flyswatter.

Mother was happy. "Why don't you take care of the rooster?" she asked me. "You seem to know what to do with him."

Excited, I said, "I'll do my best."

"It's about time you have some responsibilities, Jong-ah. You'll soon be ten," she said.

I slept little that night, occupied with my responsibility and the rooster's well-being. As I lay awake at dawn, looking at the dark ceiling, I wondered what name would be appropriate for him: Feathered Prince? Conqueror? Plumed Warrior? I couldn't think of a good name because I had never owned a rooster before. Then I heard him crowing loudly. Minutes later the rice-papered screen door became lit with grayish sunlight, and a name popped in my head. "You're Sunriser!"

"Why aren't you eating?" Mother asked.

"I'm not hungry."

"Not hungry? Are you upset because..."

"Yes!" I cut her off.

She laughed. "It's just a chicken, Jong-ah."

"He's *not* just a chicken," I blurted out. "He is my..."

"When's the funeral?" Eldest Brother teased. "Can I come?"

I stewed in silence.

Second Brother moaned in delight, "Mmmm," and licked his lips as my two older sisters laughed in unison.

Bolting from the table, I ran to the room I shared with my older sisters.

"Jong-ah," I heard Mother saying, but I didn't turn around. It was more than I could take in one day.

I don't remember how long I had been lying on my mat, an hour or two perhaps, when I heard voices in our courtyard. I listened. "Is it true? Are we at war with North Korea?" a man said.

My father replied, "The radio said that it's a border attack at the 38th parallel. Come in, come in! The twelve o'clock news will be on at any moment."

Another man said, "I hope you're right, Mr. Suh. My sons are in Seoul and I'm worried sick!"

I figured our neighbors came to listen to our Zenith radio again. None of them owned a radio. Whenever they heard rumors, they filed into our courtyard to confirm what they had heard. Five years earlier, they learned of Korea's liberation from Japan through the radio, and some time after that, the division of our peninsula was also announced on the air——with the news that the Russians were occupying the northern half and the Americans the southern half.

Pressing my ear against the thin wall facing the front room, I could hear a faint voice murmuring.

"Raise the volume," someone said, and the announcer's voice came across loudly: "…this morning, the North Korean army launched a surprise attack on the South and is now advancing on Seoul. South Korean soldiers are no match for modern Russian tanks and weapons…." The announcer paused a moment to control his emotion, then continued, speaking faster. "Our soldiers don't have helmets or army boots to wear, and their only weapons are the German rifles abandoned by the Japanese at the end of World War II. Some soldiers are fighting with farm tools—axes, shovels, hoes—and even bamboo poles." He went on to say that many South Korean army officials had been away from their posts during the weekend and that even those on duty could do nothing before ninety thousand communists mowing down everything with Russian tanks and well-equipped infantry.

The room became quiet as someone turned the radio off. Then I heard Father say, "Tea, anyone?" but no one replied. I heard them putting their shoes on and then stepping onto the porch. They didn't even say *Thank you* or *Good-bye* to my parents as they hurried away.

I grew frightened as the radio announcer's words repeated in fragments in my ears again: North Koreans…Russian tanks…38th parallel…the South Korean infantry without helmets or boots…. And then my mother's voice similarly repeated in bits and pieces too: "Your rooster…a mad rooster…brings ill-fortunes."

I had a dream that night. Sunriser was alive! He was flying again, his wings spread wide. He didn't land on the roof this time but flew over it and soared into the blue expanse above, higher and higher. Then, to my amazement, he turned into an airplane, a huge American airplane, the one that had dropped leaflets about Korea's liberation from Japan five years earlier. But this one didn't drop anything. It's wings reflecting sunlight and roaring powerfully, it disappeared into a patch of white cloud.

"Time for school," Mother's voice awakened me, and I sprang up. *Are we really at war?* I wondered. *Why did Sunriser turn into an airplane?*

At eight that morning, our fourth-grade teacher walked into the classroom, as usual, a black folder under her arm and her heels making noises on the hardwood floor. Yet, something was different about her. She looked as though she had been crying.

"Children, I have bad news," she said in a congested voice, dabbing a corner of her eye with her white handkerchief. "Yesterday morning, the North Korean communists invaded the South, and they're advancing to Seoul at this very moment. The Department of Defense announced today that all schools in Pusan must vacate their buildings immediately, because the South Korean military needs space to accommodate their injured personnel. Those of you who take trains home may leave now, but don't come to school tomorrow. We'll notify you when school resumes. The rest of you please stay and help the teachers and parents vacate the building. We don't have much time. Clear the walls immediately and empty your drawers."

We ripped off our artwork—drawings, poems, posters—from the walls, feeling sad. We then cleared out desks and moved desks and chairs out of the room and lined them up in the hallway. The teachers ran in all directions, moving boxes and giving orders at the same time. Some grownups we had never seen before shuttled back and forth in the hallway, carrying furniture or large boxes.

Early the next morning, the work continued. While some of my classmates labeled boxes, swept the floor with bristle brooms, and wiped the windows with newspapers, a few of us sat on the floor, waxing the floorboards with broken candlesticks.

Around nine, a short, round soldier wearing a white armband walked in and planted himself in the middle of the classroom. "Well!" he said, shaking his head in disappointment. "You should have finished it yesterday."

We all looked at him, not knowing what authority he had over us.

"Hey, you over there, why are you sitting on the floor?" he asked, pointing in our direction.

Teacher Kim replied nervously, "They're waxing the floor, sir."

"Waxing the floor? What for? Who told you to *wax* the floor?"

"We always wax the floor, sir." our teacher said.

"Miss, do you know men are dying out there at this moment?" the soldier said, pointing his finger to the window. "They're dying because the military hospitals have no rooms for them. Tell the kids to move this podium to the hallway and get out! That's all you need to do. We have no time!"

"Children, you heard him!" Teacher Kim clapped.

Our group rose and moved toward the podium.

"I said, we have no time!" the soldier yelled, without lifting a finger to help. *How bold he is*, I thought. As if he'd read my mind, he yelled at me. "You! What are you staring at? Didn't you hear what I said? Quick! Move that damn podium and get out of here!" He stamped the floor with his dirty boots, dropping tiny dirt clods around him.

A loud siren erupted outside, and the soldier left the room in a hurry. The drumming footsteps in the corridor intensified my fear and I looked at Teacher Kim. She moved to the window, and everyone followed her, like chicks following a hen.

A long parade of dust-covered army trucks and ambulances was crawling into our playground, sirens wailing, and within minutes, the whole place was filled with men and army vehicles. Soldiers with armbands and men and women in white gowns emerged from the ambulances and began unloading men on stretchers and wheelchairs. Voices shouted, "Doctor, this man needs help!" "Nurse, over here! He needs a transfusion!" "Water! Water..." Whistles blew. Booted feet ran. Bells buzzed.

Some men on stretchers seemed to be crying, covering their faces with their arms; some raised their feeble hands into the air in an effort to signal something to someone; and some lay lifelessly, too weak to even cry or call for help.

It was like watching a movie. *Or is this a dream?* I wasn't sure.

"Children," Teacher Kim awakened me. "This is the face of war. The men you are looking at could be your father or brother or uncle. What happened to them can happen to anyone, even to you. This is what the communists did to us."

The same soldier who had yelled at us earlier walked in again. "Miss," he said in a raspy voice, "we need some kids to give water to the soldiers."

"Follow me, children!"

Behind the building shaded by a spreading gingko tree, a sixth-grade teacher with graying hair was pumping water from the well, beads of sweat forming on his forehead. Around his feet, many wooden buckets brimming with clear water stood in line. Teacher Kim handed each of us a bucket and a gourd dipper. "Follow the soldier. Do as he tells you to!"

The soldier led us to a corner of the playground where a large group of soldiers sat under the old oak—some smoking, some resting their heads on their raised knees, and others staring faraway.

"These men are very thirsty," the soldier informed. He didn't seem rude any more. "Give each of them a dipperful, and if you run out of water, go back to the well and get more."

He assigned me to a row of men sitting on the ground, and I nervously handed water to the first soldier. He emptied the dipper instantly and said, "More, please!" As I poured more water into the dipper, some men in the back yelled to hurry up, but I couldn't move to the next one because Mother had told me again and again that I should never be impolite to older people. I waited patiently until he had three dipperfuls before moving to the next soldier. How much they each drank, and how exhausted they looked! The water ran out after five or six soldiers, and I raced back to the well for another bucketful.

On the way back, I heard some men singing. I couldn't see them, but I heard them over a loud speaker.

> March, Korean boys, blowing bugles!
> Lift your heads and fear no one.
> Glory is your aim, descendants of Tangun.
> Fight courageously, Korean boys!
>
> March, Korean boys, singing our anthem!
> Jump over rivers and climb hills.
> Unity is our aim, sons of warriors.
> Fight courageously, Korean Boys!

CHAPTER 2

▼

VICTORY USA!

All morning the next day, my mother was busy. She sat in front of her Singer sewing machine, making pockets on our underwear, mending holes in socks, and refastening loose buttons on our sweaters and Father's shirts. After lunch, wearing her white apron, she planted herself on the kitchen floor and roasted peanuts and soybeans on the cast iron skillet, steamed sweet rice cakes, and laid seasoned beef strips on bamboo baskets to dry. When finished, she went to the market and brought home boxes of Hershey bars, dried dates and chestnuts, hard candy sprinkled with sesame seeds, and a sturdy backpack for everyone except my youngest brother who was only two.

Later in the day, Father returned from his business in downtown Pusan and stayed with Mother in their bedroom for a long time, talking quietly. I heard their closet door opening and closing. After dinner, Father summoned us to their room. As we filed in, I noticed eight bulging backpacks lying in a corner and said to myself, *We're going somewhere soon.*

As usual, my two teenage brothers and my younger brother Kwon sat near Father, while my two older sisters and I sat opposite with Mother, who had Baby Brother on her lap.

Father tensed up as he began: "We're at war with our own brothers in the North. You must never forget that Korea was one nation until the Americans and Russians divided it five years ago. Now we are facing a national crisis. As soon as the communists entered our capital, they captured more than ten thousand professors, religious leaders, and government officials and took them to the North. Their plan is to make two Koreas into one as quickly as they can."

Suddenly the light went out, and Father said in the dark, "Again? Those communists! This is the second time they turned it off today. Yobo, give me a match!"

The power plant, the only one for the entire country, was in the north and the Communists controlled it. During the day, the light would stay on, but as soon as the sun went down, the light would go out, leaving us in the dark. Father had joked that if the North Koreans controlled the supply of rice, we would have starved to death a long time ago.

Father rose, ignited a match and lighted the hanging oil-lamp. I blinked, trying to see better in the dim light.

Father continued. "I know it's scary, but I want you to know the truth. If the communists take over Pusan, they'll probably kill us because they're eager to accomplish their goal as planned. There will be a time when you have to figure things out for yourselves, without anyone telling you what to do. It takes courage to take care of yourselves in a life-threatening situation such as this."

I inhaled deeply.

Father tried to smile, but his face twisted into a grimace. I couldn't tell whether he felt sorry for us or was sad for what was happening, but I knew something terrible was waiting for us.

"Let's assume we woke up one morning and found out that the communists had taken over our town during the night. What would you do?"

"We'd fight," my eight-year-old brother Kwon answered.

"How will you fight, Kwon?"

"I'll perform *tekwondo*. I'll punch and kick them until they're completely knocked down!"

"No, Kwon!" Father said, shaking his head. "You don't punch anyone with a weapon in his hand. You hide as quickly as you can."

"I thought you wanted us to be brave," Kwon said indignantly. "Didn't you say, 'If you don't have the guts to defend yourself, you're no better than a girl'?"

"I'm not talking about kids fighting," Father said. "I'm talking about war! In war, soldiers fight and civilians hide until war is over."

"But…" Kwon said but Father ignored him. "Do you know where to hide?" he asked the rest of us.

"The Crystal Cave," Eldest Brother suggested. He was a mountain climber and knew the surrounding mountains like a palm-reader knows the lines of a hand. "It's big and deep, but it's too far to walk to, especially at night."

"Hmm." Father mused, nodding.

"There's another cave near Mr. Noh's farm and it's closer," my brother offered. "But there might be some snakes."

"Snakes? Are you sure?" Father asked.

"Yes. I went there last month to collect snake skins."

Second Brother retorted. "Who's worried about snakes when we might die?"

Father said, "Usually snakes are more afraid of humans than we are of them. And not all snakes are poisonous. Anyway, we have no other choice. Make sure you know where to hide when our enemies enter the town. Your mother and I will not have time to look after all of you, even when a bomb drops. I want you to remember that! We'll just take the baby and run to the shelter, hoping for the best."

I felt like an orphan already, but Father showed no sign of sympathy as he picked up the nearest and largest backpack. "Your mother and I prepared a backpack for each of you and this is mine," he said. "Everything you need is here: clothes, blanket, food, and other things." He opened and tilted it. I saw a palm-size Bible with a black cover and knew it was Mother's idea. Although she was raised by Buddhist parents and converted to Catholicism when she married Father, she was more Catholic than Father ever was. Father rarely attended our evening prayers voluntarily, and when Mother made him sit through it, he always fell asleep before it ended.

"There're two strict rules," Father continued. "Never leave your backpack with a stranger and never tell anyone about the money hidden in your underwear pocket! If you break either of those rules, you will be sorry. Is that clear?"

"Yes, Father."

He then handed the backpack to the assigned owner, first checking the name in the front.

I inspected mine. The first thing I noticed was that there were no books or notepaper in the backpack. I couldn't believe it. Life without books and homework seemed too good to be true. Fumbling through clothes, toothbrushes, a rosary, and socks, I pulled out a large brown bag that said "10-day Food Supply."

Why only ten days? I wondered. Looking over my sisters' shoulders, I discovered that they had the same words written on their brown bags. Mother always gave my older brothers and sisters bigger portions of food or treats than she did Kwon or me. "They're older," she would say. "They need to eat more than you younger ones do." But this time it seemed we were treated equally.

"What happens when we finish our food?" I asked.

"You'll have to buy more," Mother said. "That's why we gave you money. You can buy lots of food with the money hidden in your underwear. One thing you must know is that there might not be any store open when the enemy takes over the town."

"Then what?"

"You'll have to go to a church or other charitable organization and ask for food. They'll keep their doors open for starving people, even when the communists are here."

Kwon laughed and said, "I don't mind being a beggar for one day. I think it'd be fun."

Everyone laughed. The idea of standing in line in front of a church, hoping for scrap food, failed to amuse me. I'd rather sit tight in a cave and try to stretch my ten-day supply to twenty or thirty days until stores re-open.

Kwon was now counting money. When finished, he counted again, more carefully this time. "How much money do I need to buy a boat ticket to America?" he asked.

"Probably ten times more than what you have there," Father replied. "Why do you ask, son? Do you want to go to America?"

"Someday."

"What are you going to do in America?"

"I want to be a cowboy, so you can all see me in an American movie!"

Everyone laughed, except me.

I was impressed. I couldn't wait to see my own little brother on a large screen, wearing a cowboy outfit and galloping on horseback over the prairie with a gun in his hand. "I'll write to you in America, Kwon," I told him.

Glancing at his watch, Father turned the radio on for the eight o'clock evening news. The radio announcer was reporting again: "The president of the United States, Harry Truman, declared U.S. support for South Korea today and granted General Douglas MacArthur authority to mobilize the U.S. occupation forces in Japan to South Korea immediately. He also promised the South Koreans a supply of modern artillery equipment and fighter planes. General MacArthur is believed to be flying in to inspect the situation at the 38th parallel today or tomorrow."

We cheered. Immediately, Mother told us to bow our heads. "Dear Lord," she began, "we thank you for the American president Mr. Truman and General *Macada* and every American soldier who will land in our country soon. Thank you for your angels of justice and peace."

A few days later around eleven in the morning our class leader Hwa-yong came to deliver our teacher's message: that our class was selected to greet the

American soldiers landing in Pusan the following afternoon. "Isn't it exciting?" Hwa-yong said. "We're the only fourth graders from our school who get to see them entering the city."

"That's exciting!"

"Teacher Kim wants all of us to meet her in front of the barbershop on Main Street at one. She wants us to wear short-sleeved tops and hats, because it's going to be a very long day in the sun. Don't be late. See you!" She left, waving her hand.

At one the next day in front of the barbershop, Teacher Kim gave each of us a small American flag on a wooden stick. "When everyone shouts, make sure to wave the flag in the air, okay?" she said. "It doesn't matter whether you see the Americans or not. Just do what others do." She then taught us the English slogan "Vic-to-ry USA" and had us repeat it many times. We practiced it as we followed her to a spot on Main facing the train station. The fifth graders were on our right and some unfamiliar kids on the left. Looking around, I saw many grownups standing behind us, too, each with an American flag in his or her hand.

We waited endlessly, with no place to sit down. The heat and noise were unbearable.

Finally Teacher Kim announced, "They're coming, children! Do you hear the music?" We heard a familiar military tune the radio played early every morning, but all I could see was dust churning in midair and the crowds swarming in the distance.

Then I saw them. A line of army trucks, each with an American flag flying on the hood, was approaching. Miss Kim raised her hand holding the American flag in the air and said, "Let's begin, children. Vic-to-ry USA!"

We raised ours too, shouting, "Vic-to-ry USA! Vic-to-ry USA! Victory USA! Victory USA!" Some American soldiers sitting on the back of the trucks waved at us, smiling broadly, and we shouted even louder, "Vic-to-ry USA! Vic-to-ry USA!"

The whole street boiled over in excitement. The red, white, and blue flags danced wildly everywhere, and several airplanes darted north overhead in a deafening roar, each dragging a white foamy tail behind it. Teacher Kim seemed overwhelmed: her nose turned red and her lips quivered. Other teachers cried, too.

We stood there for a long while, even after the last truck disappeared and the music stopped.

The situation worsened at the battlefront. In spite of the Americans landing in Pusan, all we heard was that the communists were defeating the U.N. forces in every town and village south of Seoul——Suwon, Ongi, Sangju. Now Taejon, one of the major cities in the South, seemed endangered.

Refugees poured into town. Men came with boxes, pots, pans, and children, all piled on wooden A-shaped frames harnessed on their backs, and women balanced bundles larger than themselves atop their heads. Dirty children, some of them crying, followed adults, each with a bundle of its own. The square in front of the train station was more crowded than it had ever been, with people camping on the ground or looking for lost family members.

One afternoon, Mother and my sisters set up a drinking stand in front of our house for the refugees, and I joined them. I couldn't help but watch each man or woman approaching the stand and drinking water. They looked pitiful in their dirty clothes, and some acted as though they were ready to hit the dirt at any moment. One middle-aged woman suddenly yelled at me.

"What are you staring at, child?" she squawked, holding the cup in her shaky hand. Her sunken eyes were scary to look at, and I stepped back. "Haven't you seen people before?" she said.

I didn't know what to say, nor did I know how *not* to stare at her.

"If you have nothing to do, go take a nap, girl! We're not entertainers!"

Mother came to my defense. "She didn't mean any harm, ma'am. She's only nine."

"Did you see how that kid looked at me?" the woman raised her voice for all to hear. "Do you know what it's like losing everything—a husband, three kids, and a home—to end up here without a thing? I'll tell you. We're cursed!" Dropping her cup and spilling water all over, she sank to her knees and wailed.

Mother quickly steered me to the house. "Go inside!" she ordered as she pushed the door open for me. "Stay there. I'm coming in, too."

Running to my room, I found myself crying. *What have I done to her?* I thought. Crawling into the closet, the only space that welcomed me with open arms whenever I had been sad or lonely, I felt safe again. I stayed there for a long time, and I eventually fell asleep in my comfort zone.

My father went to the train station twice a day, morning and late afternoon, trying to get information about our relatives in Seoul, especially our grandparents. Grandfather was a diabetic. Mother had said that without a proper diet, his chance of survival on a long journey would be slim.

Father returned home every night in stony silence. Sometimes, he smoked in the courtyard, sitting on his favorite lawn chair, until the moon rose from behind our neighbor's roof. One night, he came home drunk, his breath reeking of rice wine and mumbling something we couldn't understand. As soon as he took his shoes off, he sprawled on the floor, bursting into tears.

Mother was panicky. "What's the matter, Yobo?" she asked. "Why are you crying?"

"Han Bridge," Father slobbered his words. "It's destroyed. I'd feel better if the communists did it, but no….! It was our president."

"I don't understand! Speak clearly."

"I *am* speaking clearly," he said, raising his voice. "Not only a hundred, but more than a thousand refugees died when the bridge exploded. A thousand people!"

"Who told you this?" Mother asked.

"A young priest I met at the train station. He said he saw the whole thing from the riverbank. He said…Rhee ordered the army to blow up the bridge as soon as he and his cabinet members crossed it, and when they did it, the bridge was jam-packed with soldiers, military trucks and jeeps, civilians, livestock, children, all running from the communists."

"It's horrible!" Mother moaned.

"The priest doesn't think the soldiers warned the refugees," Father went on. "Of course they didn't. If they did, why would so many people die like that? The river was so cluttered with floating corpses, timbers, dead animals and baggage that the rescue boats couldn't even get to the survivors. What kind of man would do such a thing to his countrymen?"

"He's our president," Mother reminded.

"I wish I could shoot him."

"Shhh! The children can hear you."

"So?" he exploded. "They should know what their president did to people. He should be tried like a criminal." He began crying again. I had never seen him like this before and was scared. "Is Father alright?" I asked Mother.

She rolled her eyes. "Can't you see he's not *alright*? What more do you want to know? If you care, leave us alone."

I resented Mother for it. She could hush me and shove me away as if I were only a nuisance to her. Once when she had looked pale, I asked, "Are you all right, Mother? You don't look well," and she snapped, "I'm fine. Grownups can take care of themselves, Jong-ah! Children mustn't worry about them."

I sat there for a long time, looking at the dark courtyard and breathing summer heat. Mother helped Father into their room and my brothers and sisters all went to their corners, saying, "Good Night," but I just sat there. Crickets were chirping loudly from under the porch. It now occurred to me that no one could hush those loud insects.

I envied them.

Early next morning I heard Mother waking my two older sisters. "Girls, let's go to church and pray for your Grandparents and other relatives in Seoul!" It wasn't a Sunday so I pretended I was still asleep, but Mother woke me too.

Our parish church, Sacred Heart, was brightly lit with early sunlight filtering through the stained glass windows. An altar boy wearing a red skirt under a white top was lighting the tall candles on the altar table with a long stick. As I knelt next to Mother on the left side of the aisle, I noticed a dozen women kneeling in front of us, praying, but on the other side of the aisle, the men's side, there was no one. How strange it was that women were more religious than men, in spite of the fact that Jesus was a man!

I bent my head, folded my hands in front of me, and prayed: "Dear Lord, keep our grandparents alive and safe wherever they might be. As you know, Grandfather is ill with diabetes. Mother said he might not survive a long journey without a proper diet. Please Lord, keep Uncle Kyong, the professor, Aunt Jung-won, and their five children, safe too. And Big Uncle, Big Aunt, and their seven kids need your protection too…" I prayed for my numerous uncles, their wives, their children, and all the other relatives I could think of, and when I was done praying, I ended with, "In the name of the Father, the Son, and the Holy Spirit, amen!"

I looked at Mother, hoping she was finished praying so we could go home and eat, but she was still praying. Her eyes lifted to the ceiling above the altar where a painted angel was playing a flute, she seemed far away.

I bent my head again and prayed more: "Please God, help Kwon behave better and make him realize that I am older than he. He still doesn't call me *noona*, Big Sister, as he's supposed to, but blows his horn at me all day. He takes my pencils and crayons from my drawers, too, without asking. I can't stand him, Lord…." The Almighty seemed to be listening, so I told him about my older sisters and brothers too. "They are not as bad as Kwon, but they're giving me a hard time, Lord. They still order me around as though I'm their slave. 'Bring me a glass of water,' says one and 'Take this to Father and have him put his seal on it,' says another. They even ask me to scratch their backs! Yuck!"

I didn't exaggerate a word I said. I had been suffering quietly for only God knows how long. I could write a book about my siblings, especially Kwon. Although he was ill tempered, rude to my friends and me, and clumsy by nature,

Mother never punished him for anything because he was a boy. Plus, Kwon had an imaginary dog that hated girls. When he and I had been going to church to prepare our Confirmation a year earlier, Spear would come along. Kwon would chase me, barking, growling, and pulling my hair, leaving his dirty paw-prints all over my dress, pretending that Spear was out of control. I would finally lose my temper and ended up yelling at him to stop, but he'd laugh and act as though he was proud of Spear. Bending over, he'd say, "Calm down, Spear! We don't want to make a girl cry, do we?"

Whenever I complained to Mother about Kwon's disgusting behavior, I was asking for trouble. She could never picture what I had gone through and would lecture me instead.

"Boys are meant to be imaginative and tough to deal with, Jong-ah. That's how God made boys. If Kwon weren't the way he is, he wouldn't be a boy, would he? You're a girl. You must be patient with your younger brother." I had argued with her, saying, she favored boys over girls, but she only laughed.

My prayer ended with another "In the name of the Father, Son, and Holy Spirit, amen!" I felt peace inside. I knew Jesus was listening to my prayers, although he never lifted his head and said, "Don't worry, my beloved. I am your God and I'll protect you from all wickedness."

I lifted my eyes to Mother again. She was still the same way I had seen her earlier, her hands folded and her eyes to the ceiling, except she now had a rosary in her hands. *She could pray like this forever,* I thought. I waited patiently some more, but Mother didn't stop praying.

"I'm hungry!" I whimpered, but she said, "Shhhh," without even looking at me.

I had no choice but to wait. A fly landed on the back of the pew in front of me, making a tiny buzzing noise. I was alert. I used to love catching flies for Sunriser before he was slaughtered, and I watched it closely, wishing I had a fly-swatter. The fly seemed to be praying too, rubbing its front legs together. What could it possibly have anything to pray about? I wondered. Soon he was done praying with his front legs and lifted his rear end. He rubbed and rubbed his back legs for a long while. *It might be complaining about me,* I thought, *just the way I did about my siblings.* Carefully separating my hands, I placed one on each side of the fly. It didn't move, so I swiftly closed my hands on him, making a loud clap.

Mother finally looked at me. "What are you doing?" she demanded.

"I want to go home!" I said, sensing the feeble flutter of the wings in my hands.

CHAPTER 3

▼

REFUGEES UNDER THE SAME ROOF

Taejon fell into enemy hands on July 20, the radio announced. Losing this town located halfway between Seoul and Taegu seemed a heavy blow to the South because our parents kept sighing after hearing the news. We learned also that the North Koreans captured an American general named William Dean, who became the first American general to fall into the communists' trap. I remember hearing about him: he had been a hero to every boy and teacher at school, for General Dean had hunted down fifteen Russian tanks before he lost his chance to escape.

That evening Mother prayed again for every American soldier in our country, especially General Dean. "Dear Lord, don't let the communists hurt the American general who was captured today. And keep him safe even in a communists' prison. Look upon his wife and children in America, too, as they grieve over the tragic news. A bright star disappeared from the sky, and all we see is darkness. What will happen to us if the Reds keep defeating the Americans? And what will happen if the Reds enter Pusan? Be merciful and listen to our plea, just as you listened to the Jews at the Red Sea." She paused for a long moment, not moving. Her head still bent, she asked us, "Do you have anything to add to my prayer?"

As we looked at one another, Kwon unexpectedly said, "Dear Lord, today wasn't a good day for General Dean, but I have something to thank you for. I'm having a good time at home, without going to school. I really don't like going to school that much. Please don't hurry to send us back, please."

Everyone laughed, and our evening prayer ended in a most unusual way.

"What kind of prayer is that?" Mother asked him, a smile spreading across her face: she didn't look angry at all.

"It's true, Mother," Kwon said. "I'm surprised at myself for saying it, but that's how I feel about school."

I despised Kwon's thoughtlessness over the tragic news of General Dean. I secretly wished that Mother would scold him for saying such a stupid prayer, but she wasn't about to. If it had been *me* who had said this, she would have said, "Don't you like going to school? What do you want to be when you grow up, without an education? A maid?" But since it was Kwon who said it, she acted as though it was amusing. *How unfair!*

As more refugees came to Pusan, the city issued a new ordinance, which we heard on the radio. Officials would inspect each home and assign a number of refugees to it, according to the size of the dwelling, the number of household members, and the homeowner's income.

The day we received a notice announcing that our house would be inspected within a couple of days, Mother was furious. She said to Father, "*Yobo,* go to city hall and complain about this nonsense. The city doesn't own our home but we do! We have the right to refuse the inspection. And they can't force us to let strangers live with us! Didn't you hear that all of the prisoners were freed before the communists took over Seoul? We might end up with a murderer in our own home!"

"Do you think they'd listen to me?" Father exploded. "People think we're rich. When things are tough, rich folks become targets. If I say anything about the new ordinance, they'll begin to sniff around us, looking for dirt. It's not worth it."

Early one morning, a tall man wearing a gray uniform rode his bicycle into our courtyard. The inspector was determined not to overlook any space in our traditional-style home, including the storage room and the square opening on the back wall covered with a rusted metal plate. He admired what he saw. "Very spacious and lovely!" he said, as he walked through five bedrooms, the front room, the kitchen, and the loft in the main house. He then crossed the courtyard and entered the men's quarters known as *sarangchai*. He made a quick tour of two bedrooms, a bathroom, and Father's office, and then pronounced, while scribbling in his notebook, "You have enough living space for an army."

Father said awkwardly that we were a family of eleven, including two live-in servants, and that our refugee grandparents and uncles and aunts would soon join us, as soon as they fled the enemy occupied capital.

"Mr. Suh," the inspector said in a righteous tone. "Put yourself in a refugee's shoes for a moment. You have lost everything in the war—your home, all your possessions, and maybe your family, too—and you landed in another town where you don't know a single soul. Wouldn't you be glad if a kindhearted man offered you space in his home? Wouldn't you think there's a God somewhere, Mr. Suh?"

"Of course, but..."

The inspector cut him off. "A wealthy man has a duty to his less fortunate countrymen. This war is for all of us to suffer together, not only the victims. Those who're lucky enough to be alive and own their homes must act benevolently when the rest of the nation is collapsing. Any questions, Mr. Suh?"

"No, sir."

"Please get ready for two families!" He lifted himself onto his bicycle and rode away, ringing his bell again.

All afternoon, Father hammered, dragged furniture from room to room, and painted. He turned the dressing area in the bathhouse into a bedroom with a mirror on a wall, and removed the desks and bookshelves from our study room to convert it back to a bedroom.

The first family, a woman with a baby tied to her back, arrived later that afternoon. She was tiny compared to her bulging cargo covered with a thin blue blanket. Mother told us to welcome her and we did, but she didn't respond. Her dark, suspicious eyes shifting, she seemed uncomfortable.

"You must be exhausted with a baby on your back," Mother said, and she answered mechanically, "Yes, ma'am." "Why don't you rest for now. We can talk tomorrow." Mother told me to show her to her room and I did. I didn't see her all evening, although I heard the baby crying.

The next morning when the woman joined our breakfast table, all her secrets were revealed. The eighteen-month-old infant boy was a strange-looking thing. His head was abnormally large and soft; his dark eyes couldn't focus on anything and wandered wildly everywhere; and his mouth stayed wide open always. He cried strangely, too, more like a sheep than human: *baaa, baaa, baaa.*

"Is it a boy or a girl?" Mother asked.

"It's a boy, ma'am," she answered impassively.

"What's his name?"

"He hasn't a name yet. Just call him *Agi*-Baby."

A baby with no name? I was dying to know why he didn't even get a name, something everyone was entitled to. Mother didn't say anything for a while, her eyes glued to the baby suckling his mother's nipple. At last, she said, "It's hard for you, isn't it? I mean, raising him."

"It's a curse, I tell you," Agi-Omma said without hesitation. "He's my cross! If it weren't for him, I wouldn't be here."

I didn't know what she meant by "If it weren't for him I wouldn't be here," but I knew raising her child had not been easy for her. *What happened to the baby's father?* I wondered, but didn't dare to ask.

The woman had a huge appetite. She stuffed herself with steamed rice, beans cooked in soy sauce, and seaweed soup, occasionally dropping her gaze on the strange-looking baby glued to her breast. She seemed determined to eat for the two of them, so that through her tiny body, her son might have a chance to grow to normal size.

The second family—Mr. and Mrs. Kim and a boy my age named Teya— knocked on our door shortly after lunch. Mr. Kim, a slimly built man wearing dark glasses, didn't utter a word to Mother while his freckle-faced wife did all the talking. "We'll be here only for a couple of weeks, ma'am, I promise you," Mrs. Kim said nervously. "My husband was a schoolteacher before the war broke out, and as soon as he lands a job, teaching or something else, we'll move out. You shouldn't worry about us at all, ma'am, because he's a hard worker. All his life, he has never had difficulty finding work."

The three of them settled in the guestroom, our old study room.

"He's a strange man, Yobo," Mother reported to Father that evening. "He's hiding something."

"What did he look like?"

"I can't tell you because I don't remember anything other than his sunglasses. I wouldn't even recognize him if I saw him alone on the street without his dark glasses."

"I doubt that he's a schoolteacher," Father commented. "Most schoolteachers are big talkers. They're never shy."

Early the next morning, I heard him ordering his wife to bring water, and I saw his wife running to the well with a bucket in her hands and returning to their room. Later, she came out with a chamber pot, emptied it into the drain hole under the fence, and rinsed it.

I was curious about this *schoolteacher* who stayed in our old study room all day as if growing roots under him.

Teya was a strange boy, too. He followed his mother everywhere, even to the outhouse, as if he couldn't survive one moment without her. Kwon and I showed him plenty of hospitality, asking him to play with us and showing him our colorful American marbles, comic books, and cricket collection, but he looked neither at the toys nor us, only hung onto his mother like a tail to a dog. After trying a couple of times to draw him out, we gave up on him.

"Who needs a baby to play with?" Kwon said angrily, and I replied, "Really!"

"He'll probably live with his mother all his life," he added.

Our house had turned into a strange place, indeed.

Two days later at dusk, Father's cousin Uncle Yong unexpectedly showed up in our courtyard, wearing a jet-black wig, a fake mustache, and tinted spectacles. My sisters and I were sitting on the porch, trying to learn a new song we had heard on the radio titled "Tears of Port Mokpo" when he walked in.

"Hello girls, remember me?" he said in a low voice. "It's Uncle Yong!"

We stared at him, not believing that he was indeed Uncle Yong who had vanished before the communists invaded the South. I had never seen him with a wig and mustache before: His hair had been the color of a chestnut, not jet-black. He had taught English in some high school in Pusan before he disappeared. But this man looked like a bum looking for scraps at the market.

"You look so different, Uncle Yong. People were looking for you," I said, and my sister pinched me.

Uncle Yong's expression turned grim. "Well, is your father home?"

I hesitated to say yes, because Father didn't like him. After the CIC (Korean CIA) agents ransacked our house for the second time last June, walking everywhere with their shoes on, checking the closets, the storage room, and even the hole in the back wall covered with a metal plate, Father had said that Uncle Yong might be a communist spy. "Smoke doesn't rise from a cold furnace," was how Father put it.

"Jong-ah, let your father know I'm here, will you?" Uncle Yong pressed me. "I have something important to discuss with him." I had no choice but tell Father about him.

Father was reading the newspaper in the front room, as he always did before dinner, his reading glasses hanging by the tip of his nose, his legs crossed.

"Uncle Yong wants to see you," I said.

"Uncle Yong?" He grimaced.

"Yes. He looks different."

"How?"

"He wears a wig and mustache now. He looks like…" I stopped because I couldn't call his cousin a bum.

His eyebrows wriggling like two caterpillars, Father put aside the newspaper, rose, and stepped down to the porch, grumbling something to himself. "Well, look who's here!" he said loudly as he approached Uncle Yong. "You look quite comical, Yong. Are you in show business these days?"

"Good to see you, Elder Brother!" Uncle Yong replied timidly, and Father retorted. "Good to see me? Yong, the CIC have been here twice already! What are you doing here? Are you trying to get us arrested?"

"Not so loud," Uncle Yong whispered, lifting his shoulders like in winter. "Elder Brother, I can tell you everything about where I've been and what I've been doing, but I need to stay here for a while."

"No, not here, Yong! The CIC will show up again, I guarantee! They smell out everything."

His hands wringing in front of him, Uncle Yong begged, "Why don't you believe me, Elder Brother? I have no one to turn to if I leave here."

"That's too bad, cousin. I have to protect my family and myself against the vicious, sniffing hounds." Father moved to the door, but Uncle Yong stopped him by pulling his arm, whispering. Abruptly, Father took Uncle Yong's elbow and led him to the back. A moment later I heard the heavy wooden door to the grain storage room open and close. They didn't come out. I hoped the CIC agents wouldn't decide to show up.

Now seventeen people lived under our roof, including Teya and the strange-looking baby with no name. We had only two outhouses, one for our family and one for the servants. How could two outhouses serve seventeen people? We had already lost our school building to the soldiers, and now we were losing our home as well, at least a part of it.

What would be next? I wondered.

I woke the next morning to find a long line in front of the outhouse, everyone waiting his or her turn. Father and Uncle Yong stood there, too, not talking. The moment Mother saw me, she said, "You kids can use a chamber pot. It's too crowded here."

The idea of using a chamber pot disgusted me. Not only would it stink up the entire room, but also the chore of emptying a full pot would surely fall to me. My sisters wouldn't do it because they never dirtied their hands for anything, and the servants wouldn't do it either, because now they had seventeen mouths to feed three times a day. Then who? To make my life simple, I'd use the outhouse no matter how long I had to wait every morning, every night, and in between.

When Mother saw me still standing there, she clicked her tongue and said, "I wish you'd listen to me once in a while," but I lifted my eyes to our neighbor's rooftop, where the round sun was peeking out. *Another hot day is ahead of us,* I thought.

A few days later in the middle of the night, a strange noise woke me. At first I thought a cat was howling under the porch, but as I listened closely, I knew it wasn't our tabby cat Mimi at all. It sounded more like a woman screaming desperately into the darkness. But who could it be?

Kwon snuck into my room, clumsily stepping over my sister. "Hey, do you hear that?"

"What is it?" I whispered.

"Great!" he retorted. "Our houseguest is screaming her head off, but you don't even care! She could be murdered in our own home!"

The word "murdered" sent a shock of fear up my spine and I sprang up. "Let's find out!"

"Don't make any noise, you hear?" Kwon ordered.

We quietly opened and closed my bedroom door, tiptoed to the enclosed front porch, and then carefully stepped down to the courtyard. In the center of the sky, a full moon shone brightly like Mother's well-polished silver plate, and everything was quiet. Then I heard it again, louder this time. It came from the guestroom, our old study room.

"*Aya, aya!* Please stop," Mrs. Kim pleaded then sobbed. A thumping noise, like a heavy object falling onto the wooden floor, followed, and she cried more frantic. "Stop hitting me; it hurts! *Ayaaaa...!*" More painful sobs.

"Kwon, I'm scared. Let's go!"

"Wait!" he said. Suddenly, Kwon began to call in a strange voice, "Here, Mimi, Mimiii..."

"What are you doing?" I whispered.

"Shhh!" he said and kept calling. "Mimi...I have yum-yum for you. Don't hide, you stupid cat!"

I vaguely understood what he was trying to do, and joined him, noticing my shaky voice: "Mimi, Mimi, where are you?"

The noises stopped. Everything was silent now.

My heart raced so rapidly I thought I'd drop dead any moment.

Kwon yelled some more. "Mimi...Mimi...!" Still no sound. "Mr. Kim, did you see our cat?" he asked boldly.

He didn't respond. Mrs. Kim didn't either.

"She might be in your room, Mr. Kim. If you see her, please kick her out. She has fleas."

We heard nothing other than the crickets. We yelled "Mimiiii" some more until we were certain that whatever caused Mrs. Kim to cry had stopped, and we went back inside. Before we parted, Kwon whispered, "Mr. Kim is a wife-beater!"

"He's a schoolteacher," I said. "A schoolteacher wouldn't do a thing like that to his wife."

"Then who? The boy? He can't even make a cat cry," he said, before he slipped into the darkness.

Lying on my mat, my eyes wide-open, I thought the morning would never come. *What if Kwon is right? What would I do if I was older and my husband beat me? I'd rather jump in a lake than be beaten like a dog.*

When early sunlight touched our rice-papered screen door, I crawled out of my sleeping mat and rushed to the outhouse to beat the crowd. A line had formed there already, and I stood at the end, behind Kwon.

Father turned a tense look on Kwon. "Were you looking for Mimi last night?" he asked.

Kwon replied timidly, "Yes," and then looked back at me.

"She was in our room. Didn't you know?"

"We weren't really looking for Mimi, Father. Tell him, Jong-ah!" Kwon nudged my elbow.

"We were just pretending, Father," I reported. "Mrs. Kim was crying very hard, and we wanted to do something to help her."

"Was she, really?" Father asked, wincing.

"Positive!"

"I thought I heard something, too, but I couldn't make any sense out of it."

Uncle Yong joined in. "Actually, I heard some weird noises, too, Elder Brother. I was about to ask you if you knew about it."

"Well, your guess is as good as mine, Yong."

Mother looked puzzled. "Mrs. Kim never sleeps this late," she said, worried. "Twice she came to the kitchen early in the morning to see if we needed help. Maybe something happened to her last night."

"Like what?" Father said.

"Maybe her husband did something to her, like the children are saying. Maybe she's hurt."

"Don't let your imagination go wild, Yobo," Father cautioned. "We don't know anything yet, for sure. All we know is that the woman cried. It doesn't prove anything."

"We'll find out what happened!" Mother said.

All day long, neither Mrs. Kim nor Teya came out of their room. Around five that evening, Mother sent our servant girl Yong-ja to the Kims' room. "Tell Mrs. Kim we need help in the kitchen. Pay attention to what's going on," Mother instructed.

Yong-ja returned five minutes later and reported that no one opened the door and she heard nothing. "I think they are sleeping."

"It's only five," Mother said. "I'm suspicious now."

The next day we didn't see them either, but in the evening as we sat at the dinner table, Yong-ja cried, "There's Mrs. Kim!"

We all looked at her standing on the porch, pale as a ghost and trembling. Her eyes had purple rings around them. Her left cheek was so swollen her lips appeared crooked. Under her short sleeves, her arms looked colorful with reddish burn marks and purple bruises. Her skirt had lost some pleats and looked longer than I remembered.

Father got up and left the room, coughing to himself.

"Come in, come in!" Mother said, motioning with her hand like a traffic cop at a busy intersection.

Mrs. Kim entered and sat on the cushion next to Mother like an obedient child, without saying a word.

Mother shooed us away. "I'll see you all in the morning."

I was dying to know why Mr. Kim had beaten his wife, but knowing Mother, I went back to my room. By now I was discovering that not going to school wasn't as heavenly as I had thought earlier. I missed my friends, especially Yoja. *She will be shocked when she hears about Mrs. Kim,* I thought. I took out my notebook, opened it, and drew Mrs. Kim crying, making her teardrops as large as Mother's pearls, her hair all matted and her dress ripped. When finished, I wrote on the top of the page, "Queen of Sorrow." *Yoja will get a good idea of what I'm talking about,* I thought, and closed the notebook.

The next morning in front of the outhouse, Mother whispered to Father, "Last night, Mrs. Kim and I had a long talk, Yobo. Ever since their wedding Mr. Kim beat her regularly. Poor woman, tss, tss, tss...She needs to get away from that violent man, the sooner the better."

Father said, "Why can't she run away?"

"She has tried a dozen times," Mother said, "but he always finds her, she said. When her son was born, she gave up, which is understandable. Anyway, we should do something for her. She told me she was a seamstress before she was married, so I told her she can use my sewing machine at any time. I'll find some work for her so that she won't have to be with him all day and all night, every day."

"You're not her mother," Father said. "It's best not to get involved, Yobo. I'd rather kick them out than worry about them. We have too many problems of our own."

Uncle Yong unexpectedly said, "Yes, indeed. We all have problems, don't we?" He looked at Father, then Mother, trying to smile.

Father threw a sarcastic look at him. "Yes, Yong. You've given us plenty of problems. Twice our house was ransacked because of you, and you're now sitting in our storage room. Do you know what it feels like having you here, Yong? It's like waiting for a bomb to explode, and the bomb's sitting in your own home."

Uncle Yong's face reddened. "Do you think I like being in your storage room, smelling rat dung all day and all night?"

"Who asked you to?"

"Not you, for sure!"

"That's enough, you two!" Mother said. "Let's not argue. We must help one another at a time like this. We need one another."

"Do I need a ticking bomb?" Father said.

Uncle Yong hastily walked away toward the storage room, and a moment later I heard the heavy door sliding.

Father snorted, and Mother clicked her tongue. "Why can't you be a bit nicer to him?"

Turning toward the outhouse, Father yelled, "Who's taking so long? We don't have all day!"

That night, two men in civilian clothes came to see Father, each with a flashlight. "Is Yong Lee here, Mr. Suh?" one of them asked when Father opened the door.

"No! I haven't seen him for a long time," Father lied. "I would have let you know, officers, if he had shown up."

"Someone tipped us that he's staying with you."

"Look for him then," Father said, pushing the door wide open. "If you find him here, you're welcome to take him with you. I'm getting tired of this, gentlemen! We're entitled to some peace and quiet in our own home, but you won't leave us alone!"

The CIC agents searched the entire house again, their shoes still on, but they didn't find Uncle Yong. Instead, they found Mr. Kim in his room. The secret agents stayed there a long time.

They left just before midnight, telling Father to make sure to notify them if Uncle Yong showed up.

Early the next morning, as I lay on my sleeping mat, I heard Yong-ja's shrill voice in the courtyard. "The Kims took off!" she said. "Their room is empty."

In my sleepwear, I rushed there, like everyone else did, and saw our old study room in disarray with dirty clothes and socks, ripped linen, and the trash can overflowing with beer bottles, cigarette butts, bloody tissues, and a broken yard-stick.

"What a scum!" Father said, shaking his head. "He ran away like a dog with its tail between its legs."

I was sad for Mrs. Kim. I wished we had had a chance to play with Teya, too.

Uncle Yong didn't show up the next day or the next. Father only said, "I never believed in ghosts, but now I do. Yong is a living ghost."

Agi-Omma lived with us the longest, over two months. Once, she tried to runaway without her baby. At dawn one morning, while I slept, a policeman brought her to us, along with Mother's gold ring and clothes she had stolen. I heard later that, when the police returned her possessions, Mother lied and said that she had given them to her.

Father wasn't excited about the whole thing, Agi-Omma trying to run away, leaving the baby behind, and Mother lying about her stealing. I heard him saying at breakfast, "Stealing is a crime, Yobo. If you cover it up the guilty party will never learn what's right and what's wrong."

Mother was defensive. "I had no heart to accuse the poor woman of stealing my ring and some clothes," she said. "What value does that ring have for me, other than a sentimental one? And the clothes! They're old and I never wear them any more. I'd have given them to her, if I knew she wanted them."

"She might do it again. Watch out," Father said.

Agi-Omma showed no signs of repentance for what she had done. Once in a while, she went out at night, wearing heavy makeup, a blue western dress too large and too long for her tiny frame, and her hair neatly combed and bundled up on the back of her head. One morning, Yong-ja saw me in the well area and whispered, "Agi-Omma has a boyfriend!"

"How do you know?" I asked, and she said, "When she came back last night, her lips were smeared, her makeup gone, and her hair was a mess. Get the picture?"

"I don't get it!"

She giggled. "When you're a bit older, *Child,* I'll tell you something about a man and woman, and what they do when they're alone at night," she said and disappeared into the kitchen.

It must have been reliable news, because later, I saw Mother talking to Agi-Omma in the front room alone. I didn't hear every word they were saying, but Mother's ending statement was loud and clear. "I don't feel comfortable with the idea that you're seeing a man, a total stranger, Agi-Omma. If you're going to see him again, I'd like to meet him."

"No problem," she said. "I'll let you meet him next time."

She didn't keep her word, nor did she restrain herself from going out with him either. According to Yong-ja, she snuck out every night through the side door and didn't return before the curfew.

One evening when Agi-Omma was gone again, the cook told Mother a strange story: that Agi-Omma might be trying to starve her baby to death. Mother didn't believe her. "How can you accuse her of something like that?"

"The baby doesn't cry anymore and keeps sleeping all day," the cook said. "Knowing how crazy she is, anything is possible, ma'am."

Mother went to see the baby. Afterwards, she said, "He looks thinner, but he's breathing normally. I don't think he's dying. Let's wait another day and see if he wakes up tomorrow."

The next morning around nine, we heard a loud cry in the bathhouse. Agi-Omma emerged, bawling. "*Aigo,* my baby! My poor angel! Uhhhh…"

In shock, I ran to the servants' room.

Mother suddenly appeared. "What are you doing here?" she asked. Before I could explain, she ordered, "Go back to your room at once and stay there! There's nothing exciting here!"

I went back to the front room and looked out the window. Agi-Omma was crying, and Mother was talking to her, her hands moving. Agi-Omma kept crying, and then I heard her angry voice rising. "Leave me alone with my baby!"

Mother came back, her expression solid and solemn, so I quickly vanished to my room.

No one had died in our house before, and I had a creepy feeling whenever I looked at Agi-Omma's room attached to the bathhouse. An hour or so later, I saw her slipping out the door in her blue western dress. After ten minutes she returned with a tall porter, who had a wooden *A*-frame harnessed on his back.

Agi-Omma went back to her room and came out with a blue bundle in her arms. I knew it was the baby wrapped in the same blue blanket, which she had covered her bulging cargo with when she had moved into our house a month earlier. She gazed at the bundle for a long moment before she handed it to the porter.

The porter took off his A-frame, loaded the bundle on it, and secured it with a straw rope. After harnessing the wooden-frame to his back, he turned to her. "Shall we go, ma'am?"

To everyone's surprise, she shook her head. The servants exchanged a look with one another, but neither said anything. Agi-Omma dug into her pocket, and producing a bill, she handed it to the porter for his trouble.

Taking the money, he walked out of the courtyard, whistling a mellow tune.

In a few minutes, Agi-Omma walked out the door for the last time, in her blue dress, without telling us goodbye.

CHAPTER 4

▼

SCHOOL ON THE MOUNTAIN

Wearing his glasses, Father studied the map attached to the letter announcing the new location of the school and when classes would begin. "It's near the Buddhist temple," he said. "Do you know how to find it?" he asked Kwon and me and we said yes. The ancient, colossal temple with a pagoda in the front was easily visible from anywhere in the neighborhood, including the playground at Crystal Elementary School.

"The new school is outdoors," he said. "It's nothing like your old school. Don't be disappointed that you don't have desks and chairs or a blackboard. Considering that many people have lost their homes, family, and all their possessions, you're lucky to have a school to go to. You can learn anywhere, indoors or outdoors, standing up or sitting down."

"Yes, Father."

"One other thing," he said. "Hiking is good exercise. People pay money to go hiking, but you're doing it without spending a coin. You're lucky that way, too."

"I'm ready for school," I said.

"Good. Until next Monday, you have five days to review what you've learned before your school closed, and make sure to ask your mother to get you some new clothes and socks."

"We will."

Father dismissed us with a nod, and I went to my room. I missed my friends, especially Yoja, my best friend. It had been only six weeks since the day the soldiers took over our building, but it seemed like centuries. She was the shortest kid in our class and lived in a village near the seashore that had no public school. Her train-conductor father dropped her off at the station every morning, like a package, on his way to the main station downtown, and she walked to my house to get me. After school, she would follow me home like a stray puppy and wait for the five-thirty train, eating everything I ate and doing homework with me. Sometimes I was tired of being with her so much, but unlike Kwon who thought I wasn't worth much, Yoja respected me because she regarded me as her bodyguard. The street gangs were always looking for a tiny thing like Yoja walking alone, who might have a coin or two in her pocket. Once, when I had been sick and missed school, Yoja was attacked and came away with bruises on her face and empty pockets. "It wouldn't have happened if you were with me," she said to me when I returned to school. I hadn't been too sympathetic, because the street gangs never bothered me. They knew I could scream like an ambulance. Once I tagged along with the cook to the market, and while she was bargaining with a fish vendor, I wandered alone. As I idly admired the intoxicating smell of roasted chestnut at one corner, a hand suddenly snatched me and began dragging me away. I screamed as loud as I could. My assailant, a boy Eldest Brother's age, let go of me and vanished like the wind. I had a feast afterwards. Many vendors felt sorry for me and gave me roasted chestnuts, boiled corn, and sticky taffy to take home.

On Monday morning, I ate breakfast in a hurry and dressed. At seven-thirty I heard Yoja singing "Jong-ahhhhhhh" and rushed to the door.

"I missed you, Jong-ah!" Yoja shrieked the moment she saw me, and I said, "The vacation was awfully long without you, Miss Tiny."

She giggled. I always felt taller and older when I was with her. She showed me her new book bag—a red one with leather straps—and I showed her my new black and white canvas shoes. I wished I had a new book bag, too, but Mother said mine was only a year old and that a book bag should last for several years.

The air was crisp and the sky clear blue as Yoja and I headed for school. Many school kids walked along with us, chattering nonstop, each with a book bag in hand. For a while, walking was easy because the dirt road was wide and leveled, but when it changed into a narrow trail, we began to sweat. I helped Yoja whenever she slipped on the loose gravel and fell to her knees, and she did the same for me. By the time we reached the Buddhist temple, we were exhausted.

A wooden post bearing Chinese letters that said "Temporary Crystal Elementary School" stood on the front lawn of the temple. The view was almost surreal. In the early morning haze, our neighborhood looked like a toy village in a cartoon movie. Army trucks wormed through the streets. Houses puffed wisps of smoke through chimneys. The vendors at market were ants setting up their tiny booths. A cluster of clouds hung so low that I thought I could touch it with a long stick. At the seashore beyond, American ships glided through the calm blue water, each with a flag on its mast, blaring horns as if promising victory. We were in a different world now, broader and loftier than the one I had known.

As Father had warned us, there was no schoolhouse or jungle gyms or swing set that I could see. Instead, overgrown weeds brushed against my legs and cow paddies dried in the brilliant sunlight here and there amid rocks of all sizes and shapes. I missed our old school.

More kids showed up, wiping their foreheads and panting like dogs. Two boys next to me had crew cuts and spoke in a Seoul dialect. For some reason, they looked smarter and more mature than the local boys whose heads were shaven in the style of temple monks. One of the two boys saw me staring and snarled, "What are you looking at, girl?"

"Nothing," I said, turning away.

"Do you like me, country girl? Tell me. You were staring at me!"

Country girl? I was furious, yet I felt intimidated. I should have paid no attention to them.

The other boy, the shorter one, said, "She wants you to kiss her, dummy," and sniggered.

My face was on fire. I pretended I didn't hear what he said. The local boys would never use the word "kiss" to us girls. They would tease us, calling "fatso" or "squash flowers", but they knew better than saying such word as "kiss" at school.

"Jong-ah." Yoja suddenly awakened me, nudging my elbow. "Mia's parents died during vacation!"

"What?" I wasn't sure if I heard her right.

"Nam-hee just told me. Mia is an orphan now. Her father died during a guerrilla attack on Chiri Mountain some weeks ago and her mother was killed just last week. Can you believe it?"

I couldn't believe it. "How does Nam-hee know?"

"Why wouldn't she?" said Yoja. "She lives next door to Mia."

Poor Mia. I wasn't too surprised to hear that her father died some weeks earlier, because he was a soldier. Everyday the radio announced how many soldiers were killed and how many wounded and how many captured. But Mia's mother wasn't a soldier.

"How did she die?" I asked.

Yoja swallowed. "She was on her way to church last Sunday morning, Nam-hee said, and her long *chima* got caught in the wheels of an American truck racing by. You know how those Yankees drive."

Mia was the first girl I knew who lost both of her parents. I couldn't even imagine what it would be like not having both of my parents. What's going to happen to her? I asked, and Yoja said that her grandparents took her and her younger sister to Kim-hae, a town some distance north of Pusan.

I was sad that I would never see her again. She had many warts on her hands, which she hated. During class, she used to poke them with her nails until they bled. Still, she could do many things with her wart-covered hands that I couldn't do. She knitted with two bamboo needles and some old yarn. She could scribble some Chinese letters I was unfamiliar with. She even made dolls out of tall grass blades, using a stick to make it stand up. I couldn't believe that she would no longer be with us.

Everyone had something to talk about. I overheard that our music teacher and some others joined the military and were now fighting somewhere south of Tae-jon. Mr. Lee had a rich tenor voice and taught us to sing choir. For some reason, he used to make me sing in front of the kids, which I didn't like. I hoped he wouldn't die.

The principal appeared, wearing large, dark-rimmed glasses that made him look like an owl wearing a man's suit. Positioning himself on a huge flat rock, Mr. Owl began speaking, but we could barely hear him. Worse yet, whenever an American airplane passed overhead, we only saw his lips moving, like an actor in a silence movie.

He went on and on, and then suddenly he began shouting, throwing his arms upward. Everyone shouted, too, lifting their arms like the principal.

"Destroy communism!"

"Demolish Kim Il Sung and his Red soldiers!"

"Down with Stalin and the Soviet Union!"

"Down with Mao Tse-tung and Red China!"

"Victory, United Nations!"

"Long live President Rhee and South Korea!"

"Long live President Truman and every American soldier in our country!"

The shouting abruptly ended, and he stepped down. Teacher Kim gathered us and led us to a spot directly behind the temple.

It was quiet. The cool breeze was delightful in our lungs. We could see the back of the ancient structure and two stone Buddhist gods smiling serenely. While Miss Kim organized her books and papers for the class, we sat on the bare dirt and looked around. Some hens and chicks paraded through our classroom, pecking on our pencils, erasers, and notebooks, as if tasting them. A dozen pigs in a pen showed no interest in anything except eating, their heads buried in feed, but the cows tied to the posts in the corner welcomed us with friendly moos, bells ringing.

Everywhere I looked, there was something entertaining. A colorful funeral procession followed the mountain trail, the chanter's voice shrilling through the fields and valleys. The monks walked along the curvy trail, each with a begging-sack attached to his side. Several women at a silvery brook down below were busy, beating their laundry with wooden sticks and talking at the same time.

An old, stooped monk approached Miss Kim and they chatted for a moment. Teacher Kim turned to us.

"Children, Master Chang would like to have a word with you. He's the headmaster here at the temple. Please welcome him!" She began clapping and we all clapped.

"Good morning, children," he said in unhurried words. "Welcome to the Temple of Heaven and Earth. I'm glad I have this chance to meet you and talk to you about these mountains. When I was your age fifty some years ago, we were afraid to climb here because there was a thick forest and tigers, bears, and wolves roamed everywhere."

How amazing, I thought. *How did we lose the trees and animals?*

"In the beginning of the century the Japanese came and chopped down all of the trees and destroyed the homes of wildlife. Do you know what the Japanese did with the lumber? They made battleships, airplanes, and weapons to destroy people and civilization. It's sad, isn't it?"

"Yes."

"There's something I want you to remember while you're here. This temple is a sacred place. These two statues you're looking at are gods who watch over the mountains. Twice we found them weeping. I'm serious, children. The first time was in the early forties when the specially trained Japanese policemen butchered many Korean activists, and the second time was last June, after the North Koreans invaded South Korea."

I had never heard of Buddhist gods crying. I knew the Virgin Mary appeared to some children in Europe and told them to pray the rosary. I felt uneasy, because I didn't know how to pray to Buddhist gods.

Master Change was still talking. "Do not destroy any living things here on the mountain—trees, flowers, bugs, squirrels, frogs, anything that's alive and breathing. If you do, Lord Buddha will weep again. Do you understand?"

"Yes."

"If we take care of what we have on this earth, the heavens will bless us, and someday, these hills and valleys will be covered with thick foliage again. The god of nature will replenish what was lost if he sees that we deserve it. Keep the place clean, too, children. Do not throw away any paper or candy wrappers. I want you to enjoy the clean and fresh mountain air and peaceful surroundings, while you share this temple, the temple of gods, with us. Well, that's all I have to say today, children. Have a good day and be good to your teacher." Master Chang bowed to us and then to Teacher Kim.

Teacher Kim bowed back, and the old monk headed off toward the boys' class beneath us, the end of his ashen coat catching the gentle wind.

That first day on the mountain, we learned a valuable lesson: not having desks and chairs or blackboards wasn't a serious problem for school kids, but not having a bathroom was. We girls complained to Teacher Kim about it.

"I don't know what to tell you," she said, showing wrinkles on her forehead. "I can ask Master Chang to let you girls use their outhouse, but I doubt he'd let you. Hauling away human waste is very expensive here on the mountains. Why don't you go under big rocks or behind bushes?"

It wasn't easy finding a safe and private spot under the bright sun in an open meadow. A boy or two would suddenly appear and yell, "Look, the girls are peeing over there!" and then a bunch of them would rush toward us like mischievous puppies, yelping and giggling. We used secret codes and messages among ourselves to indicate when and where to go, but the boys always knew exactly where to find us. We had no choice but to train ourselves to delay the urge until we were safely home.

Besides not having bathrooms, we had no textbooks either. The first few days Teacher Kim had us write letters to soldiers on the front, but on the fifth day when the books still had not arrived, she taught us a new song called "To Father with Love."

> Primroses and balsams bloomed, Father,
> Along the fence we planted together,
> Reminding me of the day you left
> Turning back and back again as I waved.

You promised you'd be back with gifts
When the flowers bloom and I'm taller.
I wait by the window, my ears open
Hurry, before the flowers fade away.

On weekends, we visited our old school building, not to study there, but to entertain wounded soldiers, with songs and some gifts we made with our own hands. Every room smelled of alcohol, and soldiers lay side by side on military cots, like sardines in a can. They seemed glad to see us when we filed in and sang for them. Whenever we finished a song, they applauded loudly, and we sang every song we knew. When we left, many of them said, "Thank you, girls. Please come back!" We responded to them by smiling and waving our hands.

One afternoon, our teacher told us that we would entertain American soldiers the following Sunday. We couldn't believe it.

"Music is an international language," she said. "It's a powerful way for us to say thank you to the American soldiers fighting for us. You'll each make a thank-you card tomorrow, and the parents' association will prepare some gifts for them, too, which you're going to deliver to the soldiers on Sunday."

"They can't read what we write," the class leader pointed out.

"That's okay," Teacher Kim answered. "They will know what you mean, because the language of the heart is the same everywhere. They'll be happy to hear any song, but I think it will be nice if we can sing some American songs for them, don't you think?"

"Yes!"

Until late that afternoon, she taught us an American song titled "O Danny Boy" translated into Korean. We felt grand as we sang "O Danny Boy" over and over until we could memorize it.

The night before our grand appearance before the American soldiers, Mother ironed my Korean dress and told me to try it on. I did and stood before the mirror in the front room. Although the fabric was stiff and scratchy against my neck, I loved the red Korean dress with roomy, rainbow-colored sleeves. When I lifted my arms, I resembled a huge tropical bird soaring in the sky. When I stood erect, arms at my sides, I was a young bride in a storybook, waiting for my groom to arrive. And when I stretched my skirt wide open and whirled around the room, I was a folk dancer. Sunday couldn't come fast enough for me.

Mother said, "Make sure not to rip the hem. You're too clumsy sometimes."

On Sunday afternoon around two, we waited in front of the three-story building surrounded by a red brick fence. A long line of schoolchildren our age was there too. Two American sentries, one on each side of the black iron-gate, allowed only one group in at a time, and when our turn came, a Korean man wearing an American army uniform appeared and motioned us to follow him. In the corridor many American soldiers with long legs and big noses passed by us, smiling. We saw no Koreans, except the one leading us. The walls on both sides were white and clean. We entered a large room where many gaunt soldiers sat on benches, smoking cigarettes. We waited for a group of dancers on the stage to finish their number.

Then it was our turn. Facing the soldiers, under Teacher Kim's baton, we sang one song after another. When we sang "O Danny Boy," the soldiers applauded loudest; some even whistled with fingers in their mouths. With Teacher Kim's quick nod and broad smile, we sang "O Danny Boy" again as an encore. More applause followed.

The same Korean soldier came and ushered us to another building connected by a long corridor that had many windows on both sides. In front of a large room, we stopped.

"These men are wounded," the Korean man informed us. "Be careful not to touch any devices in the room as you go in and don't make too much noise."

Our teacher gave each of us a white silk handkerchief embroidered with delicate hibiscus, our national flower, and we filed into the room. Teacher Kim didn't follow. She stood and watched us from a window.

Awkwardly, I moved to a bed next to a wall, where a soldier with a crew cut lay, his face ghostly pale. He didn't seem much older than my Eldest Brother. I bowed to him and he smiled. I handed him the handkerchief and the thank-you note I had written on rice paper with an ink brush that I borrowed from my father's desk.

He babbled something in English. I just stared at him, uncomfortable. The soldier inspected the handkerchief, flipping it twice, before he laid it on his pillow. He then opened my note. He smiled as if he understood what I wrote. Then, he did something strange: He took my note to his lips and kissed it.

I quickly bowed to him and left his side, feeling my cheeks burning. I don't remember how I came out of the room, but I saw Teacher Kim smiling. "Very good," she said, nodding slowly. *What was very good?* I wanted to know, but I didn't ask. Riding the bus home, I kept thinking about that soldier, his pale skin, his smile, and his kiss on my note. I wondered if he had a sister or a niece or a cousin my age in America.

One day on the mountain the sky suddenly darkened and raindrops as large as American marbles began falling on our heads. Teacher Kim dismissed us immediately and we packed our bags in a hurry. Grabbing Yoja's hand, I headed for the narrow trail like everyone else. In the mad dash, I fell, dragging Yoja to the ground with me. Before I could worry about my new shoes, a bright light blinded my eyes and ear-shattering thunder followed. Pulling myself up, I helped Yoja to her feet, and together we ran again. Some men I had never seen before waited for us where the dirt trail ended and the gravel road began. "Hurry, children!" they yelled, waving us on. "The creek is rising fast."

A fierce light flashed and vanished. Thunder followed, louder than ever. I imagined that bombs were exploding on our heads. We ran faster. At the silvery brook, we jumped over together without falling, and we kept running.

Mother, holding a large bamboo umbrella, met us at the door. "Where's Kwon?" she demanded.

I had no breath left to tell her I had no idea where he was. I only blinked.

"You don't know?"

I shook my head.

"Why don't you know?"

I clamped my mouth shut. After falling and getting soaked like a mouse rescued from a drain hole, I didn't want to hear her say, "Where's Kwon?" I hoped to hear, "I'm glad you made it, Jong-ah," but "Where's Kwon"? I was of no importance to her, I thought, only another mouth she had to feed at mealtime. Angry tears burned my eyes.

"On a day like this," she lectured me, "you must pay attention to your little brother. I'm glad you remembered to bring your friend home, but next time, bring your brother, too. You hear?"

Something must have snapped inside me, for I yelled at her: "Do you want me to go back and bring him home? Do you care if I die in the rain?"

"What a silly thing to say." Her tone mellowed a little now. "Let's go inside," she said, pushing Yoja and me toward the enclosed porch.

Yoja apologized. "I'm sorry, Mrs. Suh. The rain came fast and we didn't have time to look for Kwon. But next time…"

"Alright," Mother said, without a smile. Grabbing a towel, she began to dry my hair.

I pushed her hand away.

She paused, then asked, "Do you want some barley tea and rice cakes, girls?"

"Keep them for Kwon," I muttered.

"Jong-ah!"

I took Yoja's hand and dragged her to my room.

"Why can't we have some tea and rice cake, Jong-ah?" Yoja asked but I said nothing. I buried my face in my pillow. I didn't know why I was crying, but I couldn't stop feeling sorry for myself.

Kwon came home within minutes. I heard him tell Mother that the narrow creek, which Yoja and I jumped over earlier, had swelled so much that the third-grade teachers and the neighbors had to carry each child on their backs to the other side of the creek.

The rain didn't stop for days. The wind was so strong that the gingko tree in the corner of the courtyard danced wildly, losing many of its fan-shaped leaves, and the roof tiles rattled like the teeth of giant skeletons. There was nothing wonderful about watching huge raindrops exploding in the courtyard. It was spooky.

The rain finally stopped after five days and school resumed. The mountain was ever so beautiful after a rain. Everything sparkled with renewed vitality: the hills and valleys looked greener, the sky clear blue and bottomless, and boulders whiter and luminous in the bright sunlight. The ground was still wet and soggy, so Miss Kim told us to find two large rocks each, one to sit on and one to put our notebooks on. It took an hour to find the rocks flat enough as desks and chairs.

Miss Kim said we still had no textbooks. "We've been waiting for them to get here, but they're not coming after all," she said. "Everything was lost during an air raid."

"Is that supposed to be bad news?" a girl behind me whispered and giggled, but I didn't laugh. The words "air raid" didn't sound funny at all to me.

Teacher Kim lifted a thick bundle of papers from her bag and said, "You're going to copy *Korean Literature* with your own hands, girls. I borrowed five copies from the other teachers and divided each of them into five sections. When you're done copying one section, exchange it with those who've finished another section of the book. You have three weeks to copy all ten chapters."

"What about our other subjects?" a girl asked, and Teacher Kim said, "We can work on multiplication or division without a textbook. Science isn't so bad either, but we can't learn Korean Literature without the textbook."

Coming home, Yoja and I sat at the desk and began to copy the first chapter. It was painstakingly slow, but I enjoyed watching my own handwriting fill the entire notebook page. I said, "I don't mind being a writer when I grow up."

Yoja snorted. "Writers don't make money."

"How do you know?" I asked.

"Everyone knows it."

"What do *you* want to be when you're older?" I asked.

"Me? A fashion designer! I want to make lots and lots of money making western dresses."

CHAPTER 5

▼

MY BROTHER
LOST AND FOUND

One very hot afternoon when our class was dismissed early because of the record-breaking heat wave, I rushed home to find our house empty and quiet. I didn't expect to see my sisters and brothers at this time of the day, but Mother was not there looking out for me either, asking, "How was school?"

I went to the kitchen, hoping one of the servants would tell me where Mother was. As always, Yong-ja was sitting on the floor, her face buried in a bowl of rice. Since the day she joined us two years earlier, I always found her in the kitchen, eating.

"Where's Mother?" I asked.

"She went looking for your oldest brother," Yong-ja said, barely lifting her round cheeks from her bowl.

"Why?"

"The soldiers took him."

"What soldiers?"

"How do I know? A neighbor came and told your mother that the soldiers rounded up several boys, including your brother, and took them somewhere on a truck. Your mother was crying when she left. Now go! I have work to do," she said, waving her chopsticks in the air.

I asked when she was coming back, but Yong-ja said she had no clue. "She ran out without changing her clothes!"

This seemed serious. Mother was always careful about how she looked. She never left the house without combing her hair neatly and wearing her street clothes.

I went back to the front room and sat, fanning myself with my hand. *Why would the soldiers take Eldest Brother? And where did they take him?*

Mother adored Eldest Brother and called him her "phoenix." He was tall for his age, handsome with large dark eyes, and had long earlobes, which Mother considered the sign of nobility. Twice a year, he brought Mother his report card with its ninety-five or higher score which Mother's non-phoenix children couldn't even dream of matching. Whenever Mother held his report card, her eyes gleamed like black gemstones, and she smiled unabashedly. On his fifteenth birthday the previous year, Mother awarded him with a *Leika* camera that my aunt, a medical doctor, had bought for him in Tokyo while attending a medical conference. He stole most of Mother's heart, leaving only a small portion for his five sisters and brothers to share, not counting Baby Brother.

Among her five non-phoenix children, I was the least noticeable child in our family, a mere sparrow compared to a phoenix. Nothing I did impressed my mother and nothing about me seemed right to her, even the way I walked. "Hold your shoulders back straight," she would say on the way to church. I sometimes resented Eldest Brother for his excellent academic achievement and all the good qualities that made Mother proud of him. "Why can't you do like your Eldest Brother?" she often said to Kwon and me when we brought our report cards to her.

But our phoenix brother was missing now. *What if he never comes back?* I couldn't imagine home without him.

My two sisters returned from school, arguing about something I couldn't understand. I told them about First Brother. "Mother went to find him," I said.

"What are the soldiers going to do with him?" asked First Sister to no one particular.

"Who knows," Second Sister said. "He might be having a good time somewhere. Maybe the soldiers are showing him what's like being a soldier."

"They're going to send him to the front," First Sister said. "Mother would die of broken heart, if that's what happened."

For a while, we said nothing. We were worried.

Second Sister said, "I wonder what's going to happen to his camera, if he doesn't come back."

"Is that all you can think about, his camera?" First Sister attacked her.

Second Sister said, "What's wrong to think about it? I bet you are thinking about it, too."

"I'm not as materialistic as you are, Little Sister."

"Oh yeah? You probably want the camera more than I do," Second Sister accused.

"I don't'"

"Yes, you do!"

"I said I don't."

"You do. I can see it in your eyes!"

They could argue like this until I was sick of them. I learned with time that I should never try to break up their arguments for the reason that they'd both end up blaming me for taking sides with the other.

"You want some rice-cakes?" I asked, rising.

They said yes, so I opened the tall oak cabinet in the hallway and served them each a powdered rice-cake on a plate and saved one for myself. We quietly munched, not talking to one another, but in truth, I wondered about the camera too. Once, when Eldest Brother hadn't returned from school one afternoon, I snuck into his room, found the camera on his desk, and opened the cover, my hands trembling. Removing the cover, I put the camera against my face, just the way I had seen Eldest Brother do, and looked through the lens. Everything looked small and mysterious. I wouldn't mind owning a camera like that.

Our parents returned together long after dark without Eldest Brother and not talking to one another. Mother, seeing us sitting before our dinner turning cold, ordered, "Go on, eat!" and we began eating. She didn't touch her food, though the table was loaded with grilled flounder covered with thick brown sauce, steamed vegetables, and toasted seaweed—-the dishes she loved to serve often. Suddenly, she broke into tears, covering her eyes with her hands. It took me a while but I understood why she was crying. Eldest Brother's favorite dish was flounder, the one we were eating now.

Mother didn't cry long. She said to Father, "You should have gone to city hall and talked to the mayor. Instead, you went to the police station. The police have nothing to do with it!"

Father looked hurt. He said in a low painful voice, "I did all I could."

Our parents rarely argued in front of us like this, but now they seemed completely oblivious that we were there.

"Doing all you can isn't enough sometimes. You should have done *more!*"

Father pushed his rice bowl away. "Listen, when you called me and told me what happened, I called the police immediately, although I was busy with a client. The police are civil servants; they should know something about why our son disappeared. Anyway, the line was busy, so I took a bus and went there myself. About a hundred people were screaming in front of the police station, but the guard let only one person into the building at a time, only one person! I waited there all afternoon. At four-thirty, I was still waiting, so I called your sister, the doctor. She knows many important people in government circles. What *more* could I have done? I did all I could."

"'*I did all I could!*'" she mocked Father and snorted. "Didn't you hear that the army sends boys to the front without even training them? What are you going to do if Gong lands in an army camp tonight? '*I did all I could!*' Is that what you'll say then?" She laughed cynically.

Father stared at her for a moment and rose, without saying anything.

Mother began crying again; Father coughed loudly from the front room as if saying, "Crying doesn't take care of anything!"

Before going to my room after dinner, I stepped into the courtyard and stood there for a moment. The air was hot and humid, but the stars, thousands of them, looked down at me cheerfully. They seemed to know something I didn't. I made a wish: *Please let my brother come home.*

Early the next morning, a man's voice woke me. As I listened, I recognized the voice: my aunt's new butler, a tall man with tattoos on his upper arms. "Auntie! Auntie!" he was calling.

I heard a screen door slide. "Yes, Butler!" Mother said.

"Auntie, the doctor wants you to show up at the mayor's office at nine-thirty. Lots of people will be there, she said, and she wants to see you there, too."

"What for?"

"The parents of the missing boys are protesting to the mayor and he invited some military officials to answer questions. She said you should be there no matter how busy you are!"

Within ten minutes, Father and Mother left home with my aunt's butler.

That evening Eldest Brother returned. An army truck had dropped him off in front of our home, he said. Other than some red bumps on his arms, he seemed fine: he didn't limp or wasn't bandaged all over. He even joked that the South Korean army served him and other boys a five-course meal. "See?" he said, touching his belly. "I gained some weight."

Father said, "Tell us where you spent the night."

"We were in a concrete building with a room full of boys. It was dirty but roomy. The soldiers gave us some cooked barley and bean-sprout soup for dinner, and then lectured us until our ears hurt."

"Where did you sleep?" Mother asked. "Did they give you a clean sleeping mat and a comforter?"

He laughed. "It wasn't a hotel, Mother. We slept on bare concrete, each with an army blanket. It was okay: I mean, it wasn't life threatening, except lice were crawling all over us. They had a feast, I'm sure." He rolled up his school-uniform sleeve, and we saw red bumps, the size of mung-beans, all over his arm.

"Tss, tss, tss...we'll have lice again," Mother said. "Anyway, I'm glad you're home."

"Thank you."

We talked until well past midnight.

My parents decided to hide Eldest Brother. After considering many options, they picked the crawl space under the front room. Father carefully took the nails out of two floorboards, squeezed down into the dark space with a flashlight, and removed spider webs, rotten boards, and bricks and concrete blocks that were probably left there since the day the house was built. As soon as he came up, Mother went down with rags and a freshly made straw mat. She wiped the concrete floor, which Father had cleared earlier, and laid the straw mat on it. She then took my brother's sleeping mat and comforter and spread them on the straw mat, smoothing every corner.

Watching her, I knew Mother wished she could hide her firstborn somewhere else, maybe some place with a view of the mountains or the ocean. It was torture for her even to imagine that her "phoenix" would soon be sleeping under the floor like a dog, where mice would nibble his toes or earlobes.

After dinner, Eldest Brother went down to his hiding place, taking several candlesticks, his book bag, and his Leika camera with him.

I saw Mother's eyes redden, but Father only cleared his throat and ordered us never to open the front door without making sure the floorboards were in place. "Soldiers will come looking for him without advance notice," he said. "We don't want to see anyone, not even our relatives, until it's absolutely safe for your brother, you hear?"

It was difficult to get used to the idea that my oldest brother was under my feet. When I least expected it, Eldest Brother's voice sounded from beneath me, making me jump. "Who's thumping up there? Don't you know I'm down here?"

When I'd say, "Sorry!" he would growl at me, saying that I walked like an elephant or hippopotamus and that I should be in my room doing homework. Most of the time I just ran away without saying anything, but sometimes I had an urge to thump my feet as hard as I could to show him that he had no authority over me any more. But I could never actually do it. I couldn't say what I wanted to say to him when he had been above the floorboards, and it was the same now.

Once in a while, in the middle of the night, I'd hear him crawl out of his hiding place and exercise in the courtyard with his barbells. When finished, he'd tiptoe to the kitchen and search for food, opening and closing cabinet doors and knocking down a dish or a bowl onto the floor. He then slipped back to his hiding place, and the faint light peeping through the floorboards would go out. Sometimes, he stayed awake long after we went to bed, probably reading. I knew it, because when I went to get a drink of water late at night, I could see light still shining between the floorboards.

A week later, at sundown, he liberated himself from all of his misery, along with everything he had with him, camera and books. "I've had enough," he declared, looking pale. "I'm not going down there again!"

Mother's mouth dropped. "What if they take you again, son? We might never find you next time!"

"This is no life," he said without hesitation, "sitting in a dark cage and smelling dirt and grime all day and all night. I want to live!"

Later that night my parents and Eldest Brother had a secret meeting in my father's office across the courtyard, which lasted hours. The next morning Father left home early, without eating his breakfast. Mother explained to us that Father went to see Mr. Song, the church usher who was a cook at the U.S. Eighth Army base.

"Your Father says Mr. Song knows some officers at the army base who might use your brother as an errand boy. If he can work there, no Koreans will touch him," she said.

Two days later at seven in the morning, Eldest Brother left home for an interview with a U.S. military officer. Mother was anxious all day, turning to the door whenever someone walked in.

I was anxious, too. I hoped he'd get a job in the American military base so he could bring us some American goodies every evening—Juicy Fruit, Nabisco cookies, and chocolate bars. Some American pencils would be good, too, I thought. They wrote smoothly, and unlike Korean pencils, their lead points didn't break easily.

Eldest Brother came home around four o'clock, wearing a khaki uniform, with "USA" stamped on his shirt pocket, and carrying an army duffle bag. We had been sitting in the front room, Mother, Kwon, and I, and we each gasped in amazement.

"You can fool people as an American teenager," Mother said, looking him up and down, front and back.

Eldest Brother chuckled. "Not quite," he said. "My nose isn't tall like theirs."

"Buy a rubber nose, Big Brother," Kwon said, without laughing.

"I might," he said.

Even in my own eyes, he looked smarter, taller and more handsome than ever before, and I kept looking at him.

"Is that uniform from America?" Mother asked, fingering his sleeve the way she'd feel a bolt of expensive silk at the fabric store.

"Yes. It fits well, too!"

"Very nice material," she admired. "Did they treat you well at the army base?"

"Yes, but the security is extremely tight. When I got there at seven, a long line of Korean employees stood in front of the gate, waiting, and I joined them. When it was my turn, the security guard checked all my pockets, front and back, and then had me roll up my sleeves and pant-legs and searched some more. I guess he thought he might find a grenade or a pocketknife in my trousers or in my sleeves. It was the same at the end of the day. They acted as though I stole something, touching me all over."

"Tss, tss, tss…You can't blame them for being careful," Mother said. "How many Koreans working there wouldn't steal from them? Probably only a handful. When they get to know you better, though, they won't be searching you as hard as they did today. What's your job there?"

"I work in the supply room. When a soldier needs a light bulb or a can of engine oil or a flashlight, he comes to see me, and I give it to him, writing down his name, ID number, and the unit he belongs to. It's an easy job for me, and my boss, Sergeant Bob, is a nice guy. He let me try his cigarette." Eldest Brother smiled proudly.

Mother frowned. "You shouldn't smoke!"

"But Mother, I can't be rude to my boss on my first day at my new job!"

"You never smoked. Why ruin your reputation now?"

Eldest Brother paused for a moment. "Mother, isn't there an old saying, 'With good company, Heaven is near you'? Sergeant Bob is a *really* nice guy. I like him a lot."

This time, Mother paused to think. "Do you remember the parable in the Bible where Satan tempted Jesus to sin and Jesus said, *Away with you, Satan*? Maybe that sergeant is a Satan dressed in an American military uniform!"

My brother laughed. "If he is, he's a kind devil, Mother. He makes sure I understand everything about my job, showing me around, introducing me to his co-workers."

"Were you able to understand what he was saying?"

"Yes," he said confidently.

"Say something in English."

"*Break your leg, son-o-bitch!*"

"What does it mean?"

"Have a good day, my friend!"

"That's good. Say something else!"

"'*Shove off, goddamm you!*' I just said, 'Leave me alone.' "

"I'm so proud of you, son," Mother said and smiled.

A fly suddenly came down from nowhere and sat on Mother's arm. She waved it away. Then it landed on Kwon's head.

Eldest Brother opened his bag in a hurry and produced a tall tin can. Pulling off the cap, he aimed it toward Kwon and pressed a yellow button on it. It sang, *psssss*…The fly lifted itself into the air again, then, almost immediately, it landed on the floor like a speck of dirt. I smelled a strange odor, like caustic soda, but stronger. I coughed.

Mother was terrified. "What are you trying to do, son? Is it poison gas?"

"No, it's a hand bomb," Kwon volunteered. "Isn't it, Big Brother?"

"It's insect killer," said Eldest Brother. "Sergeant Bob gave it to me when he saw the mosquito bites on my arms. It kills all kind of flying insects—flies, mosquitoes, moths, gnats, and even bees. We don't need a fly swatter or mosquito nets any more."

Mother let out a sigh. "How amazing," she said.

One afternoon, two weeks later, he returned with a long face. I knew something was wrong, but I didn't ask him because I knew he wouldn't tell me. At dinner I heard him tell our parents that Sergeant Bob's unit was assigned to join the U.N. troops at the Nakdong River area and that they'd be leaving soon.

Mother asked, "You didn't want to go with them, did you? I'm just curious."

"I did. Sergeant Bob asked me to come with him, promising he would help me go to America when the war is over, but…"

"But?" Mother pressed.

"I said no. I knew you'd be upset if I went with them."

"Upset?" Mother said. "You might end up dying at fifteen, and we'd only be *upset?*"

CHAPTER 6

▼

MY UNCLE'S DEATH MARCH

Father's effort to obtain news of our grandparents and uncles and aunts didn't diminish with time, although his focus changed from the train station to the cathedral downtown. He told us that the spacious front lawn of the cathedral was a gathering place for Catholic refugees from all over the captured territory in the South, and that there, on the bulletin board, a tree trunk, or a decorative stone, you'd see the notes people had posted with the names and descriptions of the missing.

One evening we learned that our grandparents were still in Seoul, but at least one of Father's two brothers and two of his three sisters had possibly escaped the capital.

"Where are they, then?" Mother asked. "Why do none of them come to see us?"

"I don't know," said Father, exhaling cigarette smoke through his nose. "Assuming what I heard is true, my hunch is they haven't the guts to face me. How could they, when they left their elderly parents in the ruined city full of Reds? Even dogs have some sense of duty to their parents."

"Or maybe they didn't get here yet," Mother said. "They might be anywhere, Suwon, Taejon, Sangju, who knows. Even Taegu fell into enemy hands last week."

Father only stared at the bluish threads of smoke rising toward the ceiling.

I hoped Grandparents were still alive in Seoul. In a documentary movie, which the whole school had watched in a theater near the train station, the communists were merciless, shooting people, even those handcuffed and blindfolded, and burning houses and buildings. In one scene, a dozen planes marked with red stars came down like vultures and strafed the civilians running for cover, adding more corpses to the street already strewn with bodies, broken concrete walls, and upside-down military vehicles.

Mother religiously gave drinking water to the refugees every day, and occasionally the leftovers from the kitchen as well. Some refugees in tattered clothes knocked on our door early in the morning, asking for food, and Mother made sure that we had some extra for them—a pot of steamed rice or cooked barley.

One morning while we ate, we again heard banging at the door, and Yong-ja rushed toward it with a bowl in her hand. Instead of the usual, "Thank you ma'am," a woman's screeching voice startled us. "Let us in!"

Mother looked out. "What is it?" she asked, and Yong-ja replied, "This woman wants to come in. She acts crazy, pushing and harassing me."

Then we heard it again, the same cry rising above Yong-ja's voice: "Elder Brother, please let us in!"

Our parents sprang up, dropping their spoons and chopsticks on the table, and rushed to the door. "Little Sister, is it you?" Father cried.

My appetite vanished and I followed everyone to the door. I stopped on the porch, because the woman in the courtyard, with a baby strapped to her back and four little children as dirty as field mice around her, couldn't be the slender and pretty woman we used to call Little Aunt. Had I seen her on the street, begging, I'd have dropped a coin in her hand, without paying any attention to her appearance or why she was begging.

"So good to see you, Elder Brother!" Auntie said in a quivering voice. Mother hugged her and then each of the kids who wailed in unison.

"Where's your professor husband?" Mother asked.

Touching her forehead, Auntie acted light-headed.

"What is it?" Father asked. "Why isn't Kyong with you?"

"The Reds," she barely mumbled. "They took him to the North! They're walking him and other prisoners to their death." Little Aunt buried her face in her dirty hands and wept.

Mother moaned, "No!"

Father shook his head in disbelief.

Uncle Kyong was a scientist who taught at Seoul University, but to me, he was an artist who loved to sketch anything he saw. He was the only relative who didn't notice my round cheeks or my clumsy behavior but spent time drawing pictures of me. My favorite of his artwork was the one in which I stood on the arched bridge across the pond in our old house in Taegu. I wondered what had happened to it.

My parents led Auntie and her children to the front room, where a fan whirred quietly, circulating the August heat, and for a while no one said anything. The only one making noises was the baby. He cooed while chewing his own fist, content at the wrong time and at the wrong place. I couldn't look at him: he might never see his father again, but he didn't know it.

Father asked Little Aunt many questions, and the whole story about Uncle Kyong's abduction to North Korea was revealed. On June 29 at early dawn, she and Uncle Kyong heard a man singing the North Korean anthem on the radio and knew that the communists had entered Seoul. Until the day before, President Rhee had urged citizens not to be agitated, not to worry, but trust him that Seoul was safe. He even had said that the Reds were withdrawing to the north at the moment, because the South Korean army was fighting back. But only a day later, my uncle and aunt realized that the president not only deceived his people but also fled to Suwon with his cabinet members, blowing up the Han Bridge as soon as they crossed it.

My uncle and aunt began packing. Their plan was to run to the mountain that night and hide in one of the caves there. Uncle Kyong dug a large hole in the back and buried their valuable possessions—books, sterling silver, and my aunt's jewelry. Around four, a loud banging at the door startled them as they prepared for their departure. Little Aunt told Uncle Kyong to move to the attic, but he wouldn't. "Let's be together," he said. "It might be our last day in this house."

My aunt quickly gathered the children and brought them to their bedroom. The front door burst open. Uncle Kyong whispered to the children, "If something happens to me, be good to your *Omma*, you hear?" and the children nodded innocently. Within seconds, their bedroom door was kicked open and shots blasted.

"You mean, they were shooting as they came into the room?" Father asked impatiently.

"Yes. It was louder than anything I've heard in my life, Elder Brother," my aunt said. "The chips of the plasterboard flew like birds everywhere, and the noises deafened me. My husband was brave as he said, 'Please don't hurt my family. I'll cooperate.' They stopped firing, but a hefty soldier grabbed him as if he were a wild animal and began hitting him. 'You don't need to do this,' my husband said. 'I'm not armed.'

"Another man, smaller than the first soldier, held his rifle upside down and pounded him with its butt. In front of his kids! Sang-won thought they were going to kill his dad." My aunt turned to the oldest boy, about seven, sitting next to her, and the boy looked away.

"He leapt to his dad, and a soldier kicked him. As his father reached for the boy, the hefty soldier punched him in the face repeatedly and then dragged him out to the courtyard. I saw blood dripping from his nose. The crimson of his blood made me dizzy with anger, and I threw myself in front of the soldiers.

"'Please don't take him!' I cried. 'Look at these little ones. How can you take their dad away? Don't you have kids at home? Don't you know what it's like for these kids growing up without a father?'

"The hefty guy kicked my belly really hard with his booted foot and I bent over. I heard my own scream, which sounded like an animal hit by a bullet, but I didn't feel any pain. *If I stop here*, I thought, *I'll never see him again.* 'If you take him, God will punish you,' I said. 'You'll go to hell!' Another boot kicked me, but I wasn't afraid any more. 'You might die soon, all of you...' I cursed repeatedly.

Auntie stopped to wipe her tears.

Father reached in his pocket and took out a cigarette. He struck his match, but when it didn't light, he threw away both the cigarette and the match. He just sat there, breathing heavily.

My aunt continued, but she didn't seem bitter any more. "'Take care of yourself,' were his last words to me. He wanted to say more, but a Red soldier roughly pulled him, handcuffed him, and then forced him to walk with them. I had never thought our courtyard was that large as I sat there, watching him follow his abductors, his hands bound behind him."

Little Aunt went to the guestroom to rest and Kwon and I kept the children busy, showing them around our home and playing games with them.

I was eager to help Little Aunt. I washed my cousins in the morning before I went to school, and coming home, I played with them, too. They loved the way I tickled Mimi's nose with a feather attached to a bamboo chopstick, and they laughed every time I performed the trick. They also liked rolling marbles on a wooden board that had several holes drilled in it, and we spent hours rolling marbles.

But soon I discovered that no matter how much I tried to help my aunt, and how careful I was with my little cousins, I couldn't please my aunt at all. Whenever one of the kids cried, she'd slide her screen door open and look out with a scowl on her face. "Be careful, will you?" she'd say. "Be gentle with them." Then she slammed her door shut in my face.

My little cousins weren't angels by any means. They got into everything, spilled everything, and touched everything they saw. By the end of the week, their paw prints appeared on the walls, on the scrolls, and even on Mother's mirror, which her own children weren't allowed to touch. Also, whenever I returned from school, my desk drawer was open and my pencils, crayons, and other knick-knacks I treasured were scattered on the floor.

Sang-won was the worst of all five. One day I found him playing with my rooster's feathers, plucking the fine fibers. On the floor lay my new notebook wide open, showing red circles or blue zigzags or purple railroad tracks all over. Notebooks were expensive. Mother allowed me only five of them for the entire school year.

Snatching the feather from him, I blurted, "You shouldn't touch my stuff when I'm not here, Sang-won!"

He began wailing, "Ommaaaa, ommaaaa...." His mouth was square and he was squeezing tears from his closed eyes.

Little Aunt stepped in, her uncombed hair draped on her shoulders. "What did he do?" she asked me, her icy cold eyes piercing through me.

"I don't want him to play with my stuff, Auntie. He does this everyday."

Sang-won raised his arms toward her and wailed louder, "I want the feather..."

Little Aunt took the feather from my hand and studied it, turning, and then gave it back to me. "Are you mad because he played with this dirty thing?"

"It's not dirty," I protested. I was about to say that her little boy had no business opening my drawers and scattering my treasures on the floor, but she roughly grabbed the boy's hand and pulled him up.

"Let's go," she said. "She doesn't want you any more." She then turned to me. "Listen, Jong-ah, you shouldn't touch my kids any more. You hear? I mean it. We don't need you, and that's final!" Dragging the crying boy out of the room, her chest heaving, she slammed the door behind me.

"What is this all about?" I heard Mother say through the closed door. My aunt replied cynically, "Nothing serious, Sister. I think your daughter is tired of my kids. I told her not to touch them anymore."

Mother said, "Sang-won shouldn't go in her room when she isn't there. I don't know if you noticed it or not, but he's getting into everything."

"I see!" My aunt said with finality in her voice. "You're tired of them, too, aren't you, Sister. I've noticed how you look at my kids lately. Well, it won't be much longer. I apologize for being a burden to you all."

Mother said frantically, "Wait! Can't we talk like two adults? It's difficult…"

"Don't you think I know?" my aunt said, as she dragged Sang-won to her room. Two minutes later I heard her scream at her boy, saying, "Why can't you behave? We don't have any place to go if they kick us out. What should we do then? Die together?"

Her words scared me enough that I wanted to run to her and apologize, but on second thought, I really didn't want Sang-won or other children to come into my room again, touching and scattering everything. Little Aunt should teach her kids better, I thought. Sooner or later he'd be in school: he should know what he could touch and could not.

That night I heard Mother complaining to Father how difficult it was for her to deal with five extra children running around everywhere all day, getting into everything, and Little Aunt losing her temper. "I know it's difficult for her without her husband but what about us?" Mother said. "We have seven children of our own. Doesn't she realize it?"

"What are you saying?" Father asked. "Are you suggesting that we throw them out, a woman with no husband and five kids?"

"We can help her find another place," Mother insisted. "Surely, she doesn't expect to live with us forever, does she?"

"Who'd want to rent a place to a single woman with that many kids?" Father commented. "Besides, I'm her brother: I feel responsible for her and her kids."

Mother only sighed. After a long pause, she said, "I'm a woman too, Yobo. I don't know what I'd do when my husband is no longer with me, and I have to take care of five kids alone for the rest of my life. Still, I feel I can't do anything to help your sister. The hole her husband left in her heart is so large and so deep that no one can fill it."

CHAPTER 7

▼

GRANDFATHER AND
THE REDS

In the middle of September, the <u>Pusan Daily News</u> printed a large picture of General MacArthur on a boat with other American officers, wearing sunglasses and smoking a pipe. Below the picture was the caption, "Inchon Landing! 'God is on our side,' General says." I looked at his picture for a long time. I read every printed word in the paper about him, too. He seemed more powerful than God Himself, turning around the war situation when all we heard was the gloomy news that the communists were taking over everywhere, except a small flank in the southeast corner of the peninsula.

At school later, we saw flyers coming down like snowflakes from an American airplane and landing on the field. Teacher Kim was happy. The rims of her eyes turning red, she said, "Children, our soldiers and the U.N. troops are heading to the capital at this very moment. Isn't it exciting? This is a grand triumph of the U.N. soldiers that'll be recorded in the history books."

That evening, Father was in good humor. He poured himself a glass of wine, and said, "This is for General MacArthur and every U.N. soldier involved in the Inchon landing!" He drank it in one gulp. Pouring another, he said, "This is for your grandparents, uncles and aunts, and cousins," and drank it, too. When he poured another and said, "This is for the future of South Korea…" Mother took the wine bottle away from him.

"That's enough, Yobo," she said. "By the time you're done toasting, you'll be drunk. I don't want you to spoil a good day like this with wine!"

"How else can I celebrate, then?" he asked. "Should I kneel and pray?"

"There you go!" she said.

A telegram arrived the next day, announcing that our grandparents were safe and that they were arriving at two in the afternoon on Saturday by train. Mother and Father talked with my aunt at dinner. Father told her that Grandfather and Grandmother would stay in the guestroom and that she would have to find another place. She didn't seem upset, as though she had already been thinking about it. "We'll go to Grandma's home in Masan," she said, glancing at the kids. "Grandma owns a ranch there and we can ride ponies all day, right?"

It was sad. I wished I had been kinder to her kids. She and I had been barely noticing one another at the well area or in front of the outhouse, but we had not spoken a word to each other since the day I made Sang-won cry. The thought that she would leave us, taking all her kids with her, stabbed me. *Next time I see her, I'll tell her I'll miss her and my cousins.*

On Saturday morning after breakfast, Father began ordering the servants in his booming voice, telling them to clean this and that, and move what to where, while my aunt packed her suitcases. Mother was busy in the kitchen with the cook, preparing the meal for the nearly twenty people who would come see Grandparents. I didn't know how long they would be living with us. A week? A month?

Grandfather had a booming voice even louder than my father's. He looked scary, too, like Confucius in the history books. When we had visited them in Taegu before the liberation, I was nervous about being in the same room with Grandfather. With one loud call, he'd gather all of his six servants before him and shoo away sparrows and crows from his property. He had strange attitudes about his grandkids, too: we were merely his live toys. He did whatever pleased him with us. His favorite pastime was torturing us with questions. With my older brothers, he'd ask something about Korean history or mathematics, and when the answers were correct, he would praise them, saying, "I'm proud of you!" and smile, showing his gold teeth. With my sisters, he'd ask something about school or girls' etiquette, but he never gave them the same kind of smile he gave the boys. But for me, it was worse, because I wasn't in school yet, and he knew better than to ask me a question that required a brain or education, so he could only manage to ask, "How old are you?" or "How many fingers and toes do you have?"

After answering him again and again, I was tired of his game. Instead of giving my age or saying how many toes and fingers I had, I pretended my arm itched or my foot went to sleep, only to avoid my ordeal. One day he was persistent that I answer him, so I pointed at the large mole on his chin and asked, "What's that, Grandfather? Does it hurt?" He laughed, tilting his head back, but then thought better of it. Turning to Mother and pointing at me, he said, "This one will be a problem someday if you don't raise her right!"

Mother was furious. On the way home, she lectured me about the proper demeanor of a girl my age before an elderly man like Grandfather, and what she would do next time if I behaved like I had that day.

Another thing about Grandparents coming was that Mother would make me bow at them until my forehead touched the floor. Mother disliked the way I bowed. "Don't look at the person you're bowing to, Jong-ah," she had lectured me many times. "You look like a frog about to leap! Lower your head."

I hated bowing, but Mother seemed to think that it had some traditional value which deserved to be passed on generation after generation, and insisted on it whenever our relatives visited us.

At two-thirty, my parents brought my grandparents home. But Grandfather wasn't feeling well from the long train ride and bowing was omitted. While Father carefully helped him to the guestroom, I couldn't help but smile. It was a lucky day for me.

Until dinner, my sisters and I made about two hundred meat dumplings, while our brothers went out for bicycling. Here again, Mother was never pleased about our artwork. "It's too big and shapeless," she would say.

That evening, my Big Aunt and her tall physician husband, Little Uncle and his young, sleepy-eyed wife, and about ten kids my age or older, all arrived. Little Aunt delayed her trip to Masan until the next morning, so she was there too with her five kids. Grandfather joined the crowd in his white silk Korean topcoat with delicate leaf patterns and baggy ash-gray pants. He looked dignified and wasn't as scary as I remembered. Grandmother was the same as before. She quietly sat next to Grandfather, like his shadow, nodding when Grandfather nodded and laughing when Grandfather laughed. *How boring she is*, I thought. *I'll never be like her when I'm her age.*

Little Aunt had no choice but to retell Uncle Kyong's abduction to the North, and for a while the room was filled with sniffles and the sounds of nose-blowing, while her five little kids argued among themselves.

Third Uncle, Father's younger brother, unexpectedly bent his head toward the grandparents and said, "Forgive me, Father and Mother, for not stopping by your house before we left Seoul."

"What are you talking about, son?" Grandfather asked, surprised.

"There's no excuse, no excuse at all for leaving you alone in the enemy-occupied city! Will you forgive me?"

His sleepy-eyed wife suddenly woke up and nudged his elbow. "Yobo, we had no choice. Bombs were dropping and the Reds were shooting everywhere. When did we have time?"

Third Uncle's facial muscles twisted in disgust. "Hush, woman!"

Grandfather raised his hand and said, "There's no need to apologize, Son. You have six young kids to look after. Even if you didn't have kids, who could worry about others at such a time? We're all here! We must celebrate our good fortune to be alive. Let's eat. I'm hungry."

We began eating. I saw Grandfather's hand holding the chopsticks shake violently as he reached for the meat dumplings. Father came to the rescue. Lifting one with his own chopsticks, he put it on Grandfather's plate. Grandfather took the dumpling to his mouth, but it escaped his unsteady chopsticks and landed on the table instead. Grandfather coughed to hide his embarrassment.

What's changed him so much? I wondered. Pulling Mother's sleeve, I whispered in her ear, "How old is Grandfather now?"

"Shhh!" she hissed, rolling her eyes. "You should never ask a grownup's age!"

Everyone looked at me, even the little kids. I wanted to hide. I didn't know why asking Grandfather's age was such a big deal. *It's only a number,* I thought. *He used to ask me my age, too...*

Grandfather turned in my direction. "Who wants to know my age?" He didn't seem annoyed but rather amused.

"Never mind, Father," Mother said, giving me a cold look, as she had done often. "This child doesn't know anything about manners."

Manners, manners, manners! I wanted to scream.

To my surprise, Grandfather chuckled. "I'm sixty, Jong-ah. I'm a very old man. When a man reaches my age, nothing bothers him. You can ask me anything! What else do you want to know about me?"

"Nothing," I said. If I asked another question, Mother would surely skin me alive, I thought.

"Tell us, Father," Mother said, "how did you survive in Seoul all this time? We were so worried about you."

I was relieved that everyone's eyes were now focused on Grandfather.

Narrowing his eyes, Grandfather seemed to be gathering his thoughts, while his audience waited.

"As soon as the communists entered Seoul," he began in a calm voice, "all stores and shops closed, and my house employees vanished one by one, along with our sterling silverware, cameras, watches, and anything else they could sell. I heard on the radio that thousands of politicians, religious leaders, medical doctors, and professors were captured and taken to the North, and I thought about Kyong." He looked at Little Aunt. "I prayed for him, daughter."

Little Aunt bit her trembling lips.

"Our next-door neighbors disappeared, too," Grandfather went on, "without telling us where they were going. Then came the nightmare we had been worrying about. The Red soldiers forced their entry one night and occupied our home without my consent. The first thing they said was they would send us somewhere, and I almost lost my temper. But I knew what could happen if I wasn't careful. 'I'm a sick man,' I said, acting like I was sicker. 'I might die on your truck. Please, keep us in the servants' quarter. You can have all you want in the house and the storage room. They're yours.'

"They gathered and whispered to one another. 'All right,' the tall man who seemed to be the leader said to me. 'We'll let you remain in the servants' quarter on one condition: You can't go anywhere and you can't talk to anyone other than our comrades. Is it clear?'

"'Fine,' I said. Immediately, we moved to the servant's hut next to the gate. All day we heard gunshots, bombs exploding, and tanks rumbling nearby. We were prisoners in our own home, but at least we were alive. They knocked down the front gate and widened the entryway so that their trucks could go in and out of the courtyard. The pond was filled with dirt and rocks and leveled. The trellis at the entrance of the garden covered with red roses was plucked and thrown away. All of my antique furniture, books, calligraphy, and scrolls were piled into the courtyard and burned, except the pottery collection and your grandmother's jewelry: they divided the jewelry among themselves, but my ancient jars and vases, they packed in a wooden box.

"At dinner that evening I recognized the soldier who brought the tray of food to us. It was my old tenant's son. Do you remember Chang-ho?" he asked our father.

"Yes, I do," our father said. "He was about twelve or thirteen when he lived on our property with his parents."

"Yes, that's the one. I was cautious not to make a mistake and carefully asked him if he lived in Taegu a while ago. He recognized me immediately: he whispered, 'It's so good to see you, sir.' I said, 'I thought you joined the South Korean army after the liberation,' and his answer was, 'I did, sir, but our regiment commander defected to the North in February, and we had no choice but join the Red Army. Several commanders defected to the North about the same time, dragging thousands of troops with them like cattle, sir. Kim Il-Sung lured them to the North, promising them rewards.'

"I just sat there in disbelief. He was very brave. Though he could get in trouble for helping us, he told me *not* to call him by his name but always *Comrade* and to do exactly what the Red soldiers told us to do. 'If I can do anything for you, please let me know,' he said. As he got up, I asked about his parents. He hesitated. I had a strange feeling that something happened to them.

"I'm sorry to break the bad news, but they passed away during a bombing in Taejon,' he said, then hastily left the room.

"Chang-ho brought us two meals a day, morning and at night, and we lived peacefully compared to others. He informed us what was going on outside, too, even things he shouldn't have. It was he who told us about the Inchon landing a week ago and that they were leaving that day. We were more scared than glad at hearing such news, because we had no idea what might happen to us. At dusk, the Red soldiers began packing. No food came, and we feared that Chang-ho might have already left, leaving us in others' hands. Around nine or ten that night, our rice-papered door was kicked open, and a short man entered, holding his rifle. He said, 'Get up and come with us.'

"I shook my head. 'I'm very sick, comrade,' I said. 'Why don't you shoot us now? It'd be an easy solution for you, and we don't have to die on your truck. This is our home, and we want to die here.'

"He hesitated, but when he heard a man's voice shouting outside, 'Let's go', he lifted his rifle. I heard a metallic click. Grandmother began weeping loudly, and the soldier kicked her. Then another soldier came in. 'Wait!' he said. It was Chang-ho, but I pretended that I didn't know him.

"'Why waste bullets on them?' said Chang-ho. 'They're as useless as rotten boards. Didn't Chairman Kim always tell us not to waste bullets?'

"The short soldier said they were running out of time, and Chang-ho told him to go. 'I'll take care of them!' he said. 'I'll drop them in the well or strangle them so that their lips will be sealed. Go on, comrade. Don't fall behind the regiment!'

"'Don't be late,' the short soldier told him. 'The Yankees are getting closer.' I heard his boots kick the door and run toward the gate.

"Chang-ho waited until no communists were around and took us to the loft in the storage shed. 'Don't move until the Americans get here,' he said in an urgent voice.

"I grabbed his elbow. 'How can I thank you?'

"'Don't mention it, sir,' he said. He then walked away. I cried like an orphan. A few minutes later, I heard different sounds of machine guns approaching and almost wished that the Red soldiers were still with us.

"We ate uncooked rice and raw potatoes in the storage room for the following two days. On the third day, we heard voices shouting, 'Americans are here! Americans are here!' Grandmother and I ran out to the street to see what was going on.

"The bodies of Red soldiers were strewn everywhere. I didn't see any South Korean soldiers among the dead. For some strange reason, I began searching for Chang-ho. I never wanted to find him lying among other corpses, but I couldn't stop looking for him. We walked about two blocks when Grandmother stopped me, covering her mouth, pointing.

Chang-ho lay on his back with other red soldiers, his uniform soaked in blood and his eyes fixed on the heavens. I bent down to close his eyes but straightened myself immediately, because a marching band was approaching, playing a lively military tune. I wasn't a bit glad to see an American military band or hear its music. I wanted to be alone with Chang-ho for two minutes, only two minutes, but it was impossible. People were everywhere, shouting *Manseh* (hooray) or singing our anthem.

"A few feet away, two beggar boys were talking. One of them said, pointing at the corpses, 'I found this one, this one, and that one hiding in a ruined building over there and told the police about them.' The other said the same thing, except that he showed something in his hand. "See?" he said proudly. 'I found this watch in that guy's pocket. I think it's gold.'

"I was sick to my stomach. Grabbing Grandmother's hand, I hurried home, leaving Chang-ho on the street and the boys nearby. I was afraid that the boys might get the wrong idea about me, an old man standing next to a dead Red soldier, and report to the police. I'm such a coward, compared to Chang-ho."

CHAPTER 8

▼

SANTA IN MILITARY BOOTS

By early October the temperature on the mountain dropped considerably, and even during the day we were cold. On the second weekend in October, our teachers and volunteers moved the third and fourth graders to an abandoned flourmill near the train station that had been boarded up for years. Besides too many rats and spiders, the building had a leaky roof and holes in the walls. Although we had a wood-burning stove in the middle of the room, we were still cold.

Teacher Kim taught the class wearing her wool coat and gloves, and once in a while, she had to stop teaching to blow steam into her gloved hands. In early November, the Department of Education ordered the school officials to close the building permanently.

The U.N. troops' miraculous landing on Inchon and their advance to Pyong-Yang and farther beyond seemed history now. Nearly 300,000 Chinese men had stepped into the war days earlier, ambushing the U.N. troops everywhere they went. We learned a new vocabulary on the radio——tactics, casualties, collision, and retreat.

"God wasn't on our side, after all," Father said one evening, using General MacArthur's famous line at the time of the Inchon Landing. "His *boys* can't go home for Thanksgiving, I'm afraid."

Mother said, "I'm not giving up my hopes on him yet. If it weren't for him, South Korea wouldn't exist today. He might perform another miracle."

To me, no school meant being with Kwon all day, while my older sisters and brothers were at school. My younger brother had a rare ability to exhaust me and make me sick of him at any time of the day. When we listened to the news on the radio together, he'd interrupt by interjecting, "The name of the Chinese general is *Piao!* It sure sounds like a bullet hitting something, doesn't it? I wonder if he'll die soon." Or he'd say, "Did you hear that? An American general's name is *almond.* How did he get such a strange name?"

The war must be affecting his behavior, because he amused himself for hours by lynching his imaginary Kim Il-sung, North Korea's premier, using a broomstick and a bale of hay. He'd drill his wooden sword into the hay or the bristle of the broomstick, shouting, "*Yyyyat!* You're dead, Kim il-sung! I, General *Macada* (MacArthur), killed you for good, *ha, ha, ha....*"

But Kim Il-sung never died. Even after Kwon's sword pierced him through and through, he was alive the next day, and Kwon had to kill him all over again. I sometimes wondered if Kwon really wanted Chairman Kim dead or not.

When he was bored with killing Kim Il-sung, he looked for rats to kill. He diligently checked under the firewood pile or next to the drain hole in the well area every day, and when he found a shivering critter in one of the wire traps, he'd set it on fire. Kwon called his artwork *flame throwing.* Once he insisted that I should come out to the back and watch him and I did.

"This is what Americans use on the Chinese Rats," he said, lifting the kerosene bottle so that I could see it. "First, you drench the critter with kerosene, like this!" He poured the clear fluid on the rat inside the trap, and producing a box of matches from his pants' pocket, he said, "Now we open the door and burn him."

But the rat wasn't cooperative. When I opened the door, it didn't move as if it knew what Kwon was about to do. Kwon struck a match and ignited it, and holding the burning match in one hand, he kicked the trap until the rat darted out. As the critter headed toward the outhouse, Kwon threw the match at it with precision, and instantly, the rat turned into a zigzagging fireball.

I screamed.

"What's the matter?" Kwon asked.

"You're so cruel! Look what you did!" I cried, pointing at the fireball that was now turning into a soot ball.

"We're in war, Jong-ah," Kwon said righteously. "In war, killing your enemy is considered *heroic action.* Rats are our enemies, just as the Chinese are. They steal food from us and spread diseases. They deserve to die!"

Luckily, Kwon's cruelty didn't last long. A couple of days later, the blazing rat crawled under the porch and scorched the floorboard. Mother could smell it and told Father about it. He roared to Kwon: "Are you trying to burn the house down? Don't you have better things to do than burn rats?"

In spite of the gloom and uncertainty of the future, Christmas was approaching with the cheerful tunes of *Jingle Bells* and I was excited: I would perform a Korean folk dance again at the Christmas Eve concert.

Among many fund-raising events our parish church organized each year, the Christmas Eve concert was the most publicized event, and for the last two Christmases, I had been the only Korean folk dancer among two-dozen participants. Twice, my name had been posted on the church bulletin for the month of December, and for two Christmases in a row, I danced under bright stage lights, wearing colorful makeup and a long silk Korean dress stenciled with butterfly designs. While swirling around the stage, moving my arms gracefully, hopping, skipping, and turning, I saw many smiling faces in the crowd that told me I was a promising star. Even long after the performance, girls sometimes noticed me at church and whispered, "Look, she's that little folk dancer from Christmas Eve."

I waited patiently for the first Sunday of December to come, when my name would be posted on the church bulletin again.

That Sunday morning, I left home much earlier than usual for the children's Mass and stood in front of the bulletin board. I checked all of the names but didn't find my own. I checked again, slowly and carefully, under each category: Ballet, Voice Solo, Voice Quartet, Piano Solo, Piano-for-four-hands, Acrobat, and Korean folk dance.

A different name was next to *Korean Folk Dance*. I then realized that most of the names posted there belonged to the refugee kids, who had been showing off their disgusting "talents" each Sunday afternoon in the gym, like circus monkeys. Some hung upside down on the gym set, swinging back and forth; some banged the keyboard of the old piano, while singing at the top of their voices, *do-re-mi-fa-sol-la-ti-do*"; and some performed cartwheels. A skinny girl reminded me of a cat: she could leap toward the ceiling from a six-foot high beam, flip twice in mid-air, and land on the beam again, without losing her balance.

I don't remember walking home after Mass, but I remember crawling into my bedroom closet to cry. I didn't want to see anyone, not even Mimi, nor did I want to talk to anyone. My head buried in my folded arms, I thought seriously about running away. But where could I go? I was a penniless child. I wasn't even allowed to go to the market alone.

I'm unlucky, I thought, my eyes filling. Having been born in the year of the dragon, I was supposed to be outgoing, strong, charming, and bright, but I had none of those qualities. According to Mother, I was only "average" because my report card showed mostly 80 or above: sometimes even under 80. When one of my siblings mocked or teased me, the only thing I could do was crawl into this closet, bury my head in my arms, and hope that I'd never see him or her again.

The year of the dragon brought many famous women in our history—the Yi dynasty poet Hwang, Queen Min, and astrologer Shin—but I didn't even want to be famous. In fact, I wished I had been born in the year of the snake, the creature destined to crawl on its belly all its life. The refugee kids stole everything from me today, but I didn't even have the courage to ask Sister Kim, the coordinator of the event, why I wasn't selected. I swore never to go to church again until Christmas was over and gone forever.

The next Sunday came in a hurry, in spite of my resolution not to go to church, and I made a plan. Mother would never forgive me for lying on my mat on a Sunday morning, so I got up, as usual, and wore my Sunday best—a black dress with a white collar. I didn't wait for Kwon, though we had been going to the children's Mass at nine o'clock together for two years.

With *The Children's Bible* under my arm, I headed for Unsook's house down the road. Unsook was my elder sister's classmate who belonged to the First Presbyterian Church ten blocks away. She had been fond of me, occasionally giving me a stick of Juicy Fruit or a piece of dried squid. The truth was, she wanted to lure me to her church. Many times she had told me that her church gave Nabisco cookies to every child that attended both the worship service and Bible study on Sundays, but I had never accepted her invitation. Things were different now.

Before I reached her straw thatched house facing the creek, I found her walking toward me, wearing a black wool coat and her yellow binder tucked under her arm.

"Well, are you going to join me today?" she asked me, cheerfully. "We'll have something even more special, if you care to know."

"What's that?"

"A Hershey bar for every kid. The whole bar! You don't need to share with anyone."

A whole Hershey bar, all to myself! My mouth watered.

"Well?" she said.

"I'm not sure," I said, trying to hide my appetite for a chocolate bar. "It feels funny to go to church for a treat, know what I mean?"

"How silly! It's a gift from the church on behalf of Jesus himself telling us he's glad to see his children in the House of Worship. What's wrong with that? Doesn't the Bible say 'God loves little children and widows'?"

"But I'm Catholic."

"So? Jesus doesn't discriminate against any religion. He's the God that belongs to every church."

"How do you know?"

"Because I pray everyday. And I read the Bible, too. When you're close to God, he lets you know a lot of things about himself. Anyway, there will be boxes of Hershey bars waiting for you at the church, just to show you that God loves you."

It was a convincing story. Who would turn down such a gift from Jesus himself? "Actually, Unsook Onni (sister), I've never been inside the First Presbyterian Church I've been wondering about it."

"Come on, then. What are you waiting for?" she said, pulling my elbow.

The stone building with a pointy bell tower was much taller and larger than Sacred Heart Catholic Church where I belonged, but inside, it was less ornate and didn't have as many statues. The usher, an old man with gray hair and murky fish eyes, saw me walking in with Unsook, and said, "Young Lady, the elementary school children sit in the front. Hurry, the service is about to begin."

I clung to Unsook's arm as if she were my guardian angel, and she said, "This is her first day here. I'll make sure she attends the Bible School afterwards." The usher quickly turned to find other children to send to the front. I was relieved. I sat in a middle pew next to Unsook.

As soon as the service began with the preacher's long prayer, I was miserable. He reminded me of a noisy bird with a loud metallic voice. Besides, he had no hair, like a light bulb, and whenever he lowered his head to pray, I had no choice but remember our pastor's white hair that made him appear like Saint Peter in the pictures.

How could he be God's messenger, I wondered.

The congregation sang different hymns than those I sang at my church, too, which Unsook hadn't mentioned to me. When the singing ended, they recited some prayers, and these too were different from what I knew. Doubts crept in. I didn't like this Presbyterian Church after all. I should have gone to Sacred Heart, where many familiar statues of Catholic saints and angels looked upon me with kind eyes. I missed my friends, too, who giggled with me whenever Father Yim dropped something or tripped over his long garment embroidered with gold threads.

The more I looked around me, the louder my doubts grew. Even the Jesus on the cross seemed to say, "I am the Presbyterian God. You don't belong here, child. Go to your own church at once and don't come back!"

I had no desire for Hershey bars or Nabisco cookies any more from a church I didn't belong to. *Satan's tempted me,* I thought. *He entered Unsook and talked to me in his cunning voice to disobey the Catholic God. I'm sure I'll be punished for this!*

Finding courage, I whispered, "I want to go home!"

"What?" Unsook hissed. "It just started. If you leave now, you can't get the treat!"

"I don't want the treat. I don't like your church. I'm Catholic!"

An old woman sitting before us turned and hissed, "Shhhh. Be quiet, girls!"

I had no reason to stay. I got up.

Unsook's eyes turned cold. "Leave quietly."

I left as quietly as I could, but my Sunday shoes weren't cooperative. The heels went *tap, tap, tap,* against the wooden floor, all the way to the door, and the same fishy-eyed usher wasn't pleased. Rolling his eyes, he quickly opened the heavy wooden door, as if glad to get rid of me.

Walking home, I prayed. "Forgive me, Lord, for not going to our church this morning. Satan tempted me with his cunning voice to go against you, just like in the Bible. I promise I'll never be tempted again as long as I live."

Our house was quiet at ten in the morning. Everyone had left for ten-thirty Mass and Kwon's Bible class was still in session. I played with Mimi on the porch, tickling her nose with her favorite toy—a bird feather tied to a wooden chopstick.

Kwon came home with the rest of the family around noon. He stared at me, his eyes full of questions, but I treated him as though he was an invisible boy. What I feared the most was the possibility that Mother would discover my secret, which I never wanted to reveal to anyone until I died.

At lunch, Mother asked Kwon and me, "How was Mass?"

My head lowered, I kept shoving food into my mouth.

Kwon answered, "The sermon was too long and was boring as hell."

"Watch your tongue!" Mother said.

I was grateful that Kwon didn't say, "Where were you, Jong-ah? I didn't see you at church," but the trial wasn't over yet.

"What did Father Yim talk about, Jong-ah?" Mother asked me.

"Just the usual stuff," I commented casually.

Then Kwon said, "Wasn't it so boring, Jong-ah? I mean, really! The same stuff over and over."

"Yeah, it was," I said.

"You fell asleep, didn't you? I heard you snoring from the other side of the aisle, ha, ha."

Mother flashed her eyes at Kwon. "You're being so obnoxious these days."

To my delight, Eldest brother agreed. "I've noticed it too, Mother. I found him smoking the other day." Now everyone's attention shifted to Kwon, and I knew my ordeal was over.

"Smoking?" said Mother, turning to Kwon. "Were you smoking cigarettes?"

"Not me!" Kwon said defiantly.

I tried hard not to laugh. Since reading *Tom Sawyer* that summer, Kwon had been acting strange, walking barefoot in the courtyard and pretending he was smoking a cigar with a stick of a rolled rice paper. Once I found him in a creek, mostly a bed of grass and rocks, looking for turtle eggs. But he never smoked. I only saw him strike a match and light the rolled rice paper, but when it burst into flames, he jumped and hurriedly put it out. I had no clue when Eldest Brother had seen him smoking.

Seeing my chance to help him out, I said, "It's not a real cigarette, is it, Kwon? You were just playing with a rolled rice paper, weren't you? Many boys do that for fun."

Mother seemed to buy my story. "I'll be watching you, Kwon," she said ferociously. "Getting older doesn't mean you can laugh at church or priests. In this house, we never get such ideas, do you understand?"

I thanked God for his mercy.

On Christmas Eve it rained. I was even more determined not to go to church. What joy was there in watching the refugee kids dance and sing and play the piano when I was just another face in the audience? Who'd want to walk two miles in the rain, only to be humiliated by those who had robbed me of joy and pride? I lay on my mat, coughing and complaining of a headache.

Mother came in and touched my forehead. "You don't have a fever!" she declared. "I don't want you to miss the Christmas Eve program and midnight Mass. We'll have a feast when we come home."

"I feel awful," I squeaked. "I think I'm catching a cold."

"Tonight is the most important day of the year," she went on. "We're celebrating the birth of Jesus."

"I know, but I feel really sick. I might catch pneumonia, walking in this rain."

"All right, rest for now," she said, patting my shoulder under the comforter. "I'll come back to see how you're doing in a few minutes."

You don't need to come back, Mother, I wanted to say, but I didn't. She came back in less than five minutes. She was now fully dressed in her tan cashmere coat and matching scarf, and I smelled a waft of apple blossoms from her.

"Are you still feeling sick? You're not playing hooky, are you?" she asked.

"I swear to God," I lied with a straight face.

"Well, I have no choice but to leave you, then. You'll regret it, Jong-ah! Don't blame me for not making you go with us." She rose and headed to the door. Holding the doorknob, she turned around. "Are you sure?"

"I am!"

She turned the light off and left with the rest of the family, including Yong-ja and the cook. Other than the rain's rhythmic spatter on my rice-papered screen door, everything around me stilled.

It seemed something was breathing in the corner. I sat up, trying to flick the light switch on but changed my mind. Covering my head with my comforter, I wished my family were here. There was something sad about lying in an empty house on Christmas Eve, I now realized. Mimi lay next to me, purring, warming my side, but with everyone gone I felt like the only person alive in the whole wide world. I knew my grandparents were in their room across the courtyard, but they couldn't hear me even if I screamed at the top of my lungs. I was as lonely and scared as an orphan wandering in a stormy night. The noises of the gingko branches hissing and the clothesline whistling in the wind were loud and spooky. To block the scary thoughts entering my head, I prayed: "Our Father, who art in heaven, hallowed be thy name...." Mimi suddenly got up, as if I had disturbed her, yawned, stretching all her legs, and left me cold-heartedly.

A sigh left my throat.

A long night was still ahead and I had no one to talk to. Suddenly I heard two cats howling under the porch. Mimi seemed to be in a fight again with the black alley cat, her sworn enemy. They hissed, screeched, and yowled like two soprano singers on a stage for a long time before they parted. Who won? I wondered.

I finally fell asleep, but a commotion in the courtyard woke me. I heard Kwon complaining, "I'm hungry! Where's the food?" and Mother ordering the servants to hurry up. Dishes and bowls clattered; the floorboards creaked. Finally, Mother began saying grace. And then it was quiet again. Everyone seemed to be eating.

My stomach growled. It bothered me that none of them came to see whether I was still alive. I had waited for them for what seemed like an eternity, shivering and fighting scary thoughts, but they seemed to have completely forgotten about me. If it so happened that communists had come and murdered me coldheart-edly, what would they do? Would Father and Mother shed tears of sorrow?

Would my brothers and sisters grieve over their lost little sister whom they had treated like a slave? Would Mimi remember how often I had brushed her hair? I wasn't sure.

I then heard Father say, "The kids who performed tonight were great, weren't they?"

My tongue sprang out spontaneously toward Father. I couldn't believe he could say those words when his own daughter wasn't included in the program.

"They were quite good," Mother agreed. "They did amazing things the local kids couldn't even imitate."

My lips twisted automatically.

"I liked the piano solo the best," commented First Sister. She had been talking a lot about piano lately. One of these days, I thought, she'd ask Mother to let her take piano lessons.

"The best part was," Kwon joined the conversation, "the presents Santa gave us."

My ears perked. *Presents? How could I forget about Santa's presents? Am I losing my mind completely?*

On every Christmas Eve since the liberation, a hefty American soldier dressed in a red suit and hat visited the church on Christmas Eve, his army jeep loaded with colorful packages. When the concert ended, he'd appear on the stage, laughing, "Ho, ho, ho," and motion for the children to join him. When we did, he opened a large bag and handed each of us a red sock filled with yellow American pencils, candy, and colorful marbles. Another Christmas, I got a pair of wool mitten embroidered with flowers. *It was Satan again who talked me into not going to church on Christmas Eve!*

"Did you open your present?" Mother asked. "What did you get?"

"A fountain pen. Look, it shines like gold."

A fountain pen shining like gold! I would have loved to own such a pen. *Why am I so unlucky?*

Kwon asked, "Father, do you think we'll still get a present from the Americans when the war ends?"

"Probably not. I assume they'll return to their country when the war is over."

"I don't want them to leave."

"Even if they leave," Father said, "there will be someone else giving you a present on Christmas."

"It's not the same. I can't imagine Korean Santa giving me a present."

"Now, Kwon," Mother said, "it doesn't matter who gives you the present on Christmas. The spirit of giving is what's important here."

I didn't agree with her. Santa without army boots under his bright red outfit wouldn't be the true Santa, and without the true Santa, Christmas wouldn't be the real one either. Like Kwon, I too couldn't picture a Korean man dressed in a red suit, saying, "Ho, ho, ho" as he gave out presents. I wasn't so sure if I wanted the war to end soon or not.

CHAPTER 9

▼

CHINESE ARE COMING

After Christmas Father made a couple of overnight trips, first to a small islet near the coast and then to Cheju, the largest island in the South Sea. Returning home late in the evening, he and Mother talked in their room until midnight, their screen door dimly lit from within.

The news we had heard was scary: hordes of Red Chinese were now swarming down through the mountain roads, shooting Russian-made rifles and cutting off UN supply lines. On every road leading to Pusan, American military trucks streamed down, bumper-to-bumper. Also, the American general Walton Walker died in an automobile accident a day before Christmas Eve.

Seoul was evacuated on January 4. The fate of Pusan was unknown, but the new refugees seemed to think it was the only safe place left in Korea, and poured into our town like migrating birds. More tents were pitched on public properties—some bearing English letters—and more beggars knocked on our door, begging for food. The newcomers not only took over any available spot in Pusan but also altered the view of the city as well. Everywhere I looked, I saw their crudely-built huts on steep hills, in the vacant lot near the market and near the shore, and even along the railroad tracks. It seemed to me the only place they didn't build their nests was in the treetops.

One bitterly cold evening after dinner, Father came home somewhat excited. Seeing Mother talking with us in the front room, he said, "We need to talk! It's important."

"What is it, Yobo?" she said, turning to him.

Lowering his voice a notch, Father said, "The Seoul diocese moved to Pusan today, but the Pusan diocese has no place for two hundred refugee priests and nuns. The bishop's mansion is full of refugee priests already, and even the churches are all filled up. The only hope for these religious men and women is finding Catholic families willing to share their living spaces with them."

"Who told you this?"

"Father Yim our pastor. I sat with him on the bus. He said that we'll receive a letter from the bishop asking for help. Yobo, this might be a solution for us."

"A solution to what?"

"These men and women need a place to stay and we want to move to Cheju Island. If we let them stay here, we don't need to worry about looters and vandals, and my parents will not be left alone."

"Yobo, slow down. Why are we going to Cheju Island and when? I didn't know we had a place there already."

Father seemed frustrated. "We talked about this when I returned from Cheju, remember? The only thing left for me to do is send the realtor a telegram or a letter to tell him we want the house by the shore. We can move right away, if we want to. Buying a house on a remote island isn't like buying a house in a city. It's simple. You pay cash and the house is yours the next day. Anyway, when the Chinese take over Pusan, the first thing they'll do is round up men like myself and shoot. And who knows what else they'll do. You know how much the communists hate what they call *class enemies*. I really don't want to sit and wait here to get a bullet hole in my head."

"What a terrible thing to say!"

"That's not all. The situation is a lot worse than we think. Father Yim said that the high-ranking American officers had a secret meeting with President Rhee last week at Blue House."

"What secret meeting?"

"They met to discuss evacuating the UN forces in case of an emergency and relocating the Rhee administration to Japan."

"Rhee administration to Japan? I don't believe it. The Americans know how the president feels about the Japanese. I can't imagine they would ask him to move to Japan."

"It's from a reliable source, Yobo. Father Yim knows many high-ranking soldiers at the Eighth Army. He's the one who invited them to church at Christmas."

"And did Father Yim say our president responded positively to the American generals' offer?"

"Of course not. But that's not important here. The point I'm trying to make is that the situation is serious. If we don't do something about it, we'll all end up dead. Yobo, let's go ahead with our plan and let refugee priests and nuns housesit for us. We can move our parents later, after we settle down somewhere."

Mother seemed to ponder the situation. She asked more questions and Father answered quietly. They talked for another ten or fifteen minutes and then she put her coat on. Before leaving with Father, she told the servants to clean the room in the bathhouse and make dinner for some extra people. How many extra people, the cook asked, and mother said she didn't know.

Our grandparents now occupied our guestroom, but the room next to the bathing area had been vacant since Agi-Omma left. I wondered how many people would move in with us.

We ate dinner without our parents. Just before curfew, they returned with many beggar-like people. I counted them—two men and six women, all in dirty street clothes. Mother told them to please be comfortable, and they took their shoes off and gathered in the front room, smiling uncomfortably.

I thought they were supposed to be priests and nuns but they didn't look that way at all.

Kwon must have read my mind, because he asked Mother softly, "Why aren't they wearing their *costumes*?"

"Why don't you ask them yourself, Kwon?" Mother said.

"Never mind, Mother," he said, timidly.

One of the guests, a short, round man, volunteered to answer Kwon. "I can explain, son," he said, and cleared his throat. "We can't wear our religious garb because of the communists. So many of our brothers have been killed and so many more taken to the North since last June."

"Why don't they like you, sir?" Kwon asked.

"Because we preach the Gospels. Jesus taught us to love one another as he loves us in the Bible, using many parables, didn't he?"

"Yes."

"But the communists only believe in their own power. They don't love anyone and don't trust anyone, not even their friends and families. That's why it's dangerous if the communists take over our country, and that's why so many foreign soldiers are fighting for us, so that some day, the world is a safe place to live for everyone. Did I answer your question, son?"

"Yes, sir."

Just then the servants brought our short-legged dinner table loaded with steaming bowls and dishes, and Father said, "Please enjoy, Fathers and Sisters. It's not much, but tomorrow we'll do better."

They must have been starving for days, for they shoved spoonfuls of rice and soup and pickled cabbage into their mouths, with hardly a pause. Spoons clattered and lips smacked long into the night.

Father introduced each of us to our hungry guests, and they smiled and nodded, still eating. I learned that the short and round man with a jolly face, who had volunteered to answer Kwon's question, was Father Bhang, the apparent leader of the group. The tall, scrawny man sitting next to him was Father Yoon, an author of some religious books. Whereas Father Bhang was friendly and talkative, Father Yoon seemed cold and humorless. The six women were members of the Sisters of Korean Martyred Saints, and they each seemed to have a title. The tall, masculine woman was Mother Superior. The others were Sister Benevolent, the Novice Director, the cook, the choir director, and the youngest was something called a *postulant*.

Mother Superior unexpectedly said to our parents, "Mr. and Mrs. Suh, you're blessed with such lovely daughters."

"Thank you," Mother replied, but Father said nothing. He was never comfortable when someone complimented his daughters.

Mother Superior's next words sent a cold shock up my spine. "Seriously, Mr. and Mrs. Suh, I'm looking at our three future Sisters here. I feel God is smiling upon us all."

I almost fainted. *Me, a Sister? Even if the world turns upside-down, this will not happen! They have too many rules and…all they do is pray…*

I looked at Mother, holding my breath.

Mother laughed. "I'm afraid they're not cut out to be sisters like you. They're just ordinary girls."

A sigh left my lips. *After all,* I thought, *Mother still loves us.*

CHAPTER 10

▼

FLEE TO CHEJU ISLAND

A few days later after dinner, Father gave us a long lecture. "Tomorrow morning we're leaving for Cheju Island. I've already talked to your grandparents and the Fathers and Sisters about our plan, and they all wished us a good trip. We have a place by the seashore called Pearl Bay: It's a three-bedroom house, much smaller than this one, but for the time being it's the safest place I can provide for all of us. Listen carefully and don't get lost on the way there. Kwon," he said, turning to my younger brother. "You and your oldest brother are partners. Don't lose him during the boat trip. And Gong, make sure *he* doesn't get lost."

"Yes, Father."

"And you, Jong-ah," he said. "You and Sook-ah are paired for the trip. Listen to your oldest sister and do exactly what she tells you to do. You shouldn't argue with her at all during the trip. Do you understand?"

"Of course."

"You, Hoon and Won-ah," he said turning to Second Brother and Second Sister. "I'm not worried about you middle ones. Stay close to us and pay attention to your younger brother and sister. Any questions?"

We shook our heads.

"The ship leaves at eight from the Yongdo Port. We'll take the six-thirty train to get there early enough so that we won't miss it. Keep in mind: the ship dock will be extremely crowded. It's going to be a long, strenuous day."

He then got up, slid the closet door open, and took out the backpacks, and handed one to each of us, checking the name in the front. "As I said earlier," he went on, "don't trust anyone with your backpack, hear? Don't show your money to anyone, either. If anybody sees you with money in your hands they might kill you. Money can be ugly sometimes. Do you understand?"

"Yes, Father."

"See you all in the morning. We have a long day ahead of us. Good night!"

The next morning at dawn our family slipped out of our spacious courtyard, all bundled up in wool coats, hats, and gloves. We were now refugees. I couldn't believe it.

The gray sky overhead seemed frozen solid as we walked vigorously toward the train station, each with a rucksack on his or her back. Mother was lagging behind us, and a couple times Father called out, "Are you all right?" and she replied "I'm fine," but we all knew she wasn't. She had never carried Baby Brother on her back before: it was the servant girl's job. Finally, Father untied Baby Brother from Mother's back and carried him on his backpack.

How long would we be on Cheju Island? I wondered. I didn't mind if we never came back to Pusan. I would enjoy listening to the sound of the waves at the shore and looking up at the seagulls gliding in the sky, and most of all, I would love walking on the golden sand, if the weather was warm enough.

Far away, the train station glittered golden yellow, and I had an urge to run there as fast as I could and board the train. I loved train rides. We always took trains to the beaches or to the Buddhist temples in the mountains. Although we were Catholics, our parents didn't mind taking us to ancient temples because there was so much to see and learn about our history. What I liked the most about train rides was that every passenger seemed friendly toward their traveling companions. Some of them shared their food or cigarettes with total strangers and some even told their whole life stories, laughing or crying. People never fought on the train as far as I could remember.

The train station was indeed crowded. I bumped into people as often as I did at the market. The train had already arrived, puffing and hissing, and men and women were shouting at the top of their lungs, calling their children's names or just talking.

The conductor suddenly blew his whistle sharply, adding more noise to the place.

Linking hands tightly together, First Sister and I followed Father and Mother, pushing and shoving. Kwon and Eldest Brother walked behind us and Second Brother and Second Sister behind them.

In five minutes we were in a car with screaming children. I took a seat next to the window and First Sister sat next to me, and the rest of the family sat across the aisle. People filed in with bags, boxes, and children, taking the open seats.

The train began to chug, and I heard the wheels grinding beneath me. Through the window I saw a vague outline of distant mountains and the gray sky hung very low. I hoped that it wouldn't rain.

Cheju Island had many historical places, we learned at school. For centuries, the Yi dynasty kings had banished any political troublemakers or criminals to Cheju and other remote islands in the South Sea. In some rare cases, the king would pardon them after a few years and call them back to serve him again, but most of them died in their faraway prisons that had no barred windows or doors. Some had been the scholars whom the old kings had carefully chosen to serve the kingdom by testing their poetry-writing skills. The Yi dynasty kings strictly used intellectuals to assist them in governing the kingdom because they valued art and literature much more than the physical power of warriors.

The condemned scholars left behind many beautiful *shijo*, the ancient poems that had 3-4-3-4 syllable rhythm, telling of their devotion to the king and to the dynasty, and of their devastating loneliness. The most heartbreaking shijo of all for me was "Loneliness," written by the sixth king of the Yi dynasty, a thirteen-year-old boy who took the throne after his father's sudden death. But in less than four months, his uncle, the seventh king, stole his crown by killing dozens of the palace employees, house-arresting his sister-in-law, the king's mother, and sending the thirteen-year-old to a remote, nameless island in the South Sea to die. The shijo went like this:

> Waves, rocks, wind, and sand...
> Not a soul comes by all day
> The chattering seabird overhead
> Will you sing a song of love for me?

The thought that I could actually touch the soil where those ill-fated scholars and lonely prisoners lived and died excited me. My friends would be amazed when I told them about the Yi dynasty cemeteries. "Were their ghosts whispering to you?" they'd ask, and I'd say, "Of course. They always do when someone is listening." "What did they say to you?" they'd ask again, and I'd answer, "It's a secret."

Kwon seemed lost in his own thoughts, too, his lips parted slightly and his eyes glued to the window where a new day was awakening. Mother was praying her rosary again, probably asking the Blessed Virgin for a safe trip to Cheju Island. Father was glancing at his wristwatch frequently, sitting opposite Mother. For him, everything moved intolerably slow. He always dropped his eyes to his watch, even while he ate, as though an invisible foe was after him. Someday I would tell him to relax, imitating the way he lectured us. He'd surely laugh, and say, "I must be getting old."

After passing through two dark and long tunnels that amplified the grinding of the wheels, and crawling up the side of a mountain where we could see the blue expanse of water dancing in the bright sunlight, the train pulled into the station by the seaport. We got off in pairs. Father counted our heads twice, making sure we were seven. Then we headed toward a white ship with a blue stripe, spitting smoke into the sky.

The dock was more spacious than our old school playground, which was now occupied by the soldiers. Several long lines of people stood in front of the ramp leading to the deck, and we joined them.

Father produced some yellow tickets from his coat pocket and handed one to each member of the family, except Kwon and me. "I'm afraid you younger ones might lose your ticket," he said, giving an additional ticket to my oldest brother and sister. "I think it'd be better if your partners kept them for you."

Kwon's face grew long. "When are you going to trust us, Father?" he asked boldly. "When we're twenty or thirty?"

"I hope it won't be that long, son," Father said, without missing a beat.

I was glad I didn't have to worry about losing my ticket. Things never stayed in my hands very long. Twice, I had lost my report card on the way home, and Mother had had to ask my teacher to make another one each time. Now, at Mother's request, my report card was delivered by mail, which I liked better. I trusted my sister. She kept everything—stamps, coins, smooth pebbles, buttons, broken-rosaries, and even her early teeth! Her drawer resembled a miniature junkyard, which she guarded fiercely.

We waited at the dock for a long time, shivering in the cold wind. Some people opened their lunch boxes and ate, standing and shivering; some gossiped about their landlords in Pusan and how much they hated being refugees; others sat on the ground, yawning and dozing.

As I stood next to First Sister, my hand in hers, the lines grew longer by the minute. I was sleepy and bored. I kept yawning and fidgeting.

"Stay awake," my sister ordered, yanking my hand. "I don't want to carry you up that ramp."

"I'm awake!" I said. "Don't act like you're my mother."

"Remember, you're not supposed to argue with me," she said.

Annoyed, I turned to Kwon. "I hope we can sleep on the boat. I'm sleepy."

"Me too," Kwon said, "but we might not have room to stretch our legs. It's going to be very crowded." Then, he pointed at my feet. "Look, your shoe laces are untied, Jong-ah. Do you want to fall down on that ramp?"

I wish I had ignored him.

As I reached for my shoelace, a loud voice rang through the speaker: "We are now boarding. Move forward!"

Suddenly I heard the rumble of many feet on the ground. Then, someone pushed me and I fell forward. As I struggled to rise, people walked over me with big feet. I was dizzy with fear. A hand grabbed my elbow and pulled me up, but my rescuer wasn't my sister or brother. A total stranger with a mustache said to me, "Go! Don't fall down again."

I tried to find First Sister, looking at the faces passing by, but I could only hear her muffled voice calling out, "Jong-ah, Jong-ah, over here!"

I saw her small hand waving between fast-moving heads. I tried to reach it, but too many people were crammed between us. Besides, we were being pulled away from one another. Her hand grew smaller and smaller, until all I could see were tall and big men walking toward the ramp. I turned around to find Kwon, but he wasn't there any more.

The ship honked loudly and everyone ran. There was no line of people anymore, only fleeting images of human forms and the sound of running feet. I followed them, clinging to the vague hope that my family wouldn't board the ship without me.

Two men wearing black uniforms stopped me at the foot of the ramp. "Ticket?" one of them asked. I blinked.

"Where's your ticket?" he asked, raising his voice a notch.

"My sister has it," I said in a tiny voice.

"Where's your sister?"

"I think she's on the boat!"

The ticket master rolled his eyes. "Step aside," he said, roughly grabbing my shoulder with his big, gloved hand and pulling me next to him. He then collected tickets from the people behind me and next to me, his hands moving fast like a machine.

I couldn't help but cry. Less than a minute later another loud voice resounded. "The next ship leaves at noon. The ticket booth will reopen at eleven."

"Don't leave us! We have tickets!" voices rose around and behind me, but the ticket masters turned their backs to us and climbed up the ramp. People kept yelling, only to exhaust themselves.

In the haze of bright sunlight, I saw men and women swarming on the deck of the ship ahead of me only yards away, some waving their hands, some smiling, and some wiping their eyes with their handkerchiefs. None of them looked familiar. My feet glued to the wooden floor, I didn't know what to do. My family was gone. I had never thought I could be lost in a wild place like this. Bad things had always happened to someone else, like Mia. She became an orphan some time in July because her parents had died. But my parents were alive and I had homes both in Pusan and Cheju Island. *This should never have happened to me.*

Watching the ship now pull away, with my family on it, I lifted my voice and shouted as loud as I could, "Father, Mother…" My voice cracked and I stopped.

The flag flapped loudly on the mast as if laughing at me. I called out again, "Big Sister! Big Brother! Kwon! Answer me!"

Something caught my eye. A man on the deck, whose face was partly covered by a taller man's shoulder, was waving at me, his arm making a half-circle above his head. He wore the same gray wool coat that Father had been wearing that morning, and his arm looked familiar, not too long, not too short. I didn't know exactly what he was trying to say, but somehow I understood that he wanted me to get on the next ship and not to worry.

The ship headed toward the vast horizon, making water whirl behind it. I felt as though I was looking at a crowded ship in a picture book. It finally hit me that bad things could happen to me too, like people in a storybook.

I must have been sobbing, because I felt a hand on my shoulder and heard a woman's voice saying, "Don't cry! You'll be okay." I turned to find a sympathetic face looking at me. She wore a long cashmere coat, similar to my mother's, and the fine wrinkles around her almond eyes told me she wouldn't harm me.

"We can take the next ship together, child, no big deal," she said, trying to smile. "A lot of people didn't get on that boat. You're not alone. It happens all the time."

Her words didn't cheer or comfort me. Even if I got on the next ship, how would I find my parents in a strange place? I knew we had a home by the seashore, but now I couldn't remember the address, only that it was on Pearl Bay. I kept sobbing as if crying would somehow bring back my family.

The woman took a white handkerchief from her coat pocket and dried my tears. "Come, come, it's not the end of the world," she said as if reciting a poem. "I'll help you. What's your name?"

I turned around so she could read my name and address written on my backpack.

"Suh Jong-ah. What a pretty name!" She exaggerated her smile. "Do you have a ticket for the next ship?" she asked.

I shook my head.

"Don't worry, I have an extra ticket you can use."

"You do?" I said, not believing I could be that lucky.

"Yes. I travel to Pusan every week to collect lost children like you. Sometimes they give me too many tickets and other times not enough. This time, the police officer told me he'd have twenty-two children in his custody, but when I got there, one of them had ran away and another had died, so I have some extras."

Does she think I'm an orphan? I wondered. "My parents are on that boat," I said, hiccupping between my sobs. "They'll be waiting for me at Pearl Bay near Cheju City."

"That's good," she said. "You're lost only temporarily, then."

"Yes."

"Is someone at your home here in Pusan? I'm sure I can find someone to take you there, if you want."

I shook my head. Grandparents were too old to take care of me, and I didn't trust the Sisters, especially Mother Superior. *Didn't she say she was looking at "three future sisters" when she saw me and my sisters for the first time?* I shivered.

"I want to be with my parents in Cheju," I said.

"Do you know your address there?"

"No."

"At least you know your address in Pusan," she said, patting the back of my backpack.

I sniffled.

CHAPTER 11

▼

GIRL FROM PYONG-YANG

"I see children like you every day," she said as we walked toward a group of children sitting against a wooden fence, warming themselves in the wan sunlight. "Even if you don't find your parents right away it's not the end of the world. There're a lot of people who'd like to help a little girl like you. The world is full of loving people."

If what she said was true, why were we at war? I wondered. Why were so many people dying everyday? It didn't make sense.

The kids began shouting, "Teacher Hwang! Teacher Hwang!" waving their hands. The woman walked faster. Many of the children looked sick: some coughed heavily, honking like geese, and others didn't seem to have any energy, their eyes opening and closing. *I don't belong here,* I told myself, remembering our spacious home in Pusan.

Two women, one middle-aged and one about twenty-five, both wearing black wool coats and matching scarves, stood in the middle of the children, touching the children's heads and asking questions.

Teacher Hwang planted me in front of the kids.

"Boys and girls," she said, "we have a new friend with us this morning. Her name is Suh, Jong-ah. Please say hello!"

"*Anyong,*" they barely mumbled, without even looking at me.

"Be kind to her, okay?" she continued. "She's like you. She lost her family and is going to Cheju with us. Those of you younger than her must call her *onni,* and the younger boys should address her as *noona*. Let's welcome our new friend with applause."

A feeble applause followed, then died down.

I stood there, not knowing what to do. I looked at the woman, Teacher Hwang.

"You may sit down, Jong-ah," she said, leading me to an empty spot in the first row.

Teacher Hwang now spoke to the women in black, and I felt abandoned. *No one knows me here,* I thought to myself. *Where's everybody?* New tears were gathering in my eyes.

A small hand touched my coat sleeve. When I found the owner of the hand on my left, she smiled. "It's so soft and pretty," she admired in a northern accent. She had short hair and wore a dirty old burgundy coat with matching scarf. She reminded me of Yoja, my best friend in Pusan, except that this girl's eyes were larger and prettier. "Is it from America?" she asked.

I pulled my sleeve away, shaking my head. *It's just a hand-me-down coat,* I thought. I wasn't in the mood to talk to anyone.

"How old are you?" she asked again as if she felt sorry for me. I wanted to tell her it was none of her business, but I didn't want to hurt her feelings.

"I'll be ten in February," I said, feeling a sudden loneliness. I had forgotten about my birthday, which my family would have to celebrate without me this year.

The girl smiled. "I'm your *Onni* then," she said, squinting her eyes shyly. "I'm twelve!"

What's the big deal about being older than me? I thought. *Why does everyone ask, "How old are you" whenever he or she meets someone?*

I was about to tell her that she didn't look her age, when she unexpectedly said, "Let's be make-believe sisters!"

"Huh?"

"You be my little sister and I'll be your *Onni*! What do you think?"

I felt strange to call a stranger *onni*—Big Sister. I already had two older sisters and I didn't even know where they were. Why did I need a make-believe sister?

"You don't know me at all."

"Yes, I do! Your name is Jong-ah and you're from Pusan. You got lost and you're going with us to the orphanage on Cheju Island. On second thought...if you don't want to be my sister, that's okay." She looked away.

I was curious about her. Also, I didn't know such things as "make-believe sisters" existed in the North. *Do they link their pinkies together when they make their vow, like we do here? If not, what do they do?*

"Sure, why not!" I said, lifting my pinky.

She smiled. Her face reddening a little, she wrapped her own pinky around mine, shook it up and down three times, and said, "I, Bokja, take you as my little sister and honor and cherish our sistership as long as I live."

"It's such a long speech," I said.

"It's not bad," she said and shrugged.

"But that's not how we do it here," I said.

"How do you do it?"

"We link our pinkies together, too, but we just say, 'We are sisters forever, Amen.' That's all!"

"I like it," she said. "That's a good one! It's done anyway."

"It's done?"

"Yes, you're my little sister now!"

For some weird reason, I felt close to this girl I'd just met. It wasn't such a bad idea after all, I thought, when I was lost in this strange place.

Lunch boxes were delivered, and we each got a rice roll the size of my fist covered with sesame seeds. But I had no appetite. The more I saw the dirty and sickly-looking kids around me, the quicker my appetite vanished and I just stared at the rice roll in my gloved palm. I had a sudden urge to throw it across the dock, crying, "I want to go home! I want my family!" but it was only a wild thought in my head. No matter how loudly I cried, my family wouldn't come to rescue me, and actually, I was tired. I wished I could take a nap.

"Why aren't you eating, Jong-ah?" Teacher Hwang asked me, her hand on my shoulder.

"I'm not hungry."

A dirty hand flew in and snatched the rice roll from my hand. I was stunned.

It was the boy sitting on my right. He giggled, making a funny sound through his full mouth. He had scabs all over his shaven head and his neck was black.

Teacher clicked her tongue and said, "Young-soo ya, you're as fast as a hawk snatching a chicken. Next time you should ask before you take it, okay?"

"She said she didn't want it!" the boy said, showing food in his mouth. I felt like throwing up.

"You still have to ask, Young-soo!" said Teacher Hwang firmly.

Bokja whispered to me, "I'll smack him if he steals from you again."

I said nothing. I didn't even want to think about food.

Another boat pulled into the dock within minutes, blowing its horn, and we got up. It was an older, smelly boat, but it wasn't as large as the earlier one. We formed a single-file line, pushing and shoving one another, and marched toward the ramp.

The same ticket master didn't even count the tickets when Teacher Hwang handed him the yellow stack. He just motioned us to move forward, blowing his whistle. We climbed the ramp, then walked down some stairs, and entered a large room filled with cigarette smoke. The stench of alcohol and garbage was strong. Men and women sat on the straw-mat floor, cross-legged and reading or leaning against their large bundles. A few toddlers with big bellies napped on the floor, their mouths wide-open, inviting flies.

I moved to a foggy window and Bokja sat next to me. Some kids sat across the aisle and some behind us.

Whistling sharply, the boat began to chug and I heard water hitting the sides of the ship. I wiped the window with my sleeve to look out. Waves next to my window danced, making white bubbles at the top. Seagulls glided in the air, flapping their wings gracefully, and some birds larger than seagulls kept dropping onto the water, trying to catch fish.

How happy and carefree they seemed. I wondered if they had their families somewhere. *Do they get lost too?*

Bokja asked me if this was my first time on a boat.

I told her our family once took a day trip for fishing on a small island. "And you?"

"This is my first time," she said. "I've never seen the ocean before today. It's so big!"

"You must be a refugee."

"Yes, I'm from Pyongyang."

This is big news. None of my friends would believe me when I told them I sat with a girl from Pyongyang, the capital city of the North. And we're make-believe sisters!

"Are you a communist?" I asked cautiously.

Bokja laughed, showing her dimples. "Do I look like one?"

"I don't know."

"Relax," she said, touching my elbow. "I hate the communists. When I'm older, I swear I'll fight against them."

"Why?"

"Because…the communists killed many people, including my parents. I have no one, because of them."

"I'm sorry, Bokja *Onni.* I...I didn't know."

"That's okay," she said, looking at her hands. "It happened a long time ago, and a lot of people were murdered. The communists always kill. If not, they take people somewhere and you never see them again. Everybody I know has some stories to tell."

"How did you get here, Bokja *Onni*? Who brought you to Pusan?"

"American pilots. They brought a lot of orphans from Pyongyang."

"Are you serious?" I asked enviously. "You mean, you flew in an airplane?"

"Of course I'm serious. Don't you know the Americans took over Pyongyang in October and moved on north? They went almost to the Manchurian border before the Chinese came down. That's when the Americans began to pull away from Pyongyang and my grandmother came up with an idea to get rid of me."

"What? How awful!"

"It *was* awful, Jong-ah. I had no clue what was going on that morning when she woke me and ordered me to dress warm. We had heavy snow that day. 'Where are we going?' I asked and she said, 'You'll find out.' She never acted that way to me before, you know, cold and distant, but she didn't explain anything to me. I just followed her. We walked for a long time in the snow and came to a large field. I didn't realize we were walking onto an American airstrip. The wind was blowing so hard, lifting the snow into the air, that I didn't see the airplanes parked at the far end.

"Grandmother just walked up to an American soldier drinking coffee or tea, standing next to a tent, and began bowing, blabbering in Korean. Can you imagine how embarrassed I was? She knew the soldier didn't understand a word of Korean but didn't care. 'Sir, please take my granddaughter with you and drop her somewhere in the South. I beg you,' she said.

"'Grandmother, let's go back!' I said, almost crying. Of course she paid no attention to me. She was crying too, blowing her nose into her handkerchief. I'm sure the pilots thought she was a crazy old woman, but amazingly enough, the soldier motioned her to wait. He went into the next tent and came out with another soldier much older than he. The two men talked for a brief moment in English, glancing at us once or twice. Stepping forward, the older soldier asked Grandmother in Korean, 'How may I help you, Lady?'

"Grandmother cried louder and acted as if she were seeing God. Bowing deeply, her head almost touching the snow, she said, 'Sir, please be kind and take my granddaughter to the South. I'm too old and have no money to take care of her. When I die, she'll have no one here! Please sir...' The older man seemed to be translating to the other soldier. Then Grandmother did something even worse."

"What did she do?"

"She pushed me toward them, and said to me, talking fast, 'You must go with them, Bokja! Forget about Grandpa and me. Don't even think about us, hear?' Can you imagine?"

"That's awful!"

"I clung to her arm. 'Grandma, please don't leave me here,' I begged. 'You and Grandpa need me. I'll do anything, but don't leave me here. I'm scared.'

"But she didn't flinch. Bowing to the soldiers once more, she pushed my hand off her and began walking toward where we had entered. I followed her, crying, and she turned and slapped me. 'Go, I said,' she yelled. 'Don't follow me!'"

Bokja was crying now, covering her face. I wanted to say how sorry I was, but couldn't. I was miserable, too.

I left her alone and she stopped crying. Lifting her face and wiping her tears, she said, "Actually, she did the right thing, know what I mean? How can I live in the North when they're gone? What she really wanted to tell the Americans was to take me with them to America, but she didn't know how to say it. Before Kim Il Sung became the Chairman, we had many western churches and missionaries preaching in Pyong-Yang, just like here now. My grandmother knew nothing about western religions, of course, but she figured out that the Christians were more loving to one another than the communists would ever be. So she decided to send me to America before she died. Finally she saw a chance and she handed me over to the Americans, total strangers."

"I'm glad you're here, Bokja *Onni,*" I said.

CHAPTER 12

▼

ORPHANAGE

"Dear passengers, this is Captain Choi," a loud voice came through the speakers mounted on the ceiling. "Thank you for being with us today. I hope you had a pleasant journey. Within ten minutes we'll land in Cheju City, so please gather your belongings and remain seated until the door is opened. The weather in Cheju City is mild but windy."

Cheju City! Father and Mother will be waiting for me, I thought, feeling goose-bumps on my arms. My backpack was next to my feet, where I had left it earlier, reminding me of the morning we had left home. It seemed like ages since I had been with my family, but it was only hours. Father had warned us not to get lost, but here I was, lost. *It wasn't my fault, Father,* I wanted to say when I'd see him again. *It just happened. There was nothing I could do.* The whole scene at the dock flashed back, and I was helpless and sad again.

Bokja was wide-awake, her eyes glued to the dark window. I wondered what she was thinking. She seemed far away, maybe at the airstrip in Pyong-Yang where she had seen her grandmother for the last time.

"Bokja *Onni,*" I said, nudging her elbow. "Can we ask the director to put us in the same room?"

"Let's do," she said, moving closer and grabbing my hand. "I'm sure she'll say yes." She smiled, and I told her she reminded me of my best friend Yoja. "You'll like her, Bokja *Onni,*" I said.

"Do you think she'll like me?"

"Of course. She likes everyone I like."

"That's good," she said.

After a long moment of listening to the waves rolling and hissing beneath us, we climbed up the stairs and descended onto the dock. The wind whistled sharply, and without warning, it took my hat with it. "My hat, my hat!" I cried out, but it was too late. Mingling with dried leaves and torn newspapers for a brief moment, it disappeared into the dark sky. Another girl lost her hat, too. She must have been one of the sick kids, because she honked as she wailed and coughed at the same time.

I wasn't sad at all about losing my hat, only surprised. It was a hand-me-down and I had another at home. I couldn't worry about anything other than the fact that my parents and my sister and brothers would be waiting for me somewhere in the building. I didn't know what to say to them when I finally saw them.

The lobby was crowded. Holding Bokja's hand tightly, I followed the other kids, frantically looking for familiar faces in the crowd, my head turning in all directions. A sea of people was there, but none of them looked familiar. Not a single voice called out my name either. All my energy drained out of me and my legs felt weak.

I must have let go of Bokja's hand, because she said, "Hold my hand and keep moving. We don't want to lose the others."

This angered me and I stopped walking. "I'm not going anywhere until I find my family," I said. "They're here somewhere. I just have to find them."

One of the two women, the younger one, must have heard me. She came over, grabbed my arm, and forced me to walk with her. "Don't do this, little girl!" she said, clamping my hand with her own. "We don't want to lose you!"

I tried to unclamp her hand pressing my elbow like a vise, but I couldn't. "Let go of me," I shouted, pinching her hand with my free hand, but she didn't. Pushing me abruptly to the end of the line, still holding me tight, she said to the other women, "Let's go!"

The line moved, and we were now marching toward a tall, wide glass door. I was scared. *If I walk out of that door I will never find my family*, I thought. While the woman talked to the other kids, I saw my chance. Quickly twisting and pulling my hand out of hers, I ran in the opposite direction. She followed me, yelling something I couldn't understand. I couldn't let her catch me, so I turned to my right and ran faster. She didn't give up. Through the corner of my eye, I could see the hem of her black coat dancing behind me as she followed. Something grabbed my shoulders and I jumped.

It was Teacher Hwang. "Don't run! You don't need to run like this," she said without raising her voice.

I suddenly found myself in her arms, crying. Her coat smelled like mothballs, and I cried harder. Mother's coat had the same smell, and I missed her even more. As I kept crying, she said, "Jong-ah, listen to me. If you didn't see them here, that means they're somewhere else. It doesn't do you any good waiting for someone who can't come and get you. Let's go home and find out what happened to them."

Home? Whose home is she talking about?

"They're here," I said, wiping my tears. "I know they are, because their boat left before ours did. Where else can they be?"

"All right," Teacher Hwang said. "Don't cry. Let's find out for sure." Turning to the younger woman who had been chasing me, she said, "We'll be back. Don't let the children wander away."

At the information booth, a young slender woman with heavy makeup was talking on the phone, and an old couple was waiting in front of us. She kept talking, and I wanted to scream at her to stop. I had never realized that waiting could be such torture.

I let my eyes wander, trying to calm my nerves. Posters hung everywhere: above the booth, on each side of the booth, and on the walls, each showing a large boat. On one poster, a smiling man and woman in swimsuits were sitting on a deck, holding a sign that said, "COME WITH US TO PARADISE ISLAND." I wondered where Paradise Island might be. *In the South Sea or the Yellow Sea?*

Finally the young woman dropped the receiver on the phone, and the couple moved forward. After talking with the old man briefly, she turned to us. "May I help you?" she asked.

Teacher Hwang asked her about my family, telling her the whole story. "We want to know if the ship got here okay."

The young woman's next words terrified me. "One of the ships that left Pusan this morning had some mechanical problems and landed somewhere for repairs."

"Where?"

"One of the islands, I'm sure."

"Which island? There are more than two hundred small islands between Cheju and Pusan."

"I don't know, ma'am. You might get more information about it tomorrow at the main port," the young woman said, anxious to shoo us away. "This is a privately-owned port. We only handle smaller vessels."

"At the main port?" said Teacher Hwang, showing her disappointment. "We don't have transportation."

"I don't know what to tell you, ma'am."

"Please do us a favor. Call the main port for us and find out if the passengers are safe. This little girl is very worried about her family. We'd appreciate it."

The young woman didn't seem pleased, but dialed some numbers anyway with the pencil she was holding. After talking and scratching her slender leg for a while, she hung up. "The radio system on that ship is dead, ma'am. They said they've heard nothing from the captain since early this afternoon."

"Can it be something serious?"

"I don't know, ma'am. I'm just telling you what they told me."

Another couple approached the booth, and the woman turned to them. "May I help you?"

Teacher Hwang grabbed my hand and looked at me. "We have to wait, Jong-ah!" she said. "There's nothing we can do here."

I had no energy to argue, and I merely followed her, my head full of gloomy thoughts. I knew exactly how Bokja must have felt on that airstrip watching her grandmother walk away.

I don't remember what time we got to the orphanage or what happened on that rackety bus, but I remember looking up at the half moon, shivering in the cold wind from the night's sky, thinking my family might be somewhere under that moon. I prayed, "Dear God, please don't punish me for the time I wasn't a good Catholic. I promise, Lord, I'll be better from now on." I felt better. Now for some strange reason, the moon shone brighter than earlier. If Unsook could believe that God talked to her, why should I believe differently about my prayer? I tried to focus my mind on the orphanage where we were headed, and a long forgotten memory flashed back in my mind.

Two years earlier, my mother took my sisters and me to Sacred Heart Orphanage, which belonged to our parish church. It could have been on Mother's birthday in June Full Moon Day in August, I couldn't remember. We took bags of rice cakes, apples, and candy with us. The kids sitting or lying on their sleeping mats didn't seem to be fully alive; they said nothing to us as we filed into the crowded room. They only stared at us as if we were aliens. Then suddenly, when they saw rice cakes or apples or candy, they became noisy children. They shouted, raising their bony arms into the air, "Give me, give me, give me. Please, please, please." I remember wondering what made them so hungry. How did they end up in such a horrible place called an "orphanage"? I had never imagined that one day I would end up in an orphanage, too. I had no idea what would be waiting for me when the bus stopped. One thing I knew for sure was that I'd be eating with these kids, sleeping in the same room with them, and sharing the same sickbed someday, too. I had thought I had a hard life as a middle child sandwiched between my older siblings and younger brother Kwon, but now it seemed God was eager to teach me something I didn't know.

"This is the House of Love Orphanage," Teacher Hwang suddenly announced, pointing to a dimly lit two-story house perched atop a dark hill. "When the bus stops, be careful not to slip and fall, because it's quite muddy around here. Walk slowly and carefully, and follow the person ahead of you."

I held Bokja's hand again. We got off the bus without falling and followed the kids. My canvas shoes stuck to the mud, but I managed to walk the steep hill without falling. A woman stood on the front step, holding a lamp, like an angel in a picture from Sunday School. "Be careful, children," she said in a sweet voice. "The steps are quite steep and we don't have a railing. So be very careful." The steps were wet too, and I held on to Bokja's hand even tighter.

Up close, the building was an old wooden structure that could have been a school or a government office years earlier. Even in the dim light of the lamp, the chipping paint, the cracks in the walls, and the tape on the broken windows were quite noticeable.

As soon as we were inside the door, the lamp lady gave us a short welcome speech. "We're enchanted to have you here at the House of Love. Dinner is waiting for you in the dining room, but before we go in, please take your shoes off and leave them here. We don't have enough hands to clean a thousand footprints on the floor."

We took our shoes off. My canvas shoes now looked like mud balls, and I was again reminded that I had no mother who would scold me for dirtying them.

In the dining room hung many army lamps with wire handles, their flames dancing mysteriously against the wood panels. On one wall, a large sign that said, "Welcome to the House of Love!" was written in bold letters. A low and long table decorated with cranes and flowers made of origami paper sat in the middle of the room, loaded with many pairs of bamboo chopsticks, tin plates, and tin cups filled with water.

The lamp lady clapped her hands and said, "Sit wherever you want, children, and wait until food is served."

I took off my backpack and sat next to Bokja. I was hungry and tired. Had I known I would be starving all day, I would have eaten more breakfast that morning. I had food in my backpack, but I wouldn't dare open it, for fear that everyone would want something. Unlike at lunch, I could now eat anything edible.

Bokja said, "I'm so hungry, I could eat a whole cow," she said.

I was glad that Bokja was with me. "Bokja *Onni,* what's going to happen now?" I whispered.

"Nothing bad is going to happen, Jong-ah." She seemed so mature and old. "When Grandma left me with the Yankees, I cried so much, but look at me: I'm in the South. I miss her, but I don't want to be in the North. Sometimes bad things that happen to you can turn out to be a good thing too."

The food finally came in. Two women wearing white aprons brought a large kettle on a pushcart and began serving. When we all had a bowl of soup in front of us, Teacher Hwang, standing in the middle of the room, said a mealtime prayer, her head bent and hands folded. "Dear Lord, please bless this meal we are about to receive and help our children understand your love and compassion for each of them. Thank you, Lord, for our safe trip from Pusan, too, and help one of our children, Jong-ah, to find her family soon." Everyone responded with a loud "Amen," but I sat mute. *Teacher Hwang prayed especially for me!* I was so moved I forgot to eat, but Bokja nudged me.

For a while, there was no other noise than spoons clattering against tin soup bowls. It was tasty, I thought, and wolfed it down. I could have eaten more, but I hadn't the courage to ask. A girl my age with a ponytail complained that a fly had fallen into her soup bowl. One of the women said, "Take it out, and eat it! Just because a fly jumped into your soup doesn't mean it's bad to eat. People are starving to death!" But the girl didn't touch it. The soup bowls were quickly collected and taken away on the same noisy pushcart. I felt sorry for the girl who had a fly in her soup bowl. I didn't think I could eat the soup either.

The lamp lady took us girls upstairs while the boys remained on the first floor. It was much colder upstairs. As we followed her into the corridor, I noticed that two windows had been covered with cardboard, letting in the cold outside air.

Our room was as large as the dining room downstairs. In one corner sat a stack of sleeping mats and military blankets; a bookcase loaded with old books stood in another corner; and next to it was a low table made of bare wood, cluttered with boxes of pencils, crayons, papers, and other school supplies. We heard children coughing and crying from the next room and I wondered how sick they were. I didn't want to catch cold. Luckily, heavy, dusty curtains covered every window I could see.

The lamp lady distributed a military blanket, a matching sleeping mat, and a pillow to each of us and told us to sleep anywhere in the room. "The wake-up bell will buzz at seven in the morning, girls. The washrooms are at both ends of the hallway, and the latrine is behind the building. Make sure you stand in line and wait for your turn. Don't fight! Fighting is prohibited here."

I heard girls giggling, but the lamp lady paid no attention to them and went on. "Breakfast will be served at eight in the morning in the same room where we ate dinner, and afterwards, you'll be assigned to your permanent rooms. Have a good night's rest and I'll see all of you in the morning." Before leaving the room, she told a heavily built girl about fourteen to turn the light off before she went to bed.

The room suddenly became noisy. Someone said, "Shut up, girls," and another answered, "You shut up!"

Bokja and I took our bedding to a wall and spread it on the floor. I made sure that my pillow was against the wall so that no one would walk over my head. Letting someone walk over your head was never a good idea, Mother taught me. "Your head is the most important part of your body," she had said, "and you should never let a foot be near it. Always find the safest place to lay your head, if you can help it."

I took out my own blanket from my backpack, which Mother had packed for me, and laid it under the military blanket the lamp lady had given me. I crawled onto my sleeping mat with my coat still on. The smell of home, of my family, enclosed me. *Mother, Father, everyone, where are you?* my mind called out. *I'm here with the orphans and I don't even know where you are.* My tears flowed freely.

I heard the light switch click off and listened. Other than some sniffling from the other side of the room, it was quiet.

I pushed my blanket away. A sliver of moonlight squeezed through a gap in the heavy curtain, making a long silvery line on the floor next to my mat. I stretched out my hand to let the moonlight soak through. I felt no warmth and my hand was ghostly white. Still, the moonlight comforted me. I remembered a poem about the moon that we learned in school.

> Glowing brightly in the night sky
> You're my most sincere friend
> You know what's hidden in my heart
> And I can never hide it from you.

If a Moon Goddess existed in the galaxy, like the Japanese believed, shouldn't I pray to her, too? I thought. "Dear Moon Goddess, please let my family know where I am. Tell them I miss them...."

I missed Kwon the most. Although he was rude and impossible to deal with sometimes, we had a special bond between us. We couldn't stand one another but couldn't be apart for very long, either. When he didn't return from school at his regular time, I would look for him and he did the same for me. We played "Joker" with American playing cards for hours, until one of us thought the other was cheating. I wondered where he was and what he was doing now.

I wished I hadn't complained to Mother about him so many times for not calling me *noona,* Big Sister. It bothered me now. Once, he and I had been listening to a man talking about Americans on the radio. He said that most of the Americans were God-loving people and that they respected one another in a way that we Koreans never could. "Most of them are true Christians," he said. "They know what love and respect toward fellow humans means."

Kwon was listening, so I said, "Hear that, Kwon? You have no idea what *respect* means, do you? I'm older than you and you know it, but you don't even call me *noona!* None of my friends would put up with a younger brother like you."

He laughed in my face. "That's the stupidest thing I've ever heard," he said. "Calling your older siblings Big this or Big that really stinks! You just happened to have been born a year earlier than me, that's all! Do you want a trophy for something that just happened? American people don't call their older siblings Big this or Big that, but they still *respect* one another. Forget it, Jong-ah. I'll never call you *noona!*"

He was right, I thought. It took me all this distance and time to realize that I had been stupid. *If I see him again,* I said to myself, *the first thing I'll tell him is, "Kwon, you don't have to call me 'noona' as long as you live."*

CHAPTER 13

▼

ISLAND OF THREE MANYS

I dreamed of home that night. We were all sitting in the front room with Father and Mother, each munching a rice cake and drinking barley tea and chatting, while Baby Brother played with his wooden blocks.

Father suddenly said to me, "Jong-ah, can you sing a song for us? I want to hear you sing. Sing the one that goes *Bells are tolling in the temple*. I love that song."

"Yobo, she's eating," Mother said.

"She's almost done," Father said, looking at my plate. "It's been a long time since I heard you sing that song."

Once in a while after dinner, we had a talent show. Father himself had sung many times. But compared to Second Sister who had a pretty voice, we were merely quacking ducks, including myself. When Second Sister sang, her eyes fixed somewhere on the ceiling, you would think of a canary trilling from a branch. But now, Father was asking me to sing the song I learned from the radio.

As I hesitated, hands clapped, so I wiped my mouth on my sleeve and rose. Locking my hands in front of me, I began:

> Bells are tolling in the temple.
> The monks snooze but not the guest.
> Pray, troubled soul, pray!
> 'Till your wishes come true.

"Yobo, doesn't she sing so lovely tonight?" Father said, almost sadly. "She sings with feeling." He then sang the last line, "'Till your wishes come true...'"

A metallic buzz in the hallway woke me, tearing me from my family and home. Everything disappeared——Father, Mother, my sisters and brothers, my house. A voice yelled in my ear, "Time to get up and be ready for breakfast."

I wanted to scream, "Please someone, take me home! I'm not an orphan," but instead, tears rushed to my eyes again and dampened my pillow.

A rough hand yanked my blanket. The heavyset girl was looking down at me. "Didn't you hear it?" she said. She had big nostrils like those of a horse.

I only stared.

"I'm talking to you! Did you hear the wake-up call or not?"

Bokja came to my aid. "We did," she said. "Who wouldn't? It's so loud I thought it was an earthquake alarm. Let's go, Jong-ah," she said to me. "Everyone is up." She helped me get up and fold my blanket and sleeping mat. Hers were already folded and leaning against the wall, so I put mine on top of hers. Seeing my backpack sitting next to the pile, Bokja picked it up and placed it between the folds of my blanket. "The kids might steal it," she whispered.

At the latrine behind the orphanage a long line of girls, some taller and some shorter than me, stood shivering, and Bokja and I joined them. Faraway, puffs of black smoke rose from tall chimneys. In the opposite direction, I saw a few army trucks crawling toward the port where we had come from the night before, each dragging a cloud of dust behind it. A dozen or more cows grazed along the dirt road below us, ringing bells. I wondered if the road would join the curvy shoreline at the far left where the sun was rising.

The ginkgo trees surrounding the building were shedding leaves, the same ones we'd had in our courtyard. My sister and I had often collected those fan-shaped yellow leaves and kept them between our book pages until they were too brittle to keep. Sometimes we glued them on white rice paper and used it as the background for a snapshot of a movie star, which we hung on the wall.

I must have let out a sigh because Bokja put her hand on my shoulder, whispering, "Don't worry. You'll see your family very soon."

A girl behind us mimicked Bokja's voice and said, "My darling, I'll be your mama."

Bokja paid no attention to her, as if she didn't hear her. I turned around and flashed my eyes at a tall girl with a long, freckled face.

"What's the matter, baby?" she asked, obviously making an effort to ridicule me in front of other kids.

"Stop being stupid," I said. The kids laughed, gathering around her.

"You want your mama, baby? Here, drink my milk!" Pulling her sweater out of her pants, she acted as though she was about to lift her gray sweater up to feed me. The kids laughed harder.

I thought about throwing my fist into her face for a moment, but I had no courage. I didn't know anyone here, except Bokja. What if the girl beat me? I was glad when Bokja tightened her hand on my shoulder and whispered, "Don't bother, Jong-ah. It's not worth it. Besides, we shouldn't fight."

She was right. I almost heard Mother's voice whispering, "It takes courage to walk away from a troublemaker. Would you step on feces because the smell bothered you?"

I clamped my mouth shut, acting as if I were deaf.

The tall girl laughed and snickered, calling me "stupid dwarf" but I was able to ignore her.

Inside the latrine, I gagged. It was a large pool of feces, and around the edge, several girls sat emptying themselves. The stench was intolerable. As I hesitated, the same girl behind me shouted in my ear, "Hurry up, dwarf. We don't have all day!" I didn't expect a spotless bathroom, but this was beyond anything I had seen in my life. I was glad when I found myself back outside and breathing fresh air again.

The washroom on our floor was no better. I had no pan of water to myself. A woman poured a dipperful into a pan, saying, "Girls, don't waste water, please. Only use what you need to wash your faces. Water is gold here. We have to walk a half hour each way to bring a bucketful."

The water was cold. At home, we always had plenty of water, and on a cold morning like this, our cook boiled it in a large cast iron kettle and brought it to the well area for everyone to use. But what good was there in remembering such a luxury when I only had a meager portion of cold water to share with several other girls?

I brushed my teeth with some salt from a ceramic bowl on the wooden table. I then scooped a handful of water from the pan and scrubbed my face. I skipped my neck because it was so cold and I didn't want to freeze to death before I found my family. And Mother wasn't there to scold me, either.

Besides what I had gone through in the latrine and washroom, another ordeal awaited me after breakfast——a vaccination shot for whooping cough. When the dining room was cleared, Teacher Hwang explained to us that whooping cough was spreading in the orphanage very quickly and that every newcomer must stand in line to be vaccinated.

The doctor, an old man with leathery skin and holding a syringe in his hand, wasn't sympathetic at all when I told him I had been vaccinated in the beginning of the school year.

"It couldn't have been for whooping cough."

"My aunt is a doctor," I said, desperately hoping he'd change his mind about giving me a shot.

He laughed soundlessly, but the next moment he plunged his needle in my upper arm, without even cleaning it with alcohol. When I looked at him resentfully through my tear-filled eyes, he chuckled and said, "Sorry, little one. I really don't like what I'm doing sometimes, but I'm a doctor."

Coming out of the room, I stood in a corner and let the tears flow. It wasn't the pain that made me miserable, but all the reminders that I was an orphan here. *An orphan has no protection against danger,* I said to myself. *She has no voice, either. No one believes her and no one feels for her. If Mother had been with me, she probably would have spared me this ordeal, telling the doctor the same thing I did.*

I couldn't be sorry for myself for very long. The lamp lady gathered the newcomers, including Bokja and me, and took us for a tour of the building. The kitchen was across the hallway from the dining room and was large enough to be a classroom—one side being a cooking kitchen with aluminum pots, a sink, and stove, and on the opposite side a washing kitchen where linens and baby diapers were being sterilized in a large cast iron pot. Through the glass panel on the door, I saw women's skirts and blouses, children's clothes, and diapers flapping on a clothesline in the bright sunlight. The room next to the kitchen was a nursery with four big beds: I counted six infants in one of the beds and five in another, all under about six-months old. The rest of the children were older, but not older than a year.

In the Recreation Room at the end of the lengthy hallway, an old organ with missing keys sat in the middle, and in each corner lay a stack of old sheet-music or torn picture books or a basket full of broken musical toys.

The basement was spacious but dimly lit by a bare light bulb hanging from the ceiling. The floor was cluttered with broken furniture and countless cardboard boxes filled with school supplies or canned food. In one corner was a door that had a padlock on it.

"What's this," a girl asked.

"That's the coal-storage room," the lamp lady replied. "But once in a while we use it as the detention camp for unruly kids. When you fight, we lock you up here. When you steal something, we lock you up too. We don't like troublemakers here."

Thank you, Bokja, I thought. *I could have ended up there if I had fought with the tall girl.*

During recess, Bokja and I sat on a bench in the playground surrounded by barbed wire, merely watching the boys playing basketball. We were tired and confused. As if trying to cheer me up, she said, "It's strange that I feel I've been here for a long time, but we only got here yesterday."

I felt that way too, for some strange reason, but I didn't tell her that.

"It was the same in the refugee center in Pusan. I hated that place when I got there—kids screaming and their parents trying to stop them, only making things worse. But when they told me they were sending me to an orphanage I was furious. It was the only place I knew in the South, and I couldn't stay there anymore."

I missed home so much. I even missed Yong-ja, who always ate in the kitchen. Now, she seemed luckier than me. *She'll never believe me when I tell her about this place.*

The bell suddenly buzzed, announcing it was time to go inside, and we rose and followed the big girls. We were assigned to our permanent rooms: Bokja, a dozen others, and I were in the Azalea room, two doors down from the room we had slept in the night before, and the older ones moved to the room at the end of the hallway.

The middle-aged woman who had accompanied us to Cheju Island from Pusan, was our room mother, and she told us to call her "Mother." She looked older than I had thought earlier. She could easily be our grandmother, I thought.

"For those who're new here," she began, "Cheju Island has a nickname. Do you know what it is?"

A girl in the middle of the first row raised her hand.

"Yes, Young-Sook," said the room mother.

"It's called *Sam-da-do,* 'Island of Three Manys,'"

"What are the three Manys?"

"Many winds, many women, and many rocks."

"Very good, Young-Sook," the room mother said. "Besides having many rocks and many winds, Cheju Island is mostly known for having many women. Women do everything here: farming, fishing, and harvesting sea produce, while their husbands stay home and take care of their young. It has been that way for hundreds of years. I also want you to know something about the orphanages here on the island. There are eight orphanages in this town and we are the newest. A generous American pilot single-handedly rescued lost children from Pyongyang, Shinuiju, and other North Korean towns and brought them to Seoul. But since

Seoul was evacuated last January, he moved them here to Cheju City. Thanks to him and his pilot friends, we have about two thousand children scattered in the city.

"Now we have some business to discuss. As some of you might know, we're terribly understaffed and undersupplied here at the orphanage. The Americans send us whatever they can, but it's never enough. We can use some helping hands. Some of you will go with the boys to the well twice a day, morning and evening, to fetch water and fill up the barrels in the bathrooms and kitchen. Some of you will go to the flourmills and do whatever they ask you to do and bring a bag or two of flour at the end of the day. In the cooking and washing kitchen, they always need extra hands because there are hundreds of diapers and clothes to be washed and folded everyday."

Bokja was assigned to the nursery to take care of the sick babies; some girls went to work in the kitchen or to go to the well to bring water, but I chose to go with Sookhi, a skinny girl of twelve or thirteen. She said that collecting driftwood and coal from the vacant lot was easy and fun. I had never liked crying babies: I didn't know what to do with them when they kept crying. Dirtying my hands was never a problem for me.

"Make sure to take a bucket with you," the room mother said as she handed each of us a tin pail when we left.

Sookhi and I spent all afternoon together walking around in the back and poking the mounds of dirt and debris with sticks. The wind was chilly, but Sookhi had no coat on. Wearing an over-sized green sweater over her khaki pants, she looked like a boy. She had a brown scar on the left side of her face, and every time she smiled, her mouth became crooked and her left eye seemed to be squinting in the frail sunlight. She had rough hands too, as rough as the bark of a tree. But she knew everything about digging up coal.

"Poke the dirt with a stick, like this," she said, showing me with her own stick. "When you feel something hard at the end of it, go a bit deeper and then flip the stick. Coals come out every time."

I found a stick with a pointy end and did everything Sookhi showed me. When she poked, I poked, and when she drilled the stick into the dirt, I did the same. Soon we had several broken coal pieces the size of chestnuts between us. "See?" she said, picking up a round coal and lifting it so that I could see it. "A bucketful of these coals can burn for two or three hours in the stove," she said. She looked as smart and shrewd as the coal vendors at the market.

When we couldn't find anymore chunks of coal we moved to another spot and dug for more.

By the time our buckets were full we were tired. "Let's rest," Sookhi suggested. She sat on a tree stump, ordering me to sit next to her, which I did. She then produced a box of cigarettes and a box of matches from her khaki pants, lit the cigarette, and smoked. I was stunned. I had never seen a girl smoke. In my family, only Father smoked. Once I had noticed Second Brother coming out of the storage room, his breath reeking of tobacco, but I had never seen him actually smoke. Kwon had tried with a piece of rolled rice paper, but I couldn't call it smoking.

Sookhi skillfully puffed away, sometimes blowing out two streams of smoke through her nose.

"Why do you smoke?" I couldn't help but ask.

"It's good for you when you have worms in your intestines," she said. "I used to have cramps, but not anymore. I think the smoke kills the worms. Do you want to try it?"

I shook my head. "Smoke gives me a headache."

"You get used to it. I didn't like it at first, but now I can't live without it. It makes things a bit more interesting, you know what I mean?"

"What do you mean?"

"When you smoke, it doesn't seem so bad about where you are or what you are doing everyday. I used to hate this place. I wanted to beat every girl I saw and make her nose bleed, but I don't anymore. I don't need to. Smoking really helps."

I just stared at her, amazed. She seemed alien to me, and yet she seemed to know so much about everything.

"I'll give you some helpful hints, kid," she said and spat out something I couldn't see. "Try not to fight with girls older than you. They can really beat you up. Look at me: an older girl did this to me with a spoon last year." She turned to me, so I could see her scar.

"Who?"

"She's not here any more. They sent her away."

I thought about the tall girl again. I wondered if she would beat me if she saw me alone.

"When you get in a fight, they lock you up in that coal storeroom, as the woman said this morning. I was locked in there a dozen times or more, breathing that nasty coal powder all day. It's not worth fighting."

"I won't fight."

"Have you signed up for an adoption?" Sookhi asked me, dropping the cigarette butt onto the dirt and stepping on it.

"Adoption?"

"Yeah. You know what adoption is, right?"

"Of course."

"Once in a while Americans come to the orphanage and pick the kids they want to take with them to America. Last weekend, a missionary couple came and took nine children with them, all younger than me, and the weekend before, a famous author who wrote about China took two-dozen kids with her. You better sign up. If you don't, you'll never be adopted."

"I have a family."

"Oh, you do, huh?" she said. "Where are they?"

"I lost them on the way here. They're on some island somewhere, because their boat had mechanical problems."

She snorted in my face. "When you don't live with your family, you don't have a family, it's as simple as that. Everyone here says, 'My family is in the North' or 'Mine is in Japan,' but what they're really saying is that they have no one. That's why we're in this place. It's an orphanage. Get it?"

For a moment, I hated her. But I was curious about her, too. "What happened to your parents? How did you end up here?"

The girl's expression darkened. "I have no parents. I've never had anyone who called me 'daughter' so I was born without a parent. It's a miracle, isn't it?" She laughed obnoxiously.

"No one can be born without parents."

"Who cares whether I had them or what happened to them when I'm here in this stinking place? I want to be adopted by a rich American couple and live in a big house, you know, like the American kids in movies, swimming in a big clean pool in summer and ice-skating on a huge ice-skating rink. Anything is better than being stuck at this orphanage. If I were you, kid, I would sign up immediately for adoption."

"Don't worry about me."

CHAPTER 14

▼

WHAT TOOK YOU SO LONG, FATHER?

My mind kept playing tricks on me. I heard the voices of my family in the wind and sometimes saw images that weren't real. On the fifth day, a windy day, it got much worse. Sookhi and I were again at that vacant lot, digging coal, and around eleven, I heard Father coughing behind me, just as he used to do early in the morning. My head turned automatically to find him, but there was no one, only dried leaves and torn papers swirling on the ground and then rising into the air. I felt goosebumps on my arms.

"What's the matter?" Sookhi asked, and I told her that I had heard my father coughing.

"It's the wind," she said. "It's loud and spooky, isn't it? On a day like this, you should go to the beach and drown your ears in the sound of the waves. When you come back, the wind won't bother you any more."

It didn't make sense, but I had no reason to argue with her. As I kept digging, the sound came back. It was the same cough, but this time, I knew better than to turn around.

After lunch, I had a vision. I was sitting idly on a wooden bench with other girls, merely listening to their food-talk. A girl my age who had a red polka dot ribbon on her crown said that she wished she could eat some sweet potatoes just out of the oven, and another girl, a bit smaller with a missing front tooth, said that she kept craving roasted chestnuts.

I saw Kwon's kite, the one with a red dragon on it, dancing gracefully in the sky. My brother stood in the middle of the playground, the large spool in his hand. Before I knew what I was doing, I was on my feet, calling, "Kwon!"

He disappeared, along with his kite. I kept calling, "Kwon! Kwon!" to bring him back. The girls must have thought I had gone mad because one of them said, "She's weird, isn't she?" and another girl agreed. "She's the kid who kept saying her family is coming to get her. Now she's hallucinating."

Stupid kids, I thought. It bothered me that they thought I was crazy. On second thought, they might be right. I might be losing my mind completely. And if I stayed here longer...? Rising, I went inside.

The hallway was empty, but I could hear voices murmuring from the rooms on both sides. As I passed one, I saw Teacher Hwang sitting at her desk, shuffling some papers.

It happened again. Instead of Teacher Hwang, I saw my mother sitting at her Singer sewing machine. "Mother!" I called, but I regretted it immediately because Mother disappeared and Teacher Hwang came back into view.

"What are you doing here, Jong-ah?" she asked, as if annoyed.

I had to make up a story in a hurry.

"I was wondering if you heard something about my family, Teacher Hwang. Last time, you said you called the people at the main port and left a message for them to call you when they heard something about my family, but I didn't talk to you since then. Every time I see you, you're busy with someone else."

"I'm sorry, Jong-ah," she said in the same dry tone as before. "I've been really busy. Let me call down there now and see if they know something about your family. Come in and sit down for a moment." She put the papers aside and picked up the phone.

She talked a long time, while touching the papers, rearranging her pens and pencils on the desk, and smoothing her hair. Hanging up the receiver, she said, "They hauled the boat back to Pusan, she said. I guess they couldn't fix the problem. The good news is that the passengers are safe, every one of them. No one was injured or died."

I was relieved. "When can I talk to my family, then?" I asked.

"Soon, I hope. She said some passengers are waiting to get picked up by another boat and some already left. Let's be patient a bit longer, Jong-ah, okay? I know it's been a long wait for you, but it's almost over. At least we know they're all right. Does that help?"

I wanted to tell her that an hour was like an eternity here in the orphanage, but I just stood there, my gaze dropped to the floor. I saw holes in my canvas shoes. My dusty blue wool coat had dark stains all over from digging for coal. Even if my parents saw me now they might not recognize me.

"I want to go home," I squeaked through my tight throat. But Teacher Hwang rolled her eyes. "How?" she said, her expression turning cold. "You've just heard what I said. You waited this long and you can wait a bit longer."

"If they don't get here tomorrow, I'm leaving."

"Going home by yourself?" she asked, almost amused.

"Yes."

"Certainly not. You're too young to travel by yourself. If something happens to you on the way back, I'd be responsible. Now, go to your room. We'll soon hear from them!" She virtually pushed me out of her room and closed the door behind me.

Raging with anger, I walked up the stairway and entered the Azalea Room. I couldn't believe my eyes! My backpack was on the floor, its zipper open, and the older girls were munching my Hershey bars, Nabisco cookies, beef jerky, and dried fruit. I had been careful not to leave my backpack where the girls could touch it, but they had found it. Before leaving the room every morning, I hid it between the folds of my comforter, and only when everyone was asleep would I took out a Hershey Bar or a couple of cookies to share with Bokja. And now these girls had found it and were devouring what my parents had prepared for me.

I must have momentarily lost my mind because I heard myself screaming, "Who did this? Who stole my stuff?"

No one stirred; they kept munching as if they didn't hear or see me.

"You're thieves, all of you!" I screamed like an animal.

One girl with long matted hair finally said, "I guess I'm one of the thieves," and laughed.

I stared at her, wishing I could beat her.

"Actually," said another whose lips were painted in bright red and chest was swollen, "you can't blame us for helping ourselves to your backpack. You shouldn't have kept it in the room in the first place. Did you think we'd not notice your backpack bulging with food when our stomachs are growling? How stupid can you be!"

"Yeah," said the pale-looking girl sitting in the corner, whose leg was braced with metal pieces. I didn't know her name but heard that she lost her leg in a minefield somewhere near the 38th Parallel when she escaped with her family. "Stealing food is no sin when you're hungry. Even the Bible says so. Just think you've shared something with your friends! You'll feel a whole lot better about it." She laughed disgustingly and all the others laughed too.

"You shouldn't have touched it!"

"Forget it, kid," said another girl, the one who had called me *stupid dwarf* that morning when I'd stood with Bokja in front of the latrine. "We're not sorry, okay?" she said. "Go tell the director about it: we don't care! Finders keepers."

Everyone repeated in chorus, "Finders keepers. Finders keepers."

"At least you have some leftovers," said the same girl, pointing to the floor. "We'll let you keep them. They're all yours."

Only Moon-hee, the blind girl, was quiet, sitting in her usual corner far from everyone else, her eyes blinking fast. "You nasty girls," she said in a throaty voice. "You should at least apologize for stealing the kid's food."

"Shut up, blind!" one of the thieves shouted.

I knew Moon-hee didn't touch any of my stuff, and I felt close to her. As if she could feel my glance on her, she said gently, "Hey kid, just forget it. It's not worth fighting for."

I couldn't forget it because I remembered my mother standing in the kitchen, roasting rice and soybeans and slicing fruit, packing everything for each of my brothers, sisters, and me. *Mother, they stole my food,* I said, tears brimming. She seemed to say, *Don't lower yourself to their level, Jong-ah. Rise above them.*

I knelt on the floor and scooped up the bits and pieces of candy bars, cookies, and roasted rice and soybeans, and threw them into the backpack. Then I remembered I still had money hidden in my underwear, which the girls didn't know about. I could walk to the port, buy a boat ticket, and go to Pusan. Once there, finding home would be no problem. *I'll go back the way I came,* I thought. Taking a train alone would be scary, but there must be a first time for everything. Yoja had been doing it for many years ever since she was in the first grade. I couldn't afford to wait and lose everything of home. I had to go before I lost my courage.

I put my backpack on and walked out without a word. Laughter exploded behind me. "See you around, kid," a voice said, and another added, "Come see us again, if you have more food."

I wasn't angry anymore. For the first time in my ten years, I understood what mother had tried to teach me. I was glad that I didn't lower myself to their level and fought them. I actually felt I rose above them. *I'm going home but they can't,* I said haughtily to myself.

"Jong-ah, where are you going?" Bokja asked, suddenly appearing before me in the hallway. In her white gown too large for her tiny frame, she looked older than her twelve years.

"I'm going home," I said.

"You can't go home alone."

"But I am!"

"They won't let you. Pusan is far away like Japan is."

I pushed her aside and headed to the door.

She followed. "Wait. What happened? Why are you so angry with me?"

I stopped walking. I didn't want her to think I was angry with her. As I told her what had happened, I couldn't help but cry.

Bokja held me in her arms as if I were a child. Strangely, her warm embrace comforted me.

"They're the troublemakers," Bokja said and shook her head. "I saw one of them stealing from your backpack the other day, but I couldn't tell you. I didn't want you to get upset."

"It doesn't matter now. I'm going home."

"I can't let you go by yourself," she said. "How are you going to get a boat ticket?"

"I can buy one. I have money."

"Let me go with you, then," she pleaded. "I'm on my break and I don't have to go back until four. At least I want to see you leave. Remember, we're sisters."

The idea of her coming with me made me smile, but I said, "I don't want you to get in trouble."

"I won't," she said.

Bokja was alert. "Let's see," she said, shifting her eyes. "About this time of the day the volunteer lady is sitting at the door. She'll call the director immediately when she sees your backpack."

"What should we do?"

"Let's go through the backyard. I saw some boys go in and out of the wire fence when they lose their balls. I'm sure there's a hole somewhere."

"But the boys are playing basketball right now. Maybe we should wait."

"They won't tell," Bokja said. "The big boys never pay any attention to the younger girls. They only like older girls, you know what I mean."

"If they notice us, let's just say we're looking for something, like pebbles or wildflowers to play with."

"Good idea!" she said.

The hallway was quiet, except for the voices of adults talking among themselves. Bokja and I tiptoed all the way to the back door without looking back. The wooden door let out a squeak when I pushed it, but we slipped through with no problems. About six boys were jumping up and down, catching the ball and then throwing it back into the net. None of them noticed us. Bokja nodded to me, her signal to run, and together we ran as fast as we could toward the wire fence dividing the vacant lot where Sookhi and I had collected coal, and the orphanage.

I couldn't find the hole in the fence. Panicked, I walked from one end of the fence to the other, searching for it, but all I could see was overgrown weeds and vines with thorns, tangled together.

"Jong-ah, here! In the corner!" Bokja said.

Then I saw it. I didn't know how I missed the ferocious-looking broken wire sticking out of the tall weeds with red-comb heads. Bokja helped me crawl out first by pushing the wire to one side, and I did the same for her.

We ran across the field together, holding hands. Somewhere dogs barked loudly and I shivered, but we didn't slow down. Before we reached the dirt road, the same one we had passed through on the first night here, we stopped to see if anyone was following us. We then raced like two animals.

Feather-like clouds gathered above our heads, as if it would rain soon, but the sky above the shore was clear.

"I can't believe I'm going home," I said.

"I wish I had a home to run to," replied Bokja, breathing heavily.

"Come see me in Pusan, *Onni,*" I said, already missing her. "You can stay with me as long as you want to, really!" I told her about Yoja, my best friend: how her father dropped her off at the train station every morning since we had been in the first grade and how she and I had been spending all day together, sometimes arguing, but mostly enjoying one another. I told her about Mimi, too. "She's a Tabby cat. She's the most friendly cat you ever saw."

"Does it catch mice?" she asked, showing interest.

"She does, but she never eats them. When she catches one, she just plays with it until it dies. And then she carries it around in her mouth to show off. Once she brought it in the bedroom and hid it under my comforter."

"Yuck!"

"I almost died when I saw it."

"What did you do with it?"

"My brother and I buried it next to the fence. Have you ever had a cat in Pyongyang?"

"No. My grandma is allergic to cats. But we did have chickens. Everyone had chickens to collect chicken droppings."

"Chicken droppings?" I said in astonishment. "I didn't know you can pick up chicken droppings."

"You can when it's dried."

I laughed. "What did you pick it up with? Spoons or chopsticks?"

Bokja was serious. "We used a small wooden tool with a bent tip and a dustpan to collect them. When we had enough in the dustpan we dropped it in a bucket. The commune leader collected the buckets at the end of the week, loaded them on his pickup, and took them to the district office. It was an assignment all the kids in the neighborhood had to do and I never had a second thought about it."

"What did they do with a truck full of chicken shit?"

"They made fertilizer, of course. What do you think they did with it?"

"I don't know."

We ran some more. Suddenly it began to rain. The shore was still lit with a metallic glint, but it was cloudy over our heads, and I could feel raindrops falling on me. Seeing the port only a few blocks away, I told Bokja to go back. "I can make it fine, Bokja *Onni*. I don't want them to find out you're missing."

"I'll be okay," she said.

"Please go. Soon they'll be looking for us. Please tell them you didn't see me leave, okay? You can lie, can't you?"

"Don't worry about me."

"I'll write to you as soon as I get back. Will you write to me?"

"Of course," she said. Her eyes were turning red, and I knew mine were too.

I hugged her tightly for a long moment, and then turning quickly, I ran toward the port. She said, "Goodbye, Jong-ah," but I didn't turn around, afraid I might cry or see her cry.

"Take care!" Bokja shouted again. The wind caught her voice and tossed it across the field, and I heard it echo.

"You too!" I replied and kept running.

Trucks and cars passed by me, their tires spinning and blowing dust into my face. I ran so fast I barely felt my feet touch the ground. Raindrops no longer bothered me. *I can be home in a matter of hours.*

I was about to cross a busy intersection when I saw a blue taxi heading in my direction. As it passed, it honked. I crossed the street and headed for the port. To my dismay, the taxi made a quick stop, its tires skidding on the wet surface, and turned around. It now headed toward me with its headlights on. Once Father had told Kwon and me to watch out for child abductors. "They'll approach you from behind without warning and put you in a car or a pick-up truck before you know it. Always watch for a car or truck that suddenly slows down near you. And if a man tries to grab you, yell for help as loud as you can."

There was still a good distance between the people at the dock and me. As I ran faster, trying to catch up with two women walking ahead of me, I heard a voice call, "Wait! Jong-ah!"

I turned around to make sure that I wasn't imagining it. I saw a man's hand sticking out of the taxi window and waving as the taxi followed me. I was scared. He could be someone the orphanage had sent out to get me. Seeing a small hill on my right bordered with tall hedges, I made a quick turn and ran as fast as I could toward it. I knew no car would be able to turn that quickly and follow.

Sitting between two thick hedges joined together at the top, I gasped for air. My heart pounded loudly, but I was glad that the man in the taxi, whoever it was, couldn't find me here.

I saw some stone steps on my right, leading to an elegant house adorned with flowerbeds, and I reminded myself that I would soon be at home, just as elegant as this one. Some odd-shaped rocks and stone figures stood in front of the house whose windows were mysteriously agleam, probably with reflected sunlight from the shore. I wondered who lived there. The house seemed to be empty; at least no one opened the back door to shoo me away.

I was anxious to get back to the road so I could board the ship to Pusan, but I was afraid of that taxi. I decided to wait a little longer.

Two dark figures suddenly appeared from where I had entered, giving me a cold shock. I couldn't look up. I could only see their dirty shoes walking around. I held my breath. *I can't go back to the orphanage, so help me God,* I prayed.

They were so close I could now hear their voices. "She can't be too far away, sir," a man said. "I know she's here."

"I hope so," another replied.

I wondered whether Bokja had returned to the orphanage, and the director had found out where I was headed. On second thought, I doubted that Bokja would tell her the truth.

Then I heard one of them call my name again, "Jong-ah, Jong-ah! Answer me!" The voice sounded like Father's. Then I thought, many men sounded like Father. The market was full of them.

"It's me, Jong-ah," the voice said again. "I came to fetch you."

I looked out. My father stood only two yards away, his head turning in all directions. It wasn't a dream. He wore the same coat, the one he had on when we had left Pusan together. Crawling out, I said, "What took you so long, Father?"

CHAPTER 15

▼

SWEET POTATOES AND CHESTNUTS

Father acted as though I had died and resurrected. He hurried over, pulled me into his arms, and hugged me tightly. The familiar smell of home! "I missed you," he moaned, his voice cracking. "I'm so glad that you're okay."

I couldn't say anything. I only sniffled, my lips quivering.

"Why were you running on the street?" he asked, loosening his embrace. "The clerk at the port told me you were at the House of Love orphanage. She even drew a map for me so that I could find it. Why are you not at the orphanage?"

"I ran away!"

"Why?"

"Because I hated it there. The big kids stole all my candy bars and cookies and other stuff in my backpack. Every time I asked the director if she heard anything about you, she always said, 'I'll call them tomorrow.' Nobody cared about me."

"You left because the kids stole your candy bars and cookies? I can't believe it, Jong-ah. Anyone could have picked you up from the street and taken you somewhere. It doesn't take much for an adult to kidnap a small thing like you."

"I couldn't help it, Father. I didn't know if you were coming or when you were coming. And everything I had was stolen, except for some crumbs! Look at my hands." I thrust them in his face. "We were digging coal so that we could have heat in the building."

Father showed no sympathy at all. "Go on. I'm listening."

"We didn't even have warm water to wash with in the morning. I had to share a cold pan of water with several kids. We ate thin rice soup three times a day, and that's all we ate. Why do you think I should have stayed there?"

"So tell me, Jong-ah, where were you going?"

"Home," I said without hesitation. "I was going to buy a boat ticket to Pusan, and then take a train home."

"Do you know what could have happened to you? Do you care to know? There's a wild jungle out there. There're murderers, drunkards, thieves, pickpockets, and tavern owners selling and trading young girls like you! Where did you get such a wild idea?"

I said nothing. I couldn't say my adventurism was hereditary because I'd get in more trouble.

Father's interrogation continued. "Did you tell the people at the orphanage you were leaving?"

"I was going to," I lied, "but the volunteer lady at the door fell asleep on the desk, so I just walked out." There was no way I could tell Father that I had crawled out through a hole in the barbed wire fence like a dog. He'd scold me for hours for my disgraceful behavior. The worst part would be that Mother would know about it sooner or later and tell all my aunts and uncles. Then, when they'd see me they would each say: "Jong-ah, crawling out of a barbed wire fence is nothing for a young girl to do" or "Don't give your parents too many white hairs, girl!"

"You should have at least asked the director for permission," he said. "Don't ever walk out from anywhere without telling somebody. Haven't I said this before? Did you listen when…" He went on and on. Father seemed to think that his lectures were the remedy for all my problems. Even when I was sick with a common cold, he'd say, "You shouldn't be out in the cold without your coat and hat." When I accidentally fell and scraped my knees, it was, "Didn't I tell you not to run when you can walk? Why can't you listen to me?"

I wasn't sorry for what I had done. I had no choice. As soon as I had made up my mind and was convinced that I could find my way home, I wasn't helpless anymore. My mind had crossed the ocean hundreds of times, and I had walked home from the train station, passing the market, the barbershop with its red-and-blue sign, the post office, and the bakery that opened only on weekends. There was nothing to it.

"Father, I'll be ten next month. My friend Yoja has been riding the train by herself since she was six. Why do you think I can't buy a boat ticket, go to Pusan, and then get on a train and go home?"

"You listen to me," he said, like an army officer. "There are times I might not be able to protect you, like when you were left behind at the port, but until you're an adult I'll not let you do anything that could harm you. I can't take a chance. I'm your father, if that means anything to you. You'll have plenty of time to do whatever you want to when you're old enough, but not now! Do you know what happens to a young bird that jumps out of a nest before it can fly? It falls and dies. Now get in the taxi."

"Where are we going?"

"To the orphanage."

"What for?"

"*What for?* Alright, I'll tell you what for. You're going to apologize to the director for leaving without permission. *I* need to go there too, to thank the director for keeping you in her care while we were separated. You could have ended up on the black market, and I'd never have found you."

He then ordered the taxi driver, "Please take us to the *House of Love* orphanage."

"Neh, neh!" the driver said, bowing, although Father was behind him.

I had many thoughts sprouting in my head. It was refreshing to hear Father's lecture about who he was and who I was to him when I had been lost and just been found. Most of the orphans wouldn't have anyone to claim them as their own, nor would they have to listen to long lectures on what was expected of them. I had always complained about small things, such as why Kwon never called me *noona* or who had a bigger portion of rice cake or grilled fish than I, but I had never stopped for one moment to appreciate what my parents provided for me or how much they cared for my well-being. I missed home so much. I even missed the long evening prayers. For the first time in my almost ten years, I was able to understand why parents might have to be strict with their children from time to time so that they wouldn't wander away from their tight grip. Who else in this wide world would protect me the way Father and Mother did? No one. Even though at times I wished their lectures were a bit shorter or that they wouldn't notice my imperfections so much, I knew deep inside they would never stop protecting and loving me.

Leaning on Father's sturdy shoulder, I said, "Thank you for coming to get me, Father."

He wrapped his arm around me and held me tightly as if he was afraid of losing me again. "Did you think I wasn't coming?"

"I didn't know what to think any more. I was sure that something had happened to you all."

"Something *did* happen and I'll tell you about it later. But I don't want you to forget that I'll always love you."

I rested my tired head on his chest and listened to his heartbeat. I felt safe. I secretly promised him I'd be a good daughter he could be proud of. Tears running down my cheeks, I wept quietly.

Father suddenly asked, "How many kids are there? I want to buy some treats for them."

"I'm not sure," I mumbled, acting tired. Father disliked seeing me cry. "Tears don't take care of anything but make you feel weak," was his theory.

"About thirty or forty?" he asked again.

"More, I think. Close to a hundred."

"That many?"

"Yes, but many kids are so sick they can't eat anything. And about thirty of them are babies."

"I don't know what to buy for a hundred kids. Maybe I should give some money to the orphanage, instead of buying treats."

I protested immediately. "Giving money to hungry kids isn't such a good idea, Father. If you give money to the director she'll use it for medicine or linen or other unimportant things. The kids want something to eat. They're always hungry. I heard them talking about hot sweet potatoes just out of an oven and roasted chestnuts. We had watery soup everyday, three times a day!"

"All right," Father said. "For hungry kids money doesn't mean anything. Driver," he said, raising his voice, "Is there a grocery store nearby?"

"Just around the corner, sir."

In the store an old man with a pipe in his mouth stood behind the counter, holding a fly swatter above his head, but as soon as he saw us, he quickly lowered his arm and asked, "What can I do for you?"

Father said, "Give us two crates of sweet potatoes and a bushel of chestnuts. I hope you have some fresh ones in stock."

"Immediately, sir," he said and disappeared through a curtain made of bamboo beads. When he returned with two wooden crates full of sweet potatoes and a bushel of chestnuts, Father made sure they were fresh before he paid the owner. The driver carried the sweet potatoes and chestnuts to the car and we headed to the orphanage. We took a road overlooking a sand beach where many seagulls sat in groups, squawking, and an area where women and children stood in the shallow water, digging clams.

As soon as the taxi pulled into the driveway, many kids were standing behind the barbed wire fence and watching us, like caged animals watching their audience.

While Father and the taxi driver carried the crates of sweet potatoes and chestnuts, I found myself confused. I wasn't sure anymore whether walking into the building with my father was a good idea, when the kids were looking at us. It seemed cruel.

Father came to my side and opened the door, saying,

"Lead the way, Jong-ah."

"Father, I'm not sure."

"What do you mean?"

"I don't feel like going inside. Would you please tell them that I'm sorry for leaving without permission?"

"No, I want you to tell them yourself!"

"Well…I don't want to show off my father when none of them has his or her own. At first I wanted to walk in with you to show them I wasn't lying about my family, but now it seems childish. I'd like it better if they would remember me as another orphan."

Father thought about it for a moment. "You have a point there, Jong-ah. I'm sure it'd be hard for them to see you walking in with me. All right! I'll talk to the director alone. You wait here."

I waited in the taxi for a long time. Father finally came out with Teacher Hwang. They were both smiling.

Teacher Hwang came to my side of the car, pulled me out of the back seat, and hugged me warmly. "I'm so happy for you, Jong-ah. I told you your father would come, didn't I?"

I nodded. More tears came, but I managed to say I was sorry for leaving the orphanage without telling her.

She tightened her arms and said, "I understand. I'm happy that it worked out for the best. And thank you for the sweet potatoes and chestnuts. We don't get such generous gifts very often here. Your father explained to me why you didn't want to come inside. You're such a thoughtful child, Jong-ah. I wish you my best and a happy reunion with your family."

"Thank you."

She loosened her arms and I bowed to her deeply. "Let's go!" Father ordered the driver. As the taxi pulled away, I watched her stand on the same spot, waving, until I couldn't see her any more.

Later, sitting next to Father on the homebound steamboat, I finally asked Father why he had come alone.

He cleared his throat. "I thought it would be safer to send everyone else home. It was torture even to think about boarding another ship with everyone. After I failed to find you on the boat, I regretted making the whole family move to Cheju Island. It wasn't a smart thing to do when the dock was so crowded and everyone was pushing and shoving to get ahead. Your mother and I had a touch of paranoia about losing another child, if we boarded another ship. As I said earlier, we had an emergency landing on a tiny islet called Yodo. A woman had breathing problems, and then men shouted from the bottom of the ship that smoke was coming out of the engine room. As if confirming this, many passengers came up, looking pale and coughing and gagging. We were afraid that poisonous fumes might seep through the floorboards and kill us. When something happens on a boat, there isn't much you can do.

"One man swore that he had heard crew members whispering to one another about the exhaust fan not working properly, and another said that the boat could catch fire at any moment. Everyone seemed to be making up a story, while the ship just floated in the middle of the vast ocean…."

I didn't know exactly when my head began nodding, but I knew Father stopped talking. He carefully held my head with both hands, as though he was handling a crystal vase, and pulled it toward him. I then felt his arm around my shoulder.

Heaviness weighed down on me and I heard myself snoring.

CHAPTER 16

▼

HOME AGAIN

The moment I saw our home with its upturned tile roof perched atop the gently rolling slope, my heart raced. *Am I having another dream?* I thought, blinking, but it was still there. I had never once thought seeing our home was exciting, but it was now. *I'm home: I'm finally here!*

"Jong-ah, slow down! I can't catch up with you," Father said and chuckled. He had very long legs. When we walked to church no one could get ahead of him, but it seemed now I was too fast for him.

"Walk a little faster," I said.

"Slow down for your poor father. I'm getting old and I can't walk that fast."

I ignored him. He enjoyed seeing me anxious to see everyone I had missed so much, I thought, and kept walking.

The moment I pushed the creaky, heavy wooden door and stepped into our courtyard, I shouted, "I'm home! I'm home!"

I heard Mother's rice-papered screen sliding and her voice shrieking, "Jong-ah!" I then saw her stepping out of her room barefoot. I ran and threw myself into her arms, bursting into tears. I wanted to say, "I missed you so much, Mother," but all I could do was cry.

I didn't cry for very long because all my brothers and sisters came out from their own corners of the house, making noises.

"Let me look at you, Jong-ah," I heard Eldest brother say as he gripped my shoulders and spun me around. "Hmmm, you lost some weight, didn't you, kid?" he said, acting as if I were his child.

I only smiled, sniffling. If I said anything, I'd end up crying again. I didn't want to cry; I was happy.

"Jong-ah, I'm glad you're home," said Second Brother. "Home wasn't the same without you, Kid Sister. No one can scratch my back the way you can."

I thrust my hands at him, my rough and dirty hands stained with coal powder.

"On second thought," he said, stepping back, "I can wait until you're cleaned up."

Kwon slipped something smooth and cold into my hand. "Another American marble!" I shrieked.

"Hold it against the window," he said.

I did. "I feel I'm at the bottom of the ocean, Kwon. Where did you get it?"

"I traded for my kite."

"What? Not the one with a red dragon painted on it?"

"Well, that's okay. You're worth it."

"I am?"

My brothers and sisters laughed, but I didn't think it was funny at all. I had never heard him say anything positive about me all my life, and I wanted to make sure he meant what he said.

"You are, believe me," he said and walked away.

He missed me! I was teary again. "Thanks Kwon. I never owned any marble as pretty as this one," I said to his back.

First Sister's gift was a stick of dried squid, my favorite snack. "Thanks, Big sister!" Second Sister handed me something unusual: a pink paper folded into a perfect square. "What's this?" I asked, and she said, "Open it!"

It was a poem she wrote, which she decorated with dried balsam flowers and yellow gingko leaves. I read it aloud:

> In my dream, you're still a pest,
> Messing up my desk and arguing with me
> When I'm awake you're nowhere.
> I can't pull you out of a photo, Sister
> Please come back and be my pest again.

I couldn't help but cry, and she hugged me.

Day after day, I repeated the same tale over and over, first to the two priests and six nuns, then to Grandparents, and then to our uncles and aunts who stopped by to see if what they had heard was true. I told them how I got separated from the family and ended up in an orphanage, how I escaped, and how Father found me on my way to the port. They all said, "Thank God, you're okay!" although it was my own father who had come to get me.

Father's story, however, was different each time he told it. Sometimes he'd say, "As I sat in the taxi and looked out the window, thinking where on earth she might be, I saw a young girl crossing the street. But it never occurred to me that it was Jong-ah. My mind was somewhere else, looking for her, when she was right there in front of me. Can you imagine, not recognizing your own child in broad daylight?" Other times, it was, "I spotted her immediately in a crowd. I told the driver, 'That's her! Honk your horn.' You wouldn't know it by looking at her, but Jong-ah is the Dragon Girl. She can be tough and wise too, if she chooses to be."

Then everyone would look at me, smiling, and I felt as though I was a different girl, someone bigger and smarter than me. *I will be tough and wise, Father.*

Mother made an effort to notice me and talk to me. One Saturday after breakfast, Mother said to me, "We have some business to do, Jong-ah, you and I."

"What business?" I asked.

"We'll go to the market and buy you a new coat. I can't stand looking at that dirty rag."

I didn't argue because, even in my own eyes, I looked like a beggar child. The coat that once had been dusty blue was now gray with blotches of black. It was embarrassing to look at myself in a mirror.

The market was the same as I remembered, although it seemed like ages since I had been there. The smell of hot and spicy noodle soup, sweet rice cakes, and roasted chickens glazed in thick brown sauce still made my mouth water. The heated arguments among vendors were still going on as though they had never left the market since I had seen them before. The hot item for the day seemed to be octopus.

"Octopus! Octopus! Fresh out of the sea," a woman shouted, holding the purplish, slippery creatures that had nothing but rubbery legs. Another man joined the competition, "You can slice it and eat it raw; or you can deep fry it and enjoy the crunch and chewy texture; or you can boil it and eat it with hot-pepper sauce. However you cook it, your palate will be flattered."

Mother and I snaked through the vending booths, stores, and shoppers, and entered *Children's Palace,* the largest children's garment store in town. A young woman with a painted face at the door bowed to Mother, singing, "How may I assist you, madam?"

"I'm looking for a winter coat for my daughter here."

"In aisle ten, madam!" she chirped. "The lower rack on your left is for her size. Enjoy shopping at Children's Palace!" She bowed again.

It didn't take long for Mother to go through the rack and pull out a red coat with a black velvet collar. She held it in front of me. "This will look good on you. Try it on."

It was a nice coat, but I wasn't eager to put it on. The thought that my hand-me-down coat would be discarded in a trashcan as soon as I walked out of the store bothered me. "I don't need a new coat yet," I said.

"Yes you do," Mother insisted. "Come on, put it on for me, will you?"

I just stood there, and Mother took off my old coat and put the new one on, turning me and bending my arms against my will. She then steered me toward a tall mirror on the wall and said, "Very nice. It's the perfect color and style for you."

I looked different in this red coat. *Bokja wouldn't recognize me in this. She liked my old coat.*

Turning my back to the mirror, I told Mother that I didn't like the coat. She frowned, but before she could give me another lecture, I said, "Can I wear the old one for the rest of this winter and get a new one next year?"

"But why, Jong-ah?" she said as though I disobeyed her golden rules. "I've never bought you new clothes because you have older sisters and cousins. This is a good chance for you to get a new coat. Why don't you like it? Tell me. Is there something else you'd like better than this one?"

How could I tell her that my old coat had made me feel close to home when I was away? It protected me from the cold gusty wind, too, when I had been in the vacant lot digging coal with Sookhi. I missed Sookhi. Was she still digging coal, shivering and coughing in her green sweater? Was she still smoking cigarettes? What was Bokja doing now? Still working in the nursery, wearing that long gown?

Mother was getting impatient. "If you don't see anything you like better, I'm going to get this one. It *really* looks good on you!"

"If you buy this one," I said, "are you going to throw away the old one?"

"No," said Mother. "I'll take it to a dry cleaner and have them clean it."

"Then what?"

"I'll find someone who has a daughter your age and give it to her. Why do you ask, Jong-ah?"

"It was with me the whole time I was away, Mother. I wore it even at night. I never took it off."

"I see," Mother said, her voice softening. "I can see why you don't want to see it thrown away. I promise, Jong-ah, I'll make sure that someone else will use it. If I can't find someone, a beggar would be glad to have it."

"Thank you, Mother."

As we headed home, she asked me if I had made friends at the orphanage. I told her about Bokja from Pyongyang and how her grandmother abandoned her on an airstrip last December, so that the American pilots could bring her to the South. I told her about Sookhi too; how she taught me about finding coal from a heap of dirt behind the orphanage; how she advised me never to get in a fight with the girls older than me; and how much she wanted to be adopted by an American family. But I didn't tell her about Sookhi's smoking habit, because I didn't want her to think that I might have tried to smoke too.

"You learned much about other children, didn't you?"

I nodded.

"Sometimes you learn from your own age group far more than from your parents or older siblings. While you were gone, I learned something I had never thought about before."

"Like what?"

"Like…how precious your child is or what it means to be a parent. When your child is under your wings, you don't think about those things. But when he or she is missing, you want to give the whole world in exchange for the lost one. It tears your heart when you don't even know he or she is still alive. It was a nightmare for me."

Mother reached into her purse and took out her handkerchief and wiped her eyes. I couldn't look at her eyes. If I did, I would see her pain, and I couldn't deal with it. Seeing a round and smooth rock on the ground, I kicked it, and it slid a few feet away before stopping. I followed it, kicking it again and again.

One day when the sunlight was unusually warm for February, Mother unexpectedly asked me if I would accompany her to the mountain on Saturday to pick *namool*, edible wild plants only available in early spring. When cooked and seasoned with soy sauce, sesame oil, red pepper, and chopped green onion, *namool* was a tasty side dish. It could also be brewed into tea or steamed with rice powder and chopped chestnuts and honey for a snack. Whatever you did with *namool*, everyone loved it, especially my mother. Before Baby Brother was born, Mother used to take my sisters and me to the mountain to pick *namool* in early spring, but for about three years, she hadn't been on the mountain, and I could tell she missed it.

"Just you and me?" I asked.

"Yes. Your sisters will be in school most of the day for spring cleaning, and your older brothers want to take your younger brothers to a mini-car exhibition downtown. I thought it would be a perfect time for us to go to the mountains and bring home some fresh *namool* for dinner."

This was the closest she could come to admitting that she wanted to be with me alone and that she had missed me while I was lost.

I said yes.

Early that Saturday morning, I heard Mother going to the kitchen and then dishes clattering and water splashing and knew she was making lunch for me and herself. I hoped she would make rice rolls, my favorite picnic lunch. Her rice rolls with diced shrimp were scrumptious. Everyone said so, even Teacher Kim. On the school picnic day the previous year Mother had made lunch for her, and on the way home she said, "Jong-ah, tell your mother I want the recipe for the rice rolls. I've never had such delicious rice rolls in my life."

The mountain seemed taller and broader than ever before as Mother and I walked up the curvy road, each with a bamboo basket with small garden tools inside. The sky was clear blue and the air was a bit chilly, but the sunlight was warm and pleasant on my shoulders. Wild azaleas hadn't bloomed, but forsythias had, coloring the hills and valleys into soft yellow, the color of spring chicks. After walking nearly a half hour, passing through an area where the refugees had built a village of shacks with driftwood, flattened coca-cola cans, and cardboard boxes, we reached a pond the size of our courtyard, surrounded by pale grass. It was peaceful. The water reflected the mountain peak and the clusters of white clouds above, and a family of ducks glided serenely on the mirror-like surface, trying not to disturb the mirages shimmering next to them.

"This is a perfect spot," Mother said, squatting down. Taking out a two-pronged tool with a long handle, she began pulling up spidery plants. Her hands moved fast, digging and pulling, digging and pulling, and each time, a new plant jumped into her basket, scattering new dirt. Seeing similar ones around my feet, I sat and plunged my two-pronged tool into the dirt and pulled one up.

"What's this?" I asked.

"It's *moxa*. You have to pay a fortune at the market for it when it's available. *Moxa* is an excellent remedy for arthritis and it tastes good too. But next time,

Jong-ah, be sure to dig a bit deeper and pull up the roots, too. Those roots are nutritious."

It took me a while to learn the skill, but when I finally did, Mother was happy. "See? It isn't hard, is it?" she said.

By the time my basket was half-filled, my stomach growled and my arms began aching. "I'm hungry," I said.

Mother stopped immediately and reached for her basket. Producing a white square lunchbox, she put it on a flat rock. "Let's eat," she said, opening the lid. The rice rolls filled with eggs, vegetables, and meat greeted me with their unique and irresistible aroma, and I picked one with my dirty hand and took a bite of it. It was delicious. I ate one after another, completely ignoring Mother. She would have lectured me not to eat so fast but said nothing. She only watched me.

When I was about to get up, she said, "Everything tastes good when you're on the mountain."

"It really does," I said, stuffing my mouth with another rice roll, keeping another in my hand for ducks. "I want to feed the ducks," I said. "Can I go?"

"Sure! I'll be there, too," she said.

I ran to the edge of the pond, kicked off my shoes, and stepped into the shallow water. Unlike the toasty sunlight on my back, the water was so cold I felt a knife's blade entering my feet. The ducks glided toward me as if they knew what I had for them. I broke off small pieces of the rice roll in my hand and threw them into the water. They gobbled them up fast and looked for more, turning sideways, quacking. I wished I had more but I didn't. An awkward moment passed as they inspected my hands and eyes, making sure I wasn't playing a game with them. I shooed them away, throwing my arms wildly in the air. Water murmured quietly behind them as they swam away.

The ripples grew around me, pushing the reflection of the sky to the edge of the pond. I felt as though I was riding the ripples, although I was standing like a pole, my feet planted in the water.

A jade green frog, the size of my big toe, jumped out of the water, sat on a rock, and croaked, as if preparing to sing. It had a comical grin around its mouth but its onyx-like eyes looked serious. I wanted to catch it and take it home to show it to Kwon. He loved frogs more than all the other creatures we usually found at the creek down the road—crawfish, water bugs, and baby turtles.

As if it knew my evil intention the frog leaped and hid under another rock two feet away. I looked under it, but I couldn't find it.

"What are you looking for?" Mother asked, walking toward me. "I saw a frog. It hid under that rock."

She seemed surprised. "What kind was it?"

"I don't know. It's the color of your bracelet."

"It's too early for frogs to come out," she said, squinting her eyes as she looked into the water that glittered like gold liquid against the sun. I had never thought that Mother would pay attention to such an insignificant thing as a frog but she was now. Whenever she had seen me chasing a dragonfly or a butterfly with Kwon, she'd say, "Jong-ah, what are you doing? You're not a rambunctious boy, are you?" To her, anything fun and exciting was only for boys. My brothers would go to the hills surrounding our neighbors on weekends and fly kites all day, but we girls had to make dumplings or to trim bean sprouts, even when we didn't have dinner guests.

But now, standing next to me, she wasn't the same mother I used to know. She was someone who had time and space for me, someone who could actually have fun with me. I wondered if she once had been an ordinary kid like me and innocently roamed outdoors, catching butterflies, dragonflies, and even frogs. What changed her? Who changed her? Did Grandmother lecture her that a girl should never have fun?

The frog unexpectedly leaped from under the rock and then dove back into the water, splashing, creating new ripples on the surface.

"That's a tree frog," Mother said and laughed. "I used to catch them when I was a kid. There are many kinds of tree frogs so when you're not sure, just call it a tree frog and you can't be wrong."

I stared at the spot where the frog jumped in, wishing I had met Mother when she had been my age. We could have been best friends, like Yoja and me, who knows.

"Jong-ah, let's sit down," she ordered, so we sat on a rock wide enough for the two of us.

"Look at that tree over there." She pointed at an old naked tree on the other side of the pond.

"What about it?"

"See how many branches it has? They're constantly swaying when there's hardly any wind."

"So?"

"A woman with many children has the same fate as that tree, loaded with many branches. There's not a single day you feel you're at peace. Someone always needs to curl up against your warm belly, someone brings problems from school, someone has a headache or a scraped knee, and someone wants more than you can possibly give."

Mother never talked about herself or her feelings. Actually, she had never talked to *me* about anything other than what I had done wrong or what I should have done.

I listened.

"You might think I love Kwon more than you or I pay more attention to your sisters and brothers than I do to you, but it was never my intention. All my children are equal to me, like my ten fingers are: I don't favor any one in particular. Bite any of your fingers, Jong-ah. Go on, try it."

I bit my left pinky. "Ouch," I said.

"It hurts, doesn't it? Your children each have different needs and demand different things from you, but they take up equal portions of your heart. Sometimes it's impossible to give what they want. Kwon, for instance, needed me more than you ever did. He was the youngest child for more than five years, and he still does things to draw my attention to him. But you rarely need my help. When you were only sixteen months old, Kwon came along and you had to grow up fast. And of course, having your older brothers and sisters helped you, too."

I wanted to protest that they were more like slave owners to me, but I knew she wouldn't buy it.

"Compared to the branches of a tree, Jong-ah, you're a hidden one, not very noticeable. You don't sway or rock to get my attention. There might be a time when you let other kids overshadow you or intimidate you, but a hidden branch relies on its own strength, rather than expecting someone to give it to her."

I had a strange yearning to throw myself into her arms but I resisted.

"One other thing," she continued. "Boys have their own difficulties here in our society, too. Every mother expects her son to be exceptional, best in everything, and all-capable. Kwon will have to compete with them. I was careful not to crush his spirit so that he can take the challenges in society. At the same time, you'll be a woman, Jong-ah: you'll never be a man. A woman in this society must be able to endure a harsh climate. I'm worried that your head might get too big for society to handle, and you might be an outcast. This is a serious problem for young girls today who think the sky is unlimited. When you're a woman, you'll have to give up your own family and become a part of your husband's family. It's been that way for thousands of years. That means, you must obey your mother-in-law, endure the spits and criticism of your sisters-in-law, and take care of your husband's parents as lovingly as you would your own. That's the life of a woman here in Korea. There will be times when your pillow will be drenched with your own tears, but you can't run away from your given fate."

I thought about Aunt Myong, Mother's cousin who had given birth to her fifth daughter last spring. In spite of Mother's congratulatory words, all she could do was weep, because she had no sons to show off. And Grandma Hyun, Mother's aunt…She was over sixty now but lived alone in a tiny hut in a village near Pusan. She had lost her husband to cholera when she was only fifteen, but she never remarried. In Korea, a widow never remarries because society expects her to honor her wedding vows to her dead husband.

"I'll never get married," I blurted. "I want to be in America when I grow up."

Mother didn't say anything. But for some strange reasons, her eyes were shining brightly as she gazed at the tree. I still am not sure whether what I saw in her eyes were tears or the glare of sunlight.

CHAPTER 17

▼

HOME CHURCH

My grandparents were now in Taegu. While we were gone Grandfather came down with the flu and Grandmother decided it would be better if he were near his old herb doctor who specialized in Chinese medicine. Their room, our old study room, across the courtyard was now a chapel where the two priests celebrated Mass every morning and the nuns recited their daily prayers. Father wasn't happy at all that his parents' room had been cleared and altered without his consent.

But Mother seemed exhilarated that our house was now a temple of God. "Yobo, the Sisters told me that Father Bahng and Father Yoon found some boards in the storage room and built the altar table," she reported one evening. "They made a large crucifix, too, with scrap boards, and hung it above the Lord's Table. And the Sisters! They're artists, Yobo. They embroidered a bed sheet, the one I had given them the day they arrived, with delicate flower patterns and covered the table. Did you see it?"

"I might have," Father said indifferently.

"Pay attention to it next time. They have a burning candle on each end of the table, day and night, symbolizing their yearning for peace."

"It's a waste," Father said, "burning candles all day and all night."

"There's always someone praying during the day. If it's not a Sister, it's Father Bahng or Father Yoon. We're truly blessed to have our own chapel in our own home. How many people can afford to have their own temple of God?"

"They should at least have waited until the owner of the home is back from his trip," Father said. "That's a common courtesy, I think. What else did they do while we were away?"

"Oh, there's something else they should have asked your permission."

"What?"

"They invited Jesus without asking us, along with angels and saints."

Father clamped his mouth shut. I heard him saying something through his clenched teeth, which I couldn't understand. He then got up. "I'll not be at Mass tomorrow so don't wake me up. Good night!"

"Try to be there," Mother said behind him.

Father wasn't religious like Mother. Our parish church saw him only on Sundays when it didn't rain. On a rainy Sunday, he usually came down with the flu or a cold which lasted only a few hours.

Like Father, I wasn't religious either, but I could never say to Mother, "I'll not be at Mass, so don't wake me up." I wished I could. I didn't know any kid my age that enjoyed going to church and listening to a long sermon. But I could never come down with the flu, although I had tried a couple of times. The idea that I would have to attend Mass every morning before going to school drained the life out of me. I didn't mind praying to Jesus once in a while, one-to-one, especially when I had to report about my siblings, but I didn't like the written prayers we had to memorize and recite aloud during Mass. I never could understand why saying the rosary was a big deal for Mother and the women at church, either. All they did was repeat the same sentences over and over, like parrots, until it was intolerably long and boring, but Mother always prayed the rosary, rain or shine, rolling the beads in her hands. I wondered how Jesus felt about listening to rosaries for long hours.

Confession was another problem for me. Now that two priests lived with us I feared that Mother would have me confess my numerous sins at least once a week, instead of twice a month. She was stricter with me about confession than with anyone else in the family, because, to her, sticking out my tongue at my brothers and sisters was a sin, although they deserved it. Browsing at the market after school could be a sin, too, if someone told her about it. Helping myself to a pair of socks or pencils from my sisters' drawers was also a sin, because, in Mother's book, borrowing without permission was the same as stealing.

Every time I confessed at church, kneeling in the dark, box-like space, our pastor behind the screen seemed as bored as I was. He yawned and scratched his neck and arms as I told him how many times I had stuck out my tongue at who and why and when; or what had I borrowed from my sisters without permission;

or how many times I had gone to the market with Yoja without Mother's permission. Once he fell asleep, snoring. I stopped confessing to see if he'd wake up, but he dozed on, so I said, "Father, I'm not finished yet," but he didn't hear me. I thought, *If my confession put our pastor to sleep, how would Jesus feel about it?* I had no guts to go on, so I got up and left the confessional, feeling awful about my boring confession.

The next morning at six, Mother came to our room and announced, "Time for Mass, everyone. Wake up!" I pretended I didn't hear her, and she came over and said, "Wake up, Jong-ah! I know you're awake."

"I'm tired!" I said. She clucked her tongue. "You don't know how blessed you are, having a church in your own home. If you're *really* sleepy, I have a solution for you: take your pillow with you to the chapel and sleep there. Jesus will understand."

Of course I couldn't lie down in front of the altar table, like a dog lying on the front step. Grumbling, I got up, dressed, and dragged my feet to the church. I wished I wasn't blessed so much. *None of my friends have to do this!* I complained to the Almighty on the cross, but he was silent.

Father Yoon, the humorless priest, seemed bored too. He yawned as much as I did as he mumbled some Latin words, opening and closing his arms like an accordion player, his back turned to his sleepy congregation. Except Mother and the Sisters who sang hymns, everyone was barely awake. I didn't know why God would want His beloved to suffer like this. If he enjoyed watching us torture ourselves at such an early hour of the day like we were, I was sure He wasn't the same Lord who deserved our praises.

My father didn't attend the weekday masses at all. Worse, he began drinking every evening at dinner. I gathered that, besides the fact that our house had been altered without him knowing about it, he was angry with himself for neglecting his duty to his parents by leaving them with total strangers while we were gone. Now that they weren't with us anymore, he felt guilty.

One evening Mother told Father that he was drinking too much. "What kind of example does this set for the kids?"

"Am I drinking too much, Yobo?" he asked, lifting his sleepy eyes to look at her. When Mother said, "You know better than I do," he said, "Too much for whom, you or God?" "Mostly for yourself," Mother said. "And if you're not careful with alcohol, it will swallow you before you know it."

Father never liked when Mother lectured him. "Legend has it," he said in a mocking tone, "that when a hen crows, the household collapses. There's no home that's peaceful when a hen cackles all the time."

I was surprised how calm Mother was when she said, "I'm worried about your health, that's all. Instead of torturing yourself with alcohol, why don't you go see your parents in Taegu? Spend a few days with them. They'll like it. It'll do you much good."

"Don't worry about my parents!" he snarled. He looked scary, like Grandfather once had been. "You never cared for them anyway."

It's not true, I wanted to protest on Mother's behalf. She cared for them. Since the day Grandparents had moved in with us last September and until we had left for Cheju, she spent many hours each day in the kitchen—chopping vegetables and slicing meat, and boiling them together in the cast iron pots—to make soup for Grandfather, who was on a strict diet. She also carried the tray to their room herself. While they ate, she stayed with them, informing them which one of us behaved badly and which one made the best score at school on what subject. Several times she even volunteered Kwon and me to massage Grandfather's bony arms and legs that felt like wooden logs in my hands. How could Father say that Mother didn't care for them?

Father gulped down more rice wine as if determined to show Mother that his drinking was none of her business.

The next morning at breakfast, Mother told us Father had left for Taegu earlier that morning.

Three days later at night, we waited for Father to return, all sitting in the front room lit with dim oil lamplights. Early that evening the lights had come on, but as we ate dinner, they flickered off. The wind seemed to be roaming in the courtyard because the shadows on the wall kept jerking and I could hear the gingko tree swishing and the branches knocking the side of the house. Father's train was scheduled to arrive at eight. It was now ten past nine, but there was no sign of him. I was overwhelmed at the thought that something might have happened, because the train station was only ten minutes away on foot. The curfew was at ten. Only the armed patrolmen could walk around on the street after ten, swinging rifles and barking at people who might have missed the bus home.

"Why isn't he here yet?" Mother said, wrinkling her forehead. She looked up at the wall clock again, which now indicated twenty-five after nine.

"I'm sure the train is delayed," Eldest Brother commented.

"If so, he would be better off spending the night at the station. When the security guards see him, they'll take him to the headquarters and keep him there until the curfew is over at five in the morning."

"I'm sure he knows it," Eldest Brother said. "Did I tell you, Mother, about what happened to my science teacher?" "No, what happened?" she asked. "One night he got drunk and missed his bus home. The national security guards stopped him and took him in for interrogations. They kept him there for a week."

"Why?" Mother said.

"Because he was from the North and he didn't have his teacher's certificate with him. When a guy is from the North and doesn't have relatives here, he's considered a communist spy. When he returned to school he limped badly because he was severely tortured."

"How awful!" Mother cried.

I was getting sleepy and wished Father would be home soon. I imagined that he was walking homebound, his coat collar raised against the chilly wind, taking big steps with his long legs. But the wind was so strong, lifting dust from the dirt road, that he slowed his pace. Then I saw a big dog lurching at him from behind a house, growling, and Father stepped back, covering his head with his arm. The dog bit him and they were rolling on the ground. I screamed.

Everyone was looking at me. I couldn't believe that I had fallen asleep.

Then I heard noises in the courtyard and Mother asking, "What happened to your coat?"

"I'll tell you when we're inside," Father replied.

The moment they were in Mother asked again about his coat.

"I gave it to a beggar woman at the square."

"A beggar woman! Your new wool coat?"

"That's why I'm late," Father said. "I couldn't pass her without giving her something. She was big with a baby in her belly. Only when a patrolman stopped me in front of the barbershop, I realized that my citizen card was in my coat pocket. I told him the whole story, but he didn't believe me. I said, 'I'm telling you the truth, sir. She was expecting a child and was begging for food at this hour.' You know what he said? 'Good try, sir,' and then laughed. 'Too many guys try the same trick, but when you're in the law business, you have some idea who's telling the truth. Come with me, please!' Can you believe it? I stayed at the police station almost an hour, answering questions and listening to a lot of hot air. Finally when he found my name and address in their directory, and all of the names I gave him as references were checked out, he let me go. Yobo, give me some barley tea. I'm freezing."

I was glad that Father came home safe and was in a better mood than before he left for Taegu.

CHAPTER 18

▼

RICHEST GIRL IN SCHOOL

The new school year began on a bright day in early March. As I walked alone toward the new school, my book bag in my hand, I looked for Yoja in the crowd. Now that the new school was in the backyard of a colossal mansion near the train station, she went directly to school, without coming to fetch me every morning. Some days she was a nuisance to me, only because we were together for too many hours of a day, but now I missed her; walking to school without her seemed a long, lonely journey that would never end.

In the morning sunlight, the mountains surrounding the town were cluttered with refugee shacks. I wondered what had happened to the Buddhist temple, whose backyard had been our outdoor classroom for many months the year before. Were the monks still there, chanting ancient mantras and beating their wooden prayer blocks? Were the cow and pigs there too, always eating?

The street was busy with many kids in all sizes heading for school. I noticed some Kyong-nam Girls Middle School students wearing navy blue uniforms with white stiff collars. Yoja and I would be wearing those uniforms in less than two years, if we passed the entry exam. Kyong-nam Girls Middle School was the oldest middle school in Pusan, producing some famous women in town, including my aunt, the doctor. That navy uniform said as much about you as the USA stamp on American products.

A tall brick fence surrounding a massive house twenty yards away told me I had reached my destination. The area was noisy with shops, vending booths, and stores on both sides, but once I entered the wrought iron gate, it was a different world. The fifth and sixth graders clustered here and there, each holding a book bag and talking to one another. In one corner, some boys stood around the oval-shaped pond shaded by an old weeping willow, skipping rocks, ignoring the three German shepherds barking ferociously at them from their sturdy wooden cage a few yards away.

Not finding Yoja among the kids, I walked straight toward the new wooden structure on the opposite side of the mansion. As I entered, I noticed a strong scent of fresh pine in the air. The building had a corridor in the middle and three classrooms on each side. I peeked into one room and then another, hoping to find my old classmates.

In the third room, a gaunt man sitting at the teacher's desk asked me, "Your name?" barely turning toward me. I bowed to him quickly, giving my name. "You're in my class," he said with authority. "Take the seat next to the window in the third row."

I had read about Teacher Yang in the letter sent to Father. He was a veteran who had served in the Japanese imperial army during the Pacific War, and ever since liberation six years earlier, he only taught fifth graders.

The room, smaller than the one in our old school, smelled clean, and with the morning sunlight entering through four windows and the hardwood floor under our feet, we envied no one. *Finally,* I thought.

A tiny voice whispered from behind me, "Hi, Jong-ah!" and I turned around. "Yoja! Did you have a haircut?" I asked.

Nodding, she asked, "Do you like it?" and I said I liked it a lot. She also had gained some weight, too, but I didn't tell her that.

"Let's eat together at lunch," she said in a secretive voice. "I have something to tell you."

To her, every little thing could be news material. She would probably brag about her new notebook or a kid she had met on the train, I thought.

A tall girl I had never seen before came in, talked briefly to Teacher Yang, and sat next to me. She said nothing to me as she unpacked her book bag. I only stared at the side of her face, wondering why she couldn't even give me a nod or say hello. *Is she a refugee?* She had a black mole on her chin, but her ear lobe was gracefully shaped, not too long, not too short. Had Mother been here, she'd say, "This girl will marry well someday. Look at her earlobe."

"Attention!" our teacher said, standing at the podium. I sat erect. Chairs creaked as everyone shifted and moved.

"Good morning, students. I'm glad to see no empty chairs in the room and everyone is on time. I have a feeling we'll get along just fine," he said as an introduction.

Now that I was facing him, I could see his right eye behaving strangely. It couldn't focus on anything. It wandered somewhere about the window, while his left eye, bright and dark, looked at us piercingly as if he wasn't going to tolerate any nonsense that might happen now or in the future.

Clearing his throat sonorously, he went on. "In less than two years, you'll be in middle school. How many of you will move on to the middle school? Raise your hands."

All hands went up, except three or four.

"Very well! Because of the war, the last school year was a difficult year for all of us, including the teachers. Not only did we have no school building, forcing you to study in the mountains, but we had no textbooks either, and you might have copied some books with your own hands. It's wartime, and during a war many people lose their homes or get injured or even die." He stopped to take a sip from his glass on his desk.

Mia came to my mind. Both of her parents died the year before, and she moved in with her grandparents. I didn't think about her much, only once in a while, wondering if she was still going to school.

"But now we're in a better situation," said Teacher Yang, trying to cheer us. "Donations are pouring into our country from all over the world, allowing some publishers to produce textbooks here in Pusan. Some builders are constructing the classrooms like this one with the donated materials. Isn't it nice to have a school building?"

"Yes."

"Now, come forward to get the books." Producing a large box from under his desk, he set it on top.

We each got four books—*Korean Literature, Multiplication & Division, History and Social Studies,* and *Modern Science.* The books smelled like fresh ink, Father's ink. I had never thought that holding new books was exciting, and I couldn't understand why I didn't appreciate them before. Some girls chattered loudly and some even squealed, and Teacher Yang shouted, "Be quiet!"

He had a sharp bullet-like voice and everyone stopped talking. "Go back to your seat at once, and don't talk," he said. We obeyed. Seeing that we sat quietly in our designated seats, he continued his lecture.

"There are two things I can't tolerate: you talking when I don't want you to talk, and you *not* talking when I *want* you to talk. You must eagerly participate in the class, but never talk when you aren't supposed to talk. Is that clear?"

A girl behind me mumbled, "Amen!" but I didn't think it was funny at all. We sat quietly, showing fear and respect to our teacher who might have killed many enemy soldiers during the Pacific War.

Satisfied, he smiled. "Well, if we understand one another, you'll have no problem with me, and I'll be as gentle as a Buddha. We have much catching up to do, girls. Let's begin with composition. I want you to write a one-page essay about war. What is a war? What did the North Koreans do to us on June 25 last year? Why are they our enemy? Who are our friends? Write whatever comes into your mind. You have forty-five minutes to finish it."

While pencils raced on the notebook paper, Mr. Yang walked back and forth in the aisle, his hands locked behind him, making the floorboards creak under him. Whenever he passed me, I smelled caustic soda, which most people used for laundry, including our family. I wondered if he was a bachelor. It was obvious that he didn't rinse his shirt long enough to get rid of the unpleasant smell. Mother always rinsed again and again until everything smelled clean and fresh like spring air.

It wasn't an easy essay to write, I decided after I wrote the title on my notebook, "War, Enemy, Friends." I kept rolling my pencil on the wooden desk, trying to think of what to write, and Mr. Yang hissed "shhhhh" as he passed me. Then suddenly my thoughts began to reel and I wrote:

> "In war, people destroy buildings, homes, bridges, and whatever belongs to the enemy without thinking twice about what they are doing. We are at war with the North Koreans, only because they made a surprise attack on us last June. If we don't fight back, we will become a communist country sooner or later. Because of what the Communists have done, my five little cousins lost their father, my aunt is a widow, and my friend Mia is an orphan.
>
> War brings people closer together too. The Americans in our country are our friends, because they believe that destroying civilization and human lives is wrong. They are fighting for us, risking their own lives. Because of their sacrifices in our country, someday South Korea will be a stronger nation, and the Americans will be remembered by all Koreans, as well as people all over the world."

I couldn't think of more to write, so I wrote my name, folded the paper, and handed it to Mr. Yang.

The next morning, walking into the classroom at eight, I saw my composition hanging on the back wall along with two other essays, one on each side. Mine was the second best of the three, according to the teacher's note scribbled at the bottom of my notebook paper. All day I noticed my classmates smiling at me.

Jinsook seemed pleasantly surprised that her desk partner could write an essay worthy enough to be hung on the wall. She not only began to notice me but also treated me to a handful of Nabisco cookies at recess. While talking with her, I learned that her father owned Baik's Trading Company at the market that sold strictly American merchandise, including chocolate, school supplies, canned goods, and even some clothes. Admiring her American sneakers with thick soles one day, I thought she might be the richest girl in school.

Jinsook was generous to other girls too. Once in a while, she brought a large bag of tiny marble-like American chocolate called "M&M" and shared it with the whole class. We respected her and her rich parents who allowed their daughter to bring such expensive treats to school.

Her mother, a round lady my mother's age, showed up at lunch hour occasionally, wearing a colorful American dress with bold prints and carrying a large package. I noticed the scent of lilac as she passed me on the way to our classroom, where Teacher Yang was grading our assignment papers. I wondered if that smell had come from America, squeezed into a miniature bottle, which I had seen in the show windows of fancy shops.

The grownups rarely visited school unless our teacher requested a parent-teacher conference. Since many male teachers had been recruited by the army and sent to the front, most of the teachers were busy, substituting for the absentee teachers.

One day, Jinsook's mother stayed in our classroom for a very long time, at least a half hour, before she walked out of the classroom with our smiling teacher. As they disappeared through the wrought iron gate together, Yoja said loudly, "Someone in our class will get a good report card this semester. Guess who?"

I nudged her with my elbow, but it wasn't soon enough. Jinsook heard her and turned to us, but she didn't say anything. Biting her lips, she ran into the classroom.

For a few days, Jinsook didn't talk to me, only because she knew Yoja was my best friend. I didn't know what to say to her except "Hi" in the morning. She ignored my efforts by acting as though I were her worst enemy. I didn't know how to make her talk to me. She offered me neither M&Ms nor Nabisco cookies at recess, although she offered them to others.

Jinsook didn't get her report card after all. Her mother hanged herself on a tree in their backyard one morning and Jinsook's life shattered. It was a strange morning. When I arrived at school just before eight as usual, my classmates sat in small circles, whispering to one another. Teacher Yang wasn't there, and Jinsook's chair next to mine was empty too. She was never late, though our teacher was late once in a while. A strange sensation overtook me when I saw Yoja, pale and scared, approaching my desk.

"Jong-ah, did you read the newspaper?" she asked.

I shook my head. She had never asked me such a question before and I said, "Since when did you think I read the newspaper everyday?"

Then she told me that Jinsook's mother had killed herself the night before.

I must have stared at her blankly because she added, "It's true. Ask anyone. Her father's picture was in the newspaper, hand-cuffed and all. My father gave me the newspaper on the train and I read every word of it."

"Why did she do it?" I asked.

"The American MPs attacked their shop yesterday, you know, Baik's Trading Company, and took away all of the American stuff. When her father was arrested in the late afternoon, the people who loaned him money rushed to their home and camped all night, demanding their money back. I guess she had a nervous breakdown some time before the dawn. Her next-door neighbor found her body hanging from a tree in the backyard early this morning and called the police."

It didn't seem real. She had three or four children, and Jinsook was the oldest. What would happen to her father? I had seen some Korean MPs and two or three American soldiers walking into the market in the middle of the day, blowing whistles, and some vendors shutting down their booths in a hurry and disappearing like lightning, but I had never understood the reason.

While we were still trying to understand what had just happened to our classmates' mother, Teacher Yang walked in, his eyes red and his hair uncombed, and announced grimly that Jinsook would no longer be with us because she was transferring to another school district. "If anyone wants to write to her, I have her uncle's address," he said in a low, heavy voice. Some girls cried as they copied Jinsook's address on their notebooks, but I didn't.

Teacher Yang dismissed the class early, telling us he had to attend a teacher's meeting, and coming home, I looked for the newspaper. It took me a while to finish the article because some Chinese letters popped into my view, but still, I got the whole picture in my head. Jinsook's father had been operating an illegal business, using some Korean men working for the American Eighth Army base. Besides what he had at his store, Mr. Baik owned a secret warehouse somewhere

downtown full of stolen American goods. One of his men was caught while stealing, and Mr. Baik's crime against the Americans was revealed.

In the picture, Mr. Baik didn't seem guilty or ashamed of what he had done.
He looked boldly at me from the printed page. How disgusting, I thought. He
was a thief who had been stealing from the people who came to help us. I wished
I had never taken a bite of the Nabisco cookies or M&Ms from Jinsook.

CHAPTER 19

▼

DEMONSTRATIONS
AGAINST AMERICANS

On June 25, the first anniversary of the Korean War, our school participated in a citywide anti-American demonstration in front of the U.S. Eighth Army base on the outskirts of Pusan, Somyon. Our school had been gathering frequently—sometimes at a high school campus, other times in front of the train station—since the American president had removed General MacArthur from the Korean War theater in April. But this was the first time we were gathering in front of the U.S. army base and we were excited.

Teacher Yang had explained that General MacArthur had been eager to use atomic bombs on the Chinese Communists, but President Truman was against it: President Truman wanted the war to end as soon as possible, but General MacArthur wanted to get rid of the communists from our peninsula once and for all. "If the war ends now," our teacher concluded, "our country will be permanently divided, and the two Koreas will be worst enemies forever."

The circle in front of the U.S. army base was boiling over with kids, all wearing school uniforms, in the summer heat. Our class snaked through some older boys and then some younger ones and settled near the tall wrought iron gate where several armed American MPs walked back and forth. They looked intense: they seemed sad rather than angry. I wondered if they would shoot us if we demonstrated too long.

In the center of the crowd stood a platform, and a Korean man wearing a red headband was standing on it, a microphone in his hand. It was difficult to understand what he was saying because the speaker buzzed loudly and too many vendors shouted around us. Then suddenly, everyone shouted, "We want reunification!"

"We want reunification!"

"Move out, Americans! Move out!"

"We'll fight without you!"

"The future of Asia depends on us!"

Time moved intolerably slowly in the oppressive heat as the man shouted and the crowd repeated after him. I wanted to cover my head with a wide brimmed straw hat and sit down. I wondered what the Americans had done to deserve this.

The shouting abruptly stopped and I looked up. The man with the red headband was stepping down, and another man, younger and bold-looking, was coming up. Positioning himself in the center, he lifted his arms above his head, and a white banner that said REUNIFICATION in red unfolded instantly between his hands. He stood in that position at least for ten seconds, his legs planted firmly on the wooden floor. The crowd cheered and clapped.

The man took down the banner in a swerving motion and grabbed the microphone in front of him. "Dear citizens," he said in a mellow voice, "the time has come when we must let the world's leaders know who we are and what we want." The buzzing had stopped and I could hear him now.

"If Americans don't want to fight for us any more, we'll fight with our own hands, to the last man on this land, and until we have no more blood to shed! We can't let our country be divided forever! It's been almost six years since the Americans and Russians mercilessly divided our motherland in two, like two hungry thieves dividing a cooked piglet, fairly and equally, and we have been bleeding ever since. Because of their greed, we are at war with our brothers and sisters in the North. Had the Americans and Russians left us alone after the liberation, there would be no war today."

He paused, and people began shouting, lifting their arms into the air. "Those savages!" "Damn the Russians, damn the Yankees."

The speaker raised one arm, and the crowd stopped shouting. He continued, "General MacArthur understood our sorrow and pain. He's the only man capable of granting us reunification, but the American president removed him from his duty. We want General MacArthur to reunify us!"

The crowd shouted, "We want General MacArthur! We want General MacArthur!"

The speaker's mouth moved again, but I couldn't hear him; all I could hear was "We want General MacArthur! We want General MacArthur!"

He waited until the shouting died down. "Let's sing together, Brothers and Sisters!" He began singing a song titled "Reunification" loudly into the speaker, and we all sang, holding hands, like a Gospel group.

> Come reunification!
> Make us one nation again
> You're our only hope
> Without you, we'll perish.
>
> Come reunification!
> Glue us back together
> And heal our wounds
> Never to be divided again.

My heart wasn't with the people I was singing with. It didn't make sense that we wanted to reunify with people who had killed so many innocent people. And why did we want the Americans to leave our country? When the log bridge in our neighborhood had floated away during a flood last year, the Americans had come and repaired it. Only a year earlier, we had stood on Main Street and waved American flags, shouting "Victory USA," as a long line of American army trucks entered our town. What changed?

I thought about asking the girl standing next to me, but I changed my mind. She kept eating candy, her hand traveling between her pocket and her mouth. *What can she tell me?*

During a ten-minute break, Yoja showed up. "Let's get a drink, Jong-ah," she said. "We can buy *coca-cola* here, the real *coca-cola* made in America."

I told her I wasn't thirsty. "Go ahead," I said. "I'll wait for you here." She ran toward a vending booth where a man wearing a straw hat was singing, "Ice Tea! Sweet and cold!"

Seeing Teacher Yang standing alone under a ginkgo tree, a clear glass filled with bubbly liquid in his hand, I cautiously measured my chance of being scolded for disturbing him against having my questions answered. I decided that it was worth the risk. I had seen him patiently helping my classmates solving a simple math problem without losing his temper. Although unpredictable some days, we considered him a good teacher.

"Teacher Yang, I'm confused!" I said, suddenly standing before him.

"Confused?" he said. "Who isn't confused here in Korea today?"

I knew he was drinking beer or something with alcohol because he seemed to be in a good mood.

"Tell me, what's confusing you?"

"Why are we asking the Americans to leave our country?" I asked.

"I don't know what to tell you," he said, taking a sip from his glass. "It's our president who's ordering us to do this. I don't think he really wants the Americans to pack and leave in the middle of the war, but since General MacArthur was removed from his commanding position here in Korea, he sees no chance that North and South can be one country again. That's the reason he's using many organizations—Labor Unions, women's groups, religious people—to rally against Americans, like we're doing now. We can't say 'No' to our president, can we?"

"No."

"Our president and General MacArthur were good friends, you know, playing golf or having lunch together once in a while at the presidential mansion. Who knows what General MacArthur might have promised the old man? Maybe the general told him that he could rule the entire Korea someday, undivided and reunified? Who knows. Now that General MacArthur is gone, taking his dream with him, our president is an angry man. Don't pay any attention to what we're saying. Just be there, like everyone else. Now, it's time to go back to your line. Quick!" He abruptly turned and walked away, as if he couldn't stand me any longer.

Peace-talks between the Chinese leaders and the UN delegates began that summer in a town called Kaesong near the 38th parallel. Everyday the radio reported, using big words like *armistice, ceasefire-agreement, demarcation mark, liaison.* Many anxious refugees, including our houseguests, moved back to Seoul, taking all their belongings with them. The train station became extremely crowded with people leaving town and those saying good-bye to them. Tensions eased and people seemed to think the war would end soon: some grandfathers now strode on the street again, holding their grandkids' hands; children came out of their crowded homes and jumped a rope or played ball; women on their way to the market or homes took time to exchange the latest news.

"It's time to enjoy life again," Father said one evening. "Yobo, let's have a picnic at Suyong Beach this Saturday, what do you say? It's been long since we were at the beach."

We cheered.

For several summers before the war broke out, our parents had rented a two-bedroom house by the seashore, and we spent the entire summer vacation on the beach, digging clams, swimming, and looking for pretty seashells to collect. By the time the vacation ended, we resembled a family of Peking Ducks glazed in soy sauce and baked.

That Saturday we took the train to Suyong Beach. It was a perfect day to shake off the war dust and get away from demonstrations, homework, and tests, and I was anxious to jump into the water headfirst. When we got there the sun was right above us, and tall wild sunflowers were everywhere, swaying in the ocean breeze. Many people in colorful summer outfits walked along the road leading to the beach and we joined them. Red dragonflies darted in all directions, like odd shaped specks in the air. Seagulls kited in the blue sky, squealing with joy. The salty air felt so wonderful in my lungs that I took several deep breaths.

Our favorite spot was now closed to the Korean public. A chain link fence stood before us with a sign written in English. People grumbled and moved away to find another area. Instead of Koreans, about a hundred or more American soldiers occupied the spot; several army canopies were pitched and American soldiers were having a good time—some playing volleyball, some swimming, and some walking.

We favored this spot for its endless, white sugar-like sand and seafloor rich with all kinds of clams. I used to find bright pink shells with smooth, mother-of-pearl interiors here. The view, moreover, was the best of all the other beaches surrounding Pusan. A rock island, covered with dwarf cypresses, floated only swimming strokes away from the sand beach. When the sunlight leaked through the ocean spray it gave you the illusion that you were looking at a mysterious sea animal that might rise and disappear in the blink of an eye. The only negative side of this beach was that many accidents had occurred between the beach and the rock island during high tide. Sometimes the waves, encouraged by the wind, turned into tall monumental beasts and crashed into the rock mercilessly, snatching whatever was on the rock and disappearing, including mussel hunters and picnickers.

"Let's go to the next beach," Father suggested, and we walked twenty minutes on the sand to find another area where the sand was clean and the seafloor had no deep holes. Father was particular about the safety of a beach. After wading in the water for a few minutes, while we waited, he said, "Let's stay here. It feels pretty good."

Many colorful umbrellas bloomed on both sides of us, and half-naked Korean children were busy making sand castles only a few feet away.

We had a wonderful time. We ate the rice-rolls Mother had packed for lunch; we swam in clear blue water; we dug up two-dozen clams and saved them for clam soup for dinner. We then played with a rainbow-color beach ball, including our parents, which we had rented from the booth that also sold drinks and cooked sea snails. Around four, we heard a faint siren wailing some distance away, and Mother ordered us to get dressed. "It can be a warning sign for a storm," she said.

At the train station, we heard horrible news. An American army officer, his wife, and their three-year-old daughter had drowned on the spot where we had been earlier. They had been on the rock island around noon, unaware of the wide tidal range or how quickly the water level rose in that area, and when a tall wave smashed onto the rock, their daughter rolled into the water. The soldier and his wife jumped into the water together to rescue the child. "Their bodies aren't found yet," a man told us.

All the way home, I thought about the American family drowned at our favorite beach. I wondered if they had been informed about the tidal range. I wondered why his family was there. Were they visiting him? Were they on vacation?

When the train pulled into the neighborhood station, Mother said, "I don't know why God allows such tragedy to happen to a young American family enjoying themselves at the beach."

Father retorted, "Leave God alone, Yobo. He has nothing to do with what happened today or why we're in a war with the North Koreans. Our idea of God might infuriate Him sometimes."

Still, I wished it hadn't happened.

CHAPTER 20

▼

PAINFUL GOODBYES

Autumn arrived. The sky was a sheet of tinted glass hanging overhead. It looked so transparent that I thought I could shatter it to pieces with a pebble. Leaves were turning different colors: gingko lemony yellow, pin oak brown, red maple vermilion, persimmon dark green. I loved the smell of burning leaves in the air, the smell similar to roasted chestnut. On the sunny spots in our courtyard lay bamboo baskets filled with sliced squash, strips of seasoned beef, and red peppers, each telling me winter would be here soon.

Without the priests and nuns living in our house, I felt liberated from attending daily Mass and weekly confession. Our courtyard seemed more spacious and quiet than before, since Father Yoon or Father Bahng wasn't walking and reading the Bible at the same time. The market had lost some vendors and probably some customers, too, but the noises, the smell of northern dumpling soup, or the signs bearing Seoul this or Hamhung that remained. The war introduced us to many different people and foods we didn't know about and shifted and re-arranged everything in our town—people, homes and buildings, and roads.

One morning when Mother wasn't home, I looked at my reflection in the mirror and decided that I had grown at least two inches taller since a year earlier. My cheeks weren't as plump as they used to be, and my head almost reached the top of the mirror, though I wasn't standing on my toes. My aunts and uncles would no longer tease me, squeezing my cheeks and saying, "You look like a

steam roll, Jong-ah, so plump and so chubby!" I could easily fool them now, saying, I was twelve or thirteen.

Seeing Mother's black shawl with daisy patterns hanging on a hook next to the
hallway mirror, I yanked it down and wrapped it around my face. *I'm beautiful,*
the girl in the mirror whispered to me. She looked more like my mother in her
younger days, which I saw from the yellowed pictures in her album. I had never
thought I looked like her even though some relatives had mentioned it. I tried to
picture myself being her age. Remembering that Mother kept her face powder,
blush, and lipstick in her cabinet next to her sleeping mat, I brought them and
painted my face. It wasn't easy, making a straight line with thick lipstick. Now,
the girl in the mirror didn't look like my mother in her old album at all, but more
like a circus girl with ghostly white face and crooked red lips. I laughed and she
laughed too. I covered my mouth and she did the same. *You're funny....*

First Sister's scowling face appeared in the mirror, next to the circus girl. I
froze.

"What are you doing with Mother's makeup and shawl?" she asked from the
mirror.

"What do you think I'm doing?" the circus girl asked back with a straight face.
I liked her guts.

"You look like a cat that just ate a mouse, Jong-ah!"

"So? It's none of your business, Big Sister!"

"You aren't supposed to touch anything that belongs to Mother, and you
know it!"

"Go ahead and tell her," I suggested.

"Don't worry," she said and disappeared.

I smiled to the girl in the mirror and told her I had to go. She understood and
smiled through her bright red lips.

After I cleaned myself and returned all Mother's stuff back to her drawer, I
came to my room to do homework. I then realized that I hadn't heard from
Bokja for more than a month. I had been corresponding with her since I had last
seen her in Cheju and my drawer was full of her letters. Sometimes she enclosed
some stiff dried flowers in the envelope, which she had probably picked from the
vacant lot behind the orphanage, and in response, I sent her dried clovers, poems,
and my drawings of Mimi, which I was proud of.

In her last letter, she had been frustrated because she wasn't in school. Opening my drawer, I took out her letter to read it one more time.

"My dearest," it began:

"I hope everything is well with you. Being an orphan not only means you have no home and no parents but also means you have not much hope for tomorrow. Without learning anything all day, I feel like a dog napping in the sun. What can I be when I'm older, living in a place like this? I used to complain when my grandmother woke me for school early in the morning, not knowing how lucky I was. Now the women here wake me up at seven every morning to tell me it's time to change diapers or to wash dirty clothes or to clean and dress the babies that died during the night. There's nothing I haven't done since I got here. My hands are rougher than that of construction workers. Sometimes, I'm angry and bitter at people here. If they'd send me to school, to any school, only for two or three hours a day, I would do anything for them: I'd even lick the floor.

One year when I was in Red Peony Elementary School in Pyongyang, I was named 'Chairman Kim's best student' and wore the Chairman's medal for the entire year. I'm not making it up, Jong-ah. Every teacher in school liked me then.

But what am I now? My name is orphan. But you can call me "Homeless Princess," if you like. It sounds a lot better, doesn't it? One day seems like a year for me. Pray to your Jesus so that he'll find my new home in America soon. I'm Buddhist: I can only pray to Buddha.

Missing you,
Your sister in Cheju."

I had responded to her, telling her I would pray. I also mentioned that our guest room was now available since our long-term guests had moved back to Seoul and that Mother would be glad to meet her. That was a month ago. Why wasn't she writing to me?

The days moved awfully slow for me as I waited for Bokja's letter. We demonstrated again and again, shouting the same slogans and asking Americans to move out of South Korea. Teacher Yang had been drinking lately, and sometimes he got angry with us for not answering his quizzes correctly or not understanding mathematic rules. Twice, he punished the whole class by striking each of us with a thin bamboo stick. We nicknamed him "One-eyed Communist."

One afternoon when I returned home, hating school and our mean teacher, Mother handed me Bokja's letter. I opened it immediately.

"My dearest Jong-ah," her letter began:

"Thanks for your invitation, but I can't come to meet your family. I'm going to America in three weeks, exactly on October 3. Your prayer was answered. I feel a bit strange, though, because it seems someone's bad luck brought me good fortune.

Do you remember Miya Hyun, the girl who limped badly because she stepped on a mine in Seoul? She was one of the kids supposed to go to America, but she suddenly died of diphtheria last week. Four kids died that week, believe it or not.

I didn't get the news until the following day. The director called me to her office and said I could go to America on October 3rd with Miya Hyun's passport, if I want to. I just looked at her, not believing what she was talking about. Then she said Miya died. She said that I must decide very soon because if I didn't want to go, she'd ask another girl.

Was I lucky or cursed, going to America with a dead girl's name? I don't care. This was what I have been waiting to happen and it did. I asked the director what would happen if my American parents find out I'm not Miya Hyun, and she said not to worry. She said most of the American families wouldn't care whether I'm Bokja Kim or Mia Hyun anyway. So I said I'd go..."

It was shocking news. I had vaguely expected that she would leave the orphanage someday and I might not hear from her again, but I didn't think she would go to America so soon. I couldn't imagine what it would be like going to America with another girl's name. I was worried about her. But what was there for me to do? This world belonged to grownups, not to us kids. I went on reading:

"As you know, Jong-ah, I have no one here, and no Korean family will adopt me because I'm a girl and I'm twelve. It makes me sad to go so far away from you, but...I have no choice, as you know. I want to see you so much before I leave, Jong-ah. We might never see one another again, you know. We're leaving from Pusan Airport on October 3rd by Pan Am at ten AM. You will be the only person who can see me go, so please come to wish me luck. If I don't see you again, I don't know what I would do.

Your friend and sister, Bokja

I wanted to see her as much as she did. I also wanted to encourage her to be strong in her new home in America. I wanted to give her something, too, something she could treasure for a long time, something that would make her feel close to me and her country.

I went through all of the things in my drawers. The blue marble that Kwon had given me the day I had returned from Cheju came to my mind, but I decided against it. She'd have plenty of marbles in America, prettier ones than mine. I also thought of the porcelain music box that had a ballerina dancing inside, while it played the tune of *For Elise*, but I decided against it, too. It was not only made in America, but the melody would make her cry.

Then I had an idea: Sunriser's feather. Since the day he was slaughtered a year earlier I had never looked at them because I didn't want to be reminded of how he died. Opening my drawer, I picked one, lifted it toward the window, and let the sunlight leak through it. It changed color according to the way I held it: one moment it was a fierce purple-blue, the next a metallic green, and then a crimson. Suddenly he was alive in my eyes, striding in the courtyard, head up, shifting his glass-like eyes this way and that, and pecking at the dead flies I had dropped for him.

"Bokja Onni," I began writing:

"Your letter made me so sad that I can't even cry. I wish you would change your mind, but it's your decision. I really want to give you something so that you will never forget me, and I thought this feather might do the trick. It once belonged to a rooster I was taking care of, but he died last year. He was a handsome rooster that woke me every morning like a clock before the sun came up. He even tried to tell us when the North Communists invaded the South on June 25 last year, but my mother had him slaughtered, saying that a rooster crowing at night could bring ill fortunes. But I don't believe in superstition. I think a rooster can crow at any time of a day or night, if he wants to. I promise you he will wake you up every morning, rain or shine, to announce that a new day is here for you.

I can't believe that you'll be thousands of kilometers away from me once you leave our country, but we're still sisters, remember? And who knows, Bokja *Onni,* I might be in America someday, too. Let's write to one another, okay?

Wishing you my very best in your new home,

Your sister in Pusan, Jong-ah."

On October 3rd, a Saturday, we had a drizzling rain. The gray sky hung over everything and mist-like rain came down endlessly as if the whole town was grieving for my friend's departure. I hardly ate anything for breakfast. Earlier, my sister had drawn me a map and written down on notebook paper what bus I must take to get to the airport and where to get off. Since I had never taken the bus alone, I was nervous.

Mother made me wear my new red coat, the one she bought last January, and told my sister to go with me, but I said no. Bokja would laugh, seeing me next to my big sister. Bokja had flown to Pusan by herself from Pyongyang, trusting total strangers, and I should at least show her that I was able to travel alone in my own town. I would be eleven next February.

I left home early, with the map in one pocket and my coin bag in another. I took the bus in front of the barbershop. "I'm going to the Plaza Hotel downtown," I announced nervously to an old man sitting in the driver's seat. He nodded and smiled. "Don't you worry, child. I'll tell you when to get off."

I wasn't afraid any more. The bus was only half full when we left. Through the mist-covered window, I watched the whole town pass by. On the main street, all vending booths were open, and men and women sat on tall stools, drinking steamy tea or eating hot noodle soup. Far away, a church with a tall steeple stood under the heavy gray sky, and I quietly prayed for Bokja. "Dear God, please help Bokja to be happy in her new home. Make sure her parents are kind to her and love her as their own. Guide her to do well in school, too...." I didn't ask him to bless her too much, because "blessing" could mean many different things, including going to Mass every day, and Bokja wasn't a Catholic.

Twenty-minutes later, I saw a tall western-style building with American letters written on it, amidst many other tall buildings, and I asked the driver, "Is that the Plaza Hotel?"

"Yes, it is! I was about to tell you that," he said.

I jumped off the bus, thanking the driver.

The shuttle to the airport was waiting and I got on. Many English-speaking men and woman were on the bus already, and I felt a surge of pride for going to the airport with them.

The lobby at the Pusan Airport was so crowded I bumped several times into well-dressed men and women posing for snapshots. Through the speakers mounted under the impeccable white ceiling, a man was speaking English, probably announcing the time of departure or arrival of a plane. In the middle of the lobby stood men with flowers pinned on their well-pressed suits, chattering with people without flowers. In one corner, a long line of passengers waited under a sign that said CUSTOMS, where several airport employees opened and closed huge bags and suitcases. In another corner, before a window that said, "EXCHANGE," some westerners stood in line, holding green bills in their hands.

Bokja was nowhere on the first floor. I walked up the staircase, following some grownups. I found her sitting on a bench in a corner with other girls, all younger than her. She seemed to be crying, her eyes red and puffy.

"Hi," I said cheerfully, but she didn't smile or hug me: she only looked up blankly at me as if she had never seen me before. "You look nice," I said, noticing her new green pleated dress with USA embroidered on the collar. The nametag pinned on her left shoulder had some curly letters written on it, and I wondered whether it said Bokja Kim or Miya Hyun.

Instead of smiling or saying thank you, Bokja lifted her hand holding a white handkerchief and buried her face in it. A long awkward moment followed as we just sat, she crying and I searching for words.

Two girls sitting next to her seemed to be well trained for the long trip. They didn't talk, didn't run around, and didn't pay attention to me but merely sat on the bench, like dolls in a display case. One of them smoothed the wrinkles out of her green American dress, and when she was satisfied, she sat erect again, folding her hands in front of her.

"This is for you, Bokja *Onni*," I said, handing her the envelope I had prepared. "It's something I thought you might like to have in your new home."

Her eyes wide, she said in a frightened voice, "I'm Miya, remember? Don't call me Bokja. You can get me in trouble."

"But you're not Miya," I protested. "I thought you were just using Miya's passport."

"Shhh," she said, quickly looking around. "You're not supposed to say anything about it. I'm Miya…Miya Hyun. Actually, you don't need to call me anything."

How crazy, I thought. *Does she really expect me to call her Miya when Miya is dead and buried somewhere in Cheju?* I only stared at her sadly.

Bokja opened the envelope and began reading it, her lips moving. She suddenly bent her head and began to sob.

"What is it?" I said.

"Nothing," she said, going back to the letter. It took a long time for her to finish reading, because she broke into tears again and again.

My eyes were watery, too. I was losing my make-believe sister and a friend. The day we had met at the Pusan port I had been reluctant to be her make-believe sister, because I knew nothing about her. Now I was glad that we had that special moment together and months of exchanging letters.

When she stopped reading and wiped her tears, I said, "I'll write to you, okay?"

"No, you can't," she squeaked, fighting her tears.

"Why not?"

"Because…I'm not allowed to have any contact with people who know me in Korea. I can't even write to the orphanage, the director said. The new parents can find out that the orphanage switched the kid without them knowing about it, and she doesn't want that to happen. 'Just forget everything, and move on with your new life,' she said."

"Why are you going to America, then," I blurted. "First, you lost your name, and now you're losing your connection with your own country. I can't even write to you! What's the big deal about going to America?"

She didn't look at me. With one hand, she took her handkerchief to her watery eyes again, and with the other, she reached my hand and gently squeezed it.

"Don't go, Bokja *Onni*," I said, my eyes filling. "You can live with me. I'm sure Mother will say yes. I can't let you go!"

She pulled her hand out of mine. "It's too late," she said, her voice soft but firm. "I have no choice. I'll be okay."

"You can't even try?" I said angrily.

A tall American woman with short golden hair interrupted our conversation by suddenly appearing from nowhere and clapping her big hands. Speaking something in English, she made a simple hand motion in the air and all of the kids on the bench rose and ran toward her, like puppies toward their master.

Bokja too got up. She hugged me quickly, whispering, "Bye now. Thank you for your letter and the feather." Turning her back to me, she followed the woman walking toward the wide doorway at the far end where a long line of people waited.

I stood there, waiting for her to turn around, but she didn't as if she didn't even want me to remember her.

Cupping my hands, I shouted, "Bye, Bokja *Onni*. Take care!" My voice echoed through the corridors, moving farther away.

As if God was determined to teach me something about life and death, Grandfather passed away two weeks later on a Sunday. Father had been going to Taegu almost every weekend for some time, staying there two or three days at a time. At Mother's insistence, we had prayed for Grandfather every day, before every meal and at bedtime, but our prayer and Father's devotion toward his father performed no miracles. When the telegram reached us on the following Monday, Father was already in Taegu.

Mother didn't cry much, nor did she act shocked. Making a sign of the cross on her chest, she knelt and prayed. She then began packing. I saw her white mourning dress fall into her leather suitcase, then her white rubber shoes, and then her change of clothes and makeup.

My two teenage brothers packed their bags, too, to accompany Mother and to attend the funeral Mass.

As always, Mother left us orders that we should lock the doors at night and that we shouldn't go outside at all after school until she returned. "Make sure to spend some quiet time, too," she said.

"Don't worry Mother," First Sister replied for the rest of us.

I was sad. As soon as Mother and my brothers left, I crossed the courtyard and stepped into the guestroom where Grandfather and Grandmother had stayed while they had been with us. The wooden crucifix hung on the wall just as before and I knelt under it. I could almost see Grandfather lying solemnly in his casket decorated with flowers. All my uncles, aunts, Mother, and Grandmother stood around him in mourners garb made of ramie fabric.

I tried to pray, but my mind was blank. Other than remembering his wispy voice, I couldn't remember anything about him, not even his face. All I could remember was his bony legs and arms, which Kwon and I had massaged two or three times a week. *What was it like dying, Grandfather? Was it painful to die? Where are you now? Can you see me from where you are?*

Just then, a strange sensation came over me and I thought he was in the room, lying on the floor, just as before, his herb medicine cooling next to his pillow. I could smell the medicine, the strong odor of burnt grass mixed with something old and mysterious. I could even hear his laborious breathing.

I grew teary at the thought that I'd never massage him again or watch him sleep, his mouth half open. *Had I known that you'd die like this, I'd have massaged you better and longer.* I let tears come until I couldn't cry any more. The gingko leaves whispered softly in the courtyard breeze, as if they understood how I felt.

CHAPTER 21

▼

ROUTE TO
MIDDLE SCHOOL

The following March I began sixth grade. Teacher Hahn, an old man with beady eyes under his thick eyebrows, had his own golden rules. One day he'd write on the blackboard, "Know your route to middle school, the way migrating birds know theirs," and the next day it was, "Roses bloom brighter after a storm: hard labor pays off!"

He made a large chart, too, showing our names, dates, and test-records for each subject neatly written in several columns and rows, and posted it on the front wall, so that everyone could see how well or how badly they did on what subject on what day. He also seated us according to the test results—the one with the highest score in the far most left seat in the front row, the one with the lowest in the far most right seat in the last row, and the rest in between according to the scores. We were shifted around in the classroom two or three times a day.

Once in a while, a coughing frenzy attacked Teacher Hahn and he bent over and hacked. He seemed so helpless when this happened, and we waited until his coughs subsided and he wiped his mouth to ask questions. He had poor eyesight too. He often took the book to his nose in order to read it. Still, he made us believe that we could succeed at everything we did, if we worked hard enough.

One day, entering the classroom, I found a new motto across the blackboard: "Study, study, study: you're six graders only once." An idea entered my head, and

I waited until Teacher Hahn stepped out of the room to borrow chalk from Teacher Min next door or to get fresh air, which he often did. Finally, around eleven, he left the room, coughing again and telling us to review the previous lesson.

Feeling a slight tremor, I rose silently from my seat, walked up to the blackboard, and picked up a chalk. Carefully, I replaced the word "study" with "play" and "six-graders" with "children," and returned to my desk.

My classmates laughed. Someone read it aloud, "'Play, play, play: you're children only once!' It sounds like a Bible passage, doesn't it?" "Yeah," another said, "I like it much better than the original!" I responded by waving my arm in the air and they cheered. My sense of triumph was short-lived as Teacher Hahn returned.

I pretended I was busy reading. He didn't look at the blackboard immediately, but he knew something was strange, because he asked, "What's going on?"

No one said anything. He walked to the back of the room, his hands in his pocket. I heard the floorboards creak behind me.

I was nervous: we had only had him a few weeks. He could be like Teacher Yang who loved to slash our hands with the thin bamboo stick.

"*Ahah!*" Teacher Hahn exclaimed, rushing to the front. "Who did it?" he asked.

I buried my head in the book.

Teacher Hahn walked to a girl in the front row and asked, "Who did it?"

She asked, "Who did what, sir?"

"That! Who changed my motto?"

"I don't know, sir. I was busy reading the book, as you told us. I didn't see anyone going up there."

Good liar, I thought and smiled.

He asked another girl, and she said, "I have no idea, sir. I paid no attention other than to what I was reading."

Teacher Hahn stepped up to the podium, making his footsteps heard. "The one who changed the motto, come forward!"

Someone behind me said, "Don't go, Jong-ah! Don't do anything." I toyed with her idea, but I decided against it, because he could punish us as a whole. With a quick prayer, I rose, my head hanging.

"Come to the front!"

I obeyed him. *He can't kill me,* I comforted myself.

"Read what you wrote to the class!"

"Play, play, play. You're children only once!" The classroom exploded with laughter, but he didn't laugh. He wasn't angry either. *Jesus, don't let him punish me!*

"Did you make it up or did you copy it from somewhere?" he asked me.

"I made it up, sir," I said in a tiny voice.

"Not bad!" he said.

"No?" I asked.

"No, but I have an assignment for you. Make up three more mottos that will encourage you and your classmates to study harder, and bring them to me tomorrow, understand?"

"Yes, sir."

"Here's the deal," our teacher said. "If I like your mottos, I won't punish you. If I don't like them, however, I'll give you something to remember for the rest of your life. Is it clear?"

"Like what, sir?"

"I haven't decided yet. Work on your mottos now and we'll discuss the rest tomorrow. How's that?"

"Fine."

The rest of the day I kept thinking about my unusual assignment. Yoja was worried, too. At lunchtime, she asked me if I had some ideas about the mottos.

"Not yet," I said. But soon, I had an idea, thanks to the ants I saw on the ground! "How does this sound?" I asked Yoja: 'Store your knowledge for exams, like ants storing food for winter'?"

"I like it!" she said.

Later that day, during Korean literature, another idea came when I saw nails in the floorboard. I wrote, "A carpenter drills nails into wood but a sixth grader drills words into her brains." I passed it to Yoja, and she nodded to me as her approval.

The third one didn't come easy. I had to ask Kwon to help me. "I have one for you," he said, without thinking. "Great Wall of China is the fruit of human labor."

I was surprised. "Where did you learn it, Kwon? You didn't make it up, did you?"

"Why do you care?" he retorted and walked away.

The next morning, at our teacher's request, I stood in front of the class and recited all three mottos.

Teacher Hahn was pleased. "You did your homework!"

I said I did.

"I like all of the mottos you recited, so I'll not punish you for what you did yesterday. You're forgiven."

I was elated. As I bowed to him and came to my seat, in the midst of loud cheers, I felt as though I had just stepped out of a confessional, free of all my sins. Strangely enough, I was determined to be Teacher Hahn's best student.

During each class, I diligently took notes and asked questions when something was unclear to me. Coming home, I did homework, reviewed everything we had learned that day, including the math rules, the names of the Yi dynasty kings and the capital cities of all the nations in Asia. When I had time, I read *shijo,* too. The more I read *shijo,* the more I liked history class, because *shijo* told many tales of those who lived hundreds of years before me. I always had thought history was a boring subject, but *shijo* changed my attitude entirely. The sixth-grade history book was loaded with stories of political wrangling between scholars and militants during the Yi dynasty, as well as vicious murder plots surrounding the royal families, including kings' concubines. The endless assassins, what era it happened in, and who was involved with what plot confused me at first, but after reading the lines carefully two or three times and jotting down a few important names, their titles, and what clan they belonged to, it was easy to understand.

I especially liked the *shijo* titled "Pine" written by a well-known scholar named Song Sam-moon. Emperor Yi Taejo, the first emperor of the Yi dynasty, murdered Song for not surrendering to his power after he toppled the Koryo dynasty and declared his kingship.

> What shall I be when I die?
> A tall pine tree on a mountain peak
> When snow covers the moonlit slopes.
> I'll shine ever more in my green attire.

The image of a pine standing on a mountain peak under the moonlit sky was a powerful image for me. When I was tired of studying, I closed my eyes and imagined that I was that pine on a mountain peak. A moment later when I reopened my eyes, my mind was clear and I was eager to study again.

I often took a book with me to the bathroom, and sometimes I walked in the courtyard, back and forth, with my notebook in my hand, drilling mathematic rules or the names of kings and scholars in the Yi dynasty into my head. With Mother's permission, I drank a cup of Maxwell coffee every night so that I could be as alert as an owl.

My grades improved with time. Once in a while, I made the top score and sat on the far left seat in the front row, right under Teacher Hahn's chin. I also raised my arm triumphantly at quiz hour to show off how much I knew.

Mother was glad when my first report card came in the mail. "See, I told you, you can do it," she said. It was exciting to hear my own mother complimenting me for my achievements.

The day of the exam the following February coincided with my twelfth birthday and Mother had knitted a white scarf with blue stripes for the occasion. I felt warm as I walked to Kyong-Nam Girls Middle School alone with my nametag pinned on my red coat. Yoja took the test at another location, so she couldn't be with me.

I wasn't at all nervous. I had been nervous all the while I had been preparing for the test, and finally I had nothing to be nervous about. The only thought in my head was that the battle with books would be over soon and that I would be free at last. No more studying! No more Maxwell Coffee! I could go to bed early and sleep late without feeling guilty. I didn't have to torture my brains anymore to memorize such unimportant facts as who the president of the Philippines was; which South Asian countries had been French colonies before World War II; and when the Declaration of Independence of the United States had been written.

I took a deep breath when I saw a colossal, three-story white building rise before my eyes. The South Korean army still occupied the main building surrounded by a brick fence, and the armed sentries at the wrought iron gate stood motionless like wooden soldiers. A man in a gray suit standing next to the sentry told us where to go, and a dozen of us walked toward a long wooden structure lying low behind the white building.

It was a crudely built military barrack whose roofline was crooked and sideboard had small holes. At the entrance, two middle school students in uniform checked our nametags and told us which room we belonged in.

In Room 4, I detected a moldy smell. On the front wall hung portraits of President Rhee and President Truman, and in between them was a large map of Korea showing the 38th parallel in red ink. I wondered why these two presidents had anything to do with our exam.

More girls with nametags pinned on their coats filed in, reminding me where I was and why, and I desperately looked for a familiar face but found none.

A loud metallic noise buzzed loudly, and I felt a shock of electric current passing through me. "God, help me do well on this," I prayed desperately.

Two women in black suits entered, each with a white bundle of papers under their arms. One of them, whose hair was bundled up on her crown, welcomed us and said that we would have a ten-minute break in between the tests that would go on until two. The other lady, a few years older, just stood in the back, her hands in her pockets, as if her job was catching anyone who might cheat on the test.

The papers were handed out and we began. The noises of the women walking back and forth in the aisle annoyed me. I tried hard to concentrate on what I was reading, but the letters seemed to be playing tricks on me. I couldn't understand the questions, as if reading Latin. To make the situation worse, a bright circle of sunlight landed on my paper, blinding my eyes. I moved the paper to my right to avoid the bright spot, and the older lady ordered, "Don't move. You're not supposed to move at all until you're done."

My hands were sweaty and I had a headache. My heart pounded loudly, too. I closed my eyes and pretended I was a pine, a very tall one in green attire, standing on a snow-covered slope lit by a round moon. *No more studying after today,* I reminded myself. As soon as I opened my eyes, every word on the paper leaped to my brain, like nails to a magnet, and I understood every line I read. I wrote answers diligently and neatly on the paper. When finished, I went back and read everything once more, to make sure all my answers were correct and I hadn't misspelled any words. After the papers were collected, we had a ten-minute break, but I stayed in the room to review my textbooks for the last time.

A bell buzzed again, and we read and scribbled for what seemed like an eternity.

When the test ended at two, I was tired, and all I could remember was a small circle of bright sunlight glaring at me from the paper. I began walking homeward, not a single thought in my head other than, *No more books. No more coffee. I'm free!*

I took a longer way home through the market, listening to the shouts of vendors. They were music in my ears, and I was happy to be their listener. Every vendor and shopper seemed to smile at me for no reason at all. My feet carried me to a booth that had a sign "Stone Roasted Chestnuts" in a fancy scribble. The sweet, burnt smell made my mouth water, and I suddenly realized how hungry I was. I wished I had a coin.

The vendor, an old man with a bald head and unusually large ears, seemed to recognize me. He smiled wide, showing his wrinkles and missing front tooth. "Want some?" he asked, lifting his wooden spoon with a burned handle.

"I have no money, Grandpa" I said, my feet glued in front of him.

"Don't worry, Little One," he said. "I know who you are. You mother comes here very often." He gave me a paper cone full of hot sticky chestnuts, and I bowed to him politely. "I'll bring you money next time."

"Don't worry about it," he said.

I was lucky, I thought. I bowed to him, and he said, "Watch out for rough boys. Don't lose the chestnuts!"

"Thanks Grandpa!"

Turning my back to the booth, I peeled off the brittle skin, popped the toasty chunk in my mouth, and sank my teeth into it. It melted away, and I ate one after another. How wonderful it was to taste such a delicious treasure when I was free of worry!

"How was the test?" Mother asked me from the front room as I walked into the courtyard.

"I think I did okay."

"It wasn't too hard?"

"No!"

"I'm glad. You worked very hard," she said. Digging into her cotton skirt pocket, she produced a five-*won* bill and handed it to me. "Treat yourself to something good tomorrow, Jong-ah. Today is your birthday, but we'll celebrate it next week for you and your Second Sister."

"Thanks, Mother." It was common in our family that two birthdays were celebrated together. Mother loved "two-for-one" deals, and I had no qualms about it. Everyone had a birthday. I didn't care whether I had been born on February 5th or December 5th.

"What are you going to buy with the money, Jong-ah?" Mother asked. She always had to know everything about where money went.

"I might buy me a book." I didn't tell her I might buy a comic book, which she called "trash".

"Make sure you read a couple of pages before you buy the book," she advised. "Once you bring a book home and decide that you don't like it, they won't give your money back."

"Yes, Mother."

The next morning on the way to the bookstore I saw Yoja walking up the road, and I ran to her. "I'm going to buy me a comic book. You want to come?"

"Comic book?" she said, frowning. "Aren't you sick of books? Any books?"

"I'm not going to buy a textbook, silly. I want something fun to read," I said.

"Forget the book," she said, slapping my back. "Let's go to the cinema downtown. They're showing *Waterloo Bridge*. It's a real tearjerker."

I loved tearjerkers. Many Korean movies were tearjerkers, but this one was an American movie. I had never watched an American tearjerker before. But what if Mother discovered that I went to see an adult movie without her permission? "I don't know," I said.

"Don't worry about money," she said. "My mother gave me lots of money. I'll treat you."

"It's not that. My mother might get upset when she finds out I went to see an adult movie."

Yoja laughed. "How long are you going to be an obedient child, Jong-ah? We're going to be in middle school next month. Some years ago, the girls our age got married and moved away from their parents to live with in-laws. Grow up, Child!"

"Let's go!" I said.

We took the bus and got off at the intersection where a traffic cop stood on a square stool, whistling and waving his arms in all directions. In front of the theater, we stood in line for a long time. Most of the people waiting with us were women and girls older than us.

When we entered, the theater was so dark we bumped into people, but a young woman with a flashlight came over and directed us to empty seats.

During the entire show, I couldn't take my eyes off Robert Taylor portraying an army captain madly in love with a ballet-dancer played by Vivian Leigh. How handsome he was! What would it be like falling in love with such a good-looking man? It gave me shivers on my arms. I didn't envy the dancer at all.

Yoja was right. I had never cried so much in my twelve years. Toward the end, where Vivian Leigh leaves a farewell note to Robert Taylor telling him she couldn't marry him because of what she had done while he had been considered dead and then throws herself in front of a running army truck, I wept as though my parents had died. In fact, the whole theater was filled with the sounds of sniffles and nose blowing.

When we came out of the theater, the sun was still in the center of the sky, but we were so exhausted from crying that we didn't want to do anything. We sat on a bench in front of a fountain to rest.

Yoja suddenly said, squinting in the sunlight, "You've never been to my house, have you?"

"No. You live so far away."

"My mom isn't there today, Jong-ah. We can do whatever we want. I'll show you my parents' wedding pictures."

Again, I thought about Mother. By the time I would return, it might be close to dinnertime, and Mother would certainly interrogate me, asking millions of questions.

Yoja sighed. "You're worried about your *mama* again."

Annoyed, I said, "I'm just thinking about what time I'll be back. What's so bad about it, huh?"

"Don't worry. I'll put you on the four o'clock train. You'll get home at five. Can't your mother realize that her daughter needs a break from her tight grip once in a while? You're twelve."

We took the train. I enjoyed the train ride with Yoja sitting next to me. I had known her since the day I entered the Crystal Elementary School, and we were still good friends after all these years. Someday, we'd be as old as our mothers and talk about our kids, in a small teahouse or on a park bench. Or we'd take a trip together like we were now. I couldn't picture Yoja being that old. A laugh bubbled up, and I turned my head toward the window.

"What's funny?" she asked.

I couldn't share my thought with her. Once I put it into words, it'd sound dull, and she'd mock me again, saying, *What a silly thing to think about.* I wanted to keep it to myself, so I said, "I can't believe I'm actually going to your house, after all these years," I said.

She laughed. "You think I live very far away, but I don't. It only takes fifty minutes to get there."

When the train pulled into a tiny train station surrounded by tall weeds and grasses, I felt as though I was in another country. The air was chilly as Yoja and I walked along the sandy road, listening to the ocean waves, but soon, the cold air didn't bother me. Actually, it was warmer than Pusan, and the sharp, salty smell of the ocean was pleasant in my lungs. After a few minutes, we saw an old towering wooden structure rising from a tiny islet covered with cypresses.

"Is it a lighthouse over there?"

"Not anymore," she said. "It's a ghost house."

"A ghost house! You can't be serious!"

She laughed. "Since the keeper died a few years ago during a hurricane, it's stayed empty, but lately we're seeing lights flashing at night."

"What's so unusual about that?" I remarked.

"No one lives there, that's why. My father said that there's a prison somewhere out there, and American patrolmen come to the lighthouse to look for runaway prisoners."

"Can you go there to look around?"

"No," she said. "It's closed to the public. Father said that dead bodies float up there, and no one knows where they come from. Even the police couldn't tell whether they're communists or South Koreans."

When I just stood there, lost in thoughts, she said, "Come, I'll show you the largest fish tank you ever saw." She began running toward a white concrete building on our left, and I too ran, lifting sand dust about me. For someone with short legs, she ran amazingly fast, and I told her to slow down. She ignored me. After another two minutes, I was out of breath, so I yelled, "If you don't slow down I'm going home!"

She stopped, laughing. "You can't go home until I let you. You're my hostage today. I kidnapped you, remember?"

"I'll make you pay for this!" I threatened, breathing loudly.

"Don't scare me like that, Child," she joked, acting older.

I ran, grabbed her, and put my arm around her, acting as if I'd strangle her at any moment.

"Okay, okay. I won't call you *Child.*"

"You better not!"

We then walked toward the white concrete building.

"This is Pacific Seafood Company," Yoja said as though she owned the place. "It's been here for years."

A woman standing behind the counter and weighing a large fish on a scale smiled when she saw us.

"Auntie, can I show my friend the fish tank?" Yoja asked, and the woman said, "Go right ahead, Yoja. Be careful not to fall in. The rocks are slippery sometimes."

"Don't worry, Auntie."

We passed through a large glass door facing the blue ocean, then walked along a square pool as large as a small rice paddy. The rocks bordering the pool glistened in the bright sunlight, and I walked cautiously.

"Look," Yoja said, pointing at the bottom of the pool, and I looked in. It seemed a whole population of fish had immigrated there. Some were as long as the entire length of my leg and had silvery scales all over. The middle size and smaller ones had blue or brown stripes on their backs and some had a sprinkle of yellow on the sides. There were white fish, too, their belly brown or black. I could only name the Red Fish, cod, and stingrays. They were all splashing and squirming, fighting for dear life.

"Guess, Jong-ah, how they capture them?" Yoja asked.

"They must have a large fishing boat."

"No," she said, delighted that I didn't know. "The trap is built in. See that metal grille over there? There are small squids tied to it, and during the night fish follow the tide and come in, looking for food. And then, the gate over there comes down, trapping them. I think it's so clever, the way they catch fish."

I felt sorry for them. *The ocean is their territory. Why couldn't they be smarter than humans?* I couldn't understand.

Yoja then took me to her house a few blocks away. It was much smaller than our house but had a swing on the porch. She brought her family album, and sitting on the swing together, we looked through the pages, giggling, pointing at her father's serious expression and her mother's colorful, old-fashioned Korean wedding dress. They looked ancient and strange.

Suddenly anxiety overwhelmed me. *What if I didn't pass the exam? What if I had to do another year of sixth grade?*

"What's the matter?" she asked.

"I wish I lived here," I said, making the swing creak. "I really like your house, so close to the sea."

CHAPTER 22

▼

WORK OF FORESTRY

On the first day of Kyong-Nam Girls Middle School in March, Yoja came to get me, and we left home together. Although my house was a bit out of her way to school, she didn't mind walking the extra distance so that we could go together. In the morning sunlight our three-story school building shone white and bright in the distance and I was nervous. I had sweat in my palms.

Yoja glanced at me through the corners of her eyes, a mischievous smile on her face. Annoyed, I asked, "What is it?"

"You look sharp, Jong-ah, very sharp, in that uniform."

"You too."

"Probably some boys will follow you after school, dying to get to know a new chick in Kyong-Nam Girls Middle School."

I couldn't help but laugh. I had nothing to say about boys in general. I had two bossy older brothers and one younger one who gave me enough problems every day. Why would I be interested in other boys? Strangely though, I was noticing the boys passing me. One of them, wearing a white hexagon hat and dusty blue top even smiled at me for no reason at all.

"Don't act so high and mighty," Yoja said.

"Who's acting high and mighty?"

"You are."

"Hush up," I snapped. "Don't ruin my first day at Kyong-Nam."

"Who's ruining?"

"You are!"

Fifteen minutes later, we were looking at a large sign that said, "KYONG-NAM GIRLS MIDDLE SCHOOL ASSEMBLY," followed by an arrow pointing toward the Buddhist temple.

Walking another five minutes in the direction of the sun, we saw a large flock of middle school students standing in a vacant lot, chattering. I understood why we were on this square flat surrounded by red dirt and rough edged boulders, instead of our temporary school—the army barracks. The South Korean army probably couldn't let the school use its assembly ground that served as a parking lot for their military vehicles.

The principal, a round man with a square face wearing a gray suit and a red necktie, climbed laboriously onto a huge rock and stood before us, locking his hands behind him. Unlike his rigid expression, his voice was gentle as he welcomed us. He began with the latest news of the war: that Stalin had just died and the world was ready for a change.

It was a very long speech, which took at least an hour. Although the sunlight was pleasant on my shoulders, its brightness gave me a headache and I wanted to sit down. But he kept on talking.

He said that we must prepare ourselves for the day the war would suddenly end and the Americans return to their country, leaving us alone to take care of war debris, the wounded, and the homeless. He told us how the Germans had risen from the ashes of World War II and rebuilt a new nation with almost empty hands. He talked about how the Hindus, Moslems, and Sikhs in India had fought among themselves after World War II, killing one another, but now they were learning to accept one another. He talked about Japan, too, how the Japanese rebuilt their new nation after atomic bombs had incinerated Hiroshima and Nagasaki.

"Freedom is never free," the principal suddenly shouted, his voice rising above us all. "It demands a price, a lofty price. Nearly a million men lost their lives during the last three years, including foreigners, and barrels of human blood were spilled here on Korean soil. How could we pay back such a huge debt to those who fought for us at the cost of their lives? Should we cut off our arms and legs and spill our own blood to make up for what they've lost? Should we pluck out our eyes for those who lost their sight?"

No one moved.

"The only sensible payment is our hard work," he continued. "We must rebuild what was destroyed, recover what was lost, and strengthen what was weakened. Only by working until our hands blister and sweat drips from our foreheads, can we truly pay back those who sacrificed their lives in our country."

He then announced that our school would be participating in a campaign called *Plant for the Future*. "The Department of Education decided that it would be educational for all middle school children to participate in the work of forestry. It will be meaningful labor for you, something you'll remember. When we were your age, our country was under the Japanese regime, and we had to use Japanese names, speak Japanese, and learn Japanese history at school, without mentioning the harsh punishment we endured for accidentally speaking Korean in front of the Japanese teachers. We couldn't even sing our songs, the Korean songs.

"Today, we have no excuse for not working hard and proving to ourselves what we are capable of. We owe it to ourselves. This work of forestry is the beginning of our new path as a nation and we must succeed at it."

He stopped. After a long moment of silence, he asked, "Are there any questions?" and looked at us, his eyes sweeping over the heads.

No hands came up that I could see.

"Then, your homeroom teacher will give you the details for tomorrow—when and where to meet, what to wear, what to bring..."

Coming home, I looked for the hand gardening tools in the storage room. Finding a small spade and short-handled hoe, I put them in a brown bag for the next day. Mother found my First Sister's old workpants and gave them to me.

She said, "Your older brothers and sisters did hard work too before the liberation. The Japanese teachers asked them to bring anything that's made of rubber or metal from home, and when they did, they shipped it to Japan. Your brothers dug trenches, too, just in case Americans came and bombed our towns, and everyday they came home with dirt all over them. But you're working for your own country. There's a huge difference between what your brothers and sisters did and what you're doing now."

The next morning, Yoja and I left for school at seven, each with a lunch box and hand tools. After crossing a creaky log-bridge lying over a foamy stream, we reached a cliff where we could see a large square pool of water glinting under our feet and an arch of a waterfall spouting white water from the opposite hill. With a sharp whistle and an arm gesture, our homeroom teacher Mr. Lee assigned our spots and we scattered. Yoja, three others, and I were a team. We began digging holes on our assigned spot near a small family grave lot. When we had each dug several holes, Teacher Lee came, inspected the holes, making sure they were deep and wide enough, and gave us a bundle of barren twigs. We dropped a twig in each hole and filled it with dirt. Then the watering crew came to spill a gourd full of water in each hole.

It was fun. When whistles blew sharply in my ear, signaling lunchtime, I couldn't believe how fast time had flown. As I looked at my schoolmates wiping their foreheads and washing their hands, I felt a surge of pride. Someday, these naked mountains would be covered with tall, thick green trees, providing us with shade. Some animals might return to their old homes too. I suddenly realized that the future was there with us.

CHAPTER 23

▼

COMMUNISTS IN
OUR HOUSE

On a warm Saturday evening in early June, Father again poured himself a glass of rice wine, while giving us his version of the armistice.

"I don't blame President Truman at all for not wanting to waste another American life here in Korea, not at all," he said. "But I wonder if he really knows who Kim Il-Sung really is. Now that Stalin is dead and gone, Truman considers Kim a tiger without a head, but he'll be surprised: Kim might be a two-headed tiger, who knows. I'm sure he's chuckling now, thinking, 'Let's do what the Yankees want for now, but who knows what tomorrow might bring.' See the difference between the American president and the North Korean chairman on the same issue?"

A loud banging startled us all. Annoyed, Father roared, "Who's there?"

"Open the door," a man's voice demanded.

Frowning, Father shifted his dark eyes to Eldest Brother, and he rose. After two minutes, my brother returned. "Two National Guards are here, Father. They want to see you."

"National Guards? What do they want?"

"I don't know, sir, but they brought two strange guys with them."

"What strange guys?"

"They look like beggars to me. I have no idea who they are."

Father put his shoes on and stepped into the courtyard. I tried to listen to the conversation, but everything was muffled: all I could hear was my father's nervous responses, "Is that so? I can't imagine!"

Then he said loudly, "Yobo, bring some tea to my office! We have guests."

Mother became alert. Smoothing out her well-combed hair, she rose. "Don't move until I'm back," she said as she left the room.

I looked at Eldest Brother, hoping he'd tell us something, but he gave me no clue. His gaze glued to the door, it seemed he was trying to hear something none of us could. After a long moment, we heard footsteps in the courtyard, and we knew the National Guards were leaving.

"We'll return soon," a deep voice said with authority. "Please make them feel comfortable while they're in your hands. We'll be back in a couple of days."

"Make *who* feel comfortable," Kwon asked impatiently, and Eldest Brother silenced him with a quick "Shhh!"

Mother came back, her cheeks flushed. "Listen carefully," she whispered. "The men in Father's office are two North Korean prisoners just released from a prison."

"North Korean prisoners!" we chorused.

"Shhhhh, not so loud," Mother cautioned us. "We're in a strange situation here. Don't repeat what I say to anyone. The guards said that our president set free today altogether twenty-six-thousand North Korean prisoners from every major city in the South, without telling American officials about it. These men are supposedly anti-communists."

"I don't believe it," Eldest Brother said so unexpectedly that my head automatically turned to him. "You mean, thousands of men escaped from the sturdy American prisons and the guards didn't know about it? Even if the guards were all asleep, surely some of them heard something when thousands of feet marched out of the gate. Two hundred men might try to escape together, but thousands? It doesn't sound right."

Mother seemed frustrated. "I'm just telling you what the guards told us. How can we really know what happened in prisons all over the South? What I'm saying is, we have problems here at home: we're hiding the communists. It's not a laughing matter at all!"

Eldest Brother only shrugged.

"Can we meet them?" Kwon asked.

"No!" Mother replied.

"Why not? I've never met a communist before."

"Be glad that you haven't met them. If you had, you weren't be here."

Kwon only stared at Mother.

I didn't want to meet the communists. Besides killing people and burning homes, they were terrible to women, which I learned from a movie. In one scene, two communists dragged two screaming women to an abandoned shack, knocked them down amid broken concrete pieces and splintered wood, and got on top of them, one on each. A moment later, they dragged them out and tied them to the trunk of a tree, and then, walking back a few feet, shot them without blinking an eye. I would never forget those women's blood-smeared faces and their piercing screams that lasted only two seconds before they became still.

Mother awakened me, saying, "I don't want you to go to school tomorrow. That's an order for all of you."

"I can't miss school," Eldest Brother said.

"I have a test tomorrow," First Sister complained too.

"All right then!" Mother said, without hesitation. "You older ones can go to school, but I want to keep Kwon and Jong-ah with me tomorrow. It's not at all uncommon that soldiers use children to find out information they need. The Japanese did it, the Germans did it, and why do you think the Americans wouldn't do it?"

The next day around noon, I was bored. I missed Yoja and my new friends at school. I didn't even know where the communists were hiding, and Mother wouldn't tell me when I had asked her. Some time during the night, I had heard the heavy storage room door open and close and thought they might be hiding there, like Uncle Yong. But it was only a guess. All morning, it had been quiet.

I knew Kwon was sitting atop the firewood pile, looking out for Americans. I hoped he wouldn't fall asleep and roll off the pile.

Around four that afternoon, when Mother and I were in the front room, my brothers returned together as usual.

"Mother, the American MPs are near the market," Eldest Brother reported. "Going around with Korean translators, they were stopping people and asking questions."

"Did they stop you, too?" Mother asked.

"Of course."

"What did they ask you?"

"*Where do you live? Have you seen any strange-looking fellows walking around?* I tried to speak some English, and they let go of me. But they weren't so easy with other people."

An hour later, Yong-ja walked in with a basket full of leafy vegetables and announced that the Americans were getting closer.

Mother tried to be calm, but her eyes shifted nervously as she checked the front door, the courtyard, and the porch where Baby Brother's toys were strewn.

"We have nothing to be frightened about, children," Mother said, but her voice was shaky. "We're not doing anything wrong. Let's just be the way we are and do things we normally do everyday. This is another phase of war, where the leaders play vicious games with one another." She hastily walked to the kitchen, brought a small bamboo basket full of bean sprouts, and began plucking their roots.

I sat against the wall and opened the Sears catalogue, which Mother had brought from the market. Flipping through the pages, I tried to be calm.

Kwon took out *hwatoo* (Korean playing cards) from a cabinet drawer and began shuffling, making clapping noises. "You want to play *Go-Stop?*" he asked me.

I shook my head.

Eldest Brother was reading the newspaper, his belly on the floor, and Second Brother was polishing Father's black leather shoe with an old sock. My two sisters were in their room, doing homework or arguing.

A hand banged on our door and everyone stiffened.

Mother's eyes swept the room once more, and seeing that we were all there, doing things we normally did, she rose, scattering a few bean sprouts onto the floor.

"May I help you?" Mother asked politely as soon as the door creaked open.

"We're the U.S. military police looking for fugitives," a Korean man said to Mother, talking fast. "Is anyone staying with you other than your family?"

"No, sir," Mother said. "You're welcome to search, if you like." She stepped aside to give them room to walk in.

I was nervous. *What if they did?* But luckily, they didn't.

Mother asked, "Is it true that our president has something to do with why you're here?"

"We aren't sure yet," the Korean answered and then translated to the Americans. One of them said something in English, and the Korean asked Mother, "Have you seen strangers asking for food or money?"

"Not a soul," Mother said, "other than a few beggars we feed every morning. I hope we'll never see them. Are they armed, the men you're looking for?"

"No, ma'am, but they can be dangerous even without weapons."

"We know, sir. We know how horrible the communists have been, killing innocent people and destroying what little our country has. Trust me, gentlemen, we'll be the first to report when strangers show up here."

The Americans seemed satisfied. They said "Thank you" in English, and left, babbling among themselves.

Mother came back, sat down again, and began picking up the bean sprouts scattered on the floor as if nothing had happened. I was amazed how calm she was. I wanted to be like her when I was older, strong and wise.

As soon as Father returned, our parents had a secret meeting in their room, door closed. I figured they might let the prisoners leave that night, probably through the secret opening in the back wall. Because, if they didn't, they could get in serious trouble with the Americans.

Later, while I lay in my bedroom lit with pale moonlight filtering through the thin rice-paper door, I heard Father's footsteps in the back, and then the storage room door sliding quietly.

The chirruping of the crickets under my screen door suddenly got louder, and I was annoyed. Then I heard faint footsteps coming in my direction. Licking my forefinger, I gently pressed it into the rice paper screen door facing the back, and when it made a hole about the size of a silver coin, I looked out.

Three shadows emerged. "Good luck, gentlemen," Father whispered. "When you reach the end of the tunnel, you'll see a trail going right. Follow it until the road splits into two, one going toward the mountain and the other to the main part of the town. Take the road to the town and try to find the nearest market. Mingle with vendors and shoppers there, and nobody will pay attention to you. Be careful with your northern accent, though. You can make people suspicious."

"Thank you, sir, for everything," the second shadow replied. The third one only shook hands with Father. "Hurry, before they get here." Father ordered. The metal door opened, squeaking, then closed.

Father stood there for a long moment, casting a long shadow in front of him.

I fell asleep, but some noises awoke me: *Tan, tan, tan…Who's shooting?* I wondered.

My parent's door slid open, and I heard footsteps going to the front room. I knew it was Father, probably worried about the prisoners. The floorboards creaked nervously under him. More noises rang out. Besides the gunshots, dogs were barking and cars were sputtering too. I heard Father stepping down to the porch and then to the courtyard. My ears followed him all the way to the back and to the secret opening. Slipping out of my sleeping mat, I snuck out.

I found Father where I had thought he would be, standing like a straight post under the gray sky, his back turned to me. Suddenly a man's voice rose from behind the brick fence, giving me a chill. "Check this hole! They might be hiding in here!" Dogs barked again.

Then, Father did something I never expected he'd do. He ran to the back wall, yanked the metal plate, and crawled into the dark space as quick as a rat. "Hey," I heard him call in a hushed voice, "if you're still there, come back down. It's not safe!"

"Father! Don't go away!"

An explosion of bullets echoed in the tunnel, followed by dog barking and many voices shouting at the same time. I froze.

Mother appeared from nowhere and asked me, "What happened, Jong-ah? Where's your father?" I stared at her, unable to speak, as though two hands were wringing my neck.

"Jong-ah, what happened?" She shook me, her grip tight on my shoulders and the whites of her eyes larger than I'd ever seen before. I couldn't squeeze a sound out of my throat. I remembered everything—the dogs barking, a man shouting about the hole, Father going into the opening, the deafening gunshots—but how could I tell her when I couldn't talk?

"Jong-ah," Mother yelled. "What are you trying to hide?"

I felt helpless as though I had just asked her another annoying question. But now, she was the one who needed my answer, not the other way around. I was light-headed. All I could think was to hide in my closet again, away from everything, and sleep.

Not only was I unable to talk, I couldn't see well either: my eyes were blurry. My knees buckled, and I hit the ground hard. Dirt jumped to my face.

I had no idea how long I had been lying in my room when my eyes suddenly opened. For a moment, I didn't know where I was. Loud voices penetrated through the wall next to me and I could hear a man asking Mother, "Mrs. Suh, what was he doing in the tunnel? Where were you when he crawled into that hole? Tell us about that opening in the back too…"

It slowly came to me that I was lying in my room alone, and everyone else was in the front room with some strangers. I shivered as I remembered the metallic blast in my ears and Father disappearing into the secret opening. It seemed ages ago, yet it was vivid and clear. I was tired. I wanted to drift away somewhere, without knowing where, and keep drifting until I could find my way back.

I fell asleep again and had many dreams, white and vague dreams, the kind you couldn't remember when you woke up.

A hand touched my arm, and I jumped.

Mother was looking at me, and I saw my sister and my brothers encircling me. "How're you feeling, Jong-ah," Mother asked me.

"Fine." My voice was rusty and I was still tired.

"You slept a long time," she said, her eyes sad and worried. "Do you know where you are?"

"Yes."

"Can you see everyone here?"

"Of course!"

"Do you know what happened to Father, too?"

I froze. *Is she going to tell me that he died?* I shook my head.

"The Americans arrested him for hiding the communists in our home. But he'll be back soon."

"Did they kill...the communists?" I asked, and she said no. "They found a couple hundred of them hiding in people's homes and took them back to the prisons. It's over now and no one's killed."

I let out a sigh of relief.

Father came home a week later. He looked thinner and was unshaven, but he seemed to be in a good mood.

"Were you tortured?" Mother asked him the moment he stepped into the front room where we waited for him.

"Of course not," he said. "Why would they when the war is about to end?"

"Then why did they keep you for so long?"

"They wanted to make sure I wasn't one of the communists. After a session with one officer, I was sent to another, and he asked me the same questions all over again, only in a different tone of voice. This went on almost everyday. They kept me in a room separated from others, and I had a good time, listening to lively American music and eating at their cafeteria. One of the questions they asked over and over was, why I was in that tunnel with the prisoners. I told them I felt some sense of duty to my countrymen and that I wanted to help them escape. No one was impressed about my speech. I guess it was difficult for them to understand why I was helping the communists. They kept asking, and asking, and...."

"How did you communicate with them? I know you can't speak a word of English."

"Through a translator, of course. You won't believe this!"

"What?"

"My translator was my cousin Yong!"

"Yong?"

We couldn't believe it.

"Does he still wear a wig and moustache?" I asked.

"No. He has a crew cut, just like the Americans, and he looked good. He seemed younger and healthier than two years ago when he stayed with us."

"How did he end up in the American army base?" Mother asked.

"That's exactly what I asked him, Yobo. He said that, after he left our house, he took the bus and went straight to the U.S. army base. At the gate, he explained to the guard that he was in trouble with the South Korean authorities and that he needed protection. A moment later, a soldier came to get him. To make a long story short, the Americans liked him, especially because Yong spoke quite decent English, and employed him as a translator. Isn't it ironic? The man the Korean police hunted for is safe in the American army base."

"Have you asked him why the secret police was looking for him?" Mother asked.

"That idiot," Father muttered. "He signed a paper at some teachers conference that spring, without knowing that he was committing himself to Kim Il-Sung's underground Workmen's Party. A lot of men did it, he said, including students, laborers, soldiers, and teachers like himself. The Red spies were everywhere, camouflaged as soldiers or students or laborers. When the North Korean communists entered Seoul, these men went out to cheer them, shouting *mansei,* but they were the first ones to die, because the Reds didn't have time to sort out who's who and shot them all. Yong is lucky to be alive."

CHAPTER 24

▼

FAREWELL AMERICANS!

The war officially ended a month later, on July 27th, the day the Chinese and U.N. leaders signed the armistice. But to me, the war ended a few days later, the day the first group of Americans left Pusan. I remember that day far better than the day some papers were signed by the people who meant nothing to me.

Unlike when the Americans had entered our city three years earlier, there was no mention of us children going to the Main street to say farewell to our departing heroes, so I went there alone. A large crowd had gathered on both sides of the street, some drinking coca-cola, some chewing gum, and others merely talking to one another.

Somewhere a band was playing the American anthem over and over, and on every building, a large American flag flapped in the wind. Five American airplanes were darting in the vast blue overhead, each dragging a white foamy tail, and I hoped those were flown by the Korean pilots saying thank you to the Americans Air Force for teaching them how to fly American air fighters. I learned somewhere that several American pilots had each received a purple medal from our president for their outstanding performance in training the Koreans, who had previously flown only Japanese planes during World War II. As a result, our own pilots participated in the air battle along with the American pilots.

People began applauding, their heads turned to the left. I saw American army trucks, probably twenty or more, were crawling toward us, each with a red-white-blue flag on the hood, just like the day they had arrived three years earlier. The crowd shouted, "Thank you, Americans! Have a good trip home!"

"We'll never forget you, GI Joe!"

"You'll be forever in our hearts!"

The trucks moved slowly as if hesitant to leave.

Some women were crying, wiping tears with their bare hands or blowing their noses into their handkerchiefs.

I waved my hand too, and the soldiers sitting in the back of the trucks waved back to me, smiling, as if they remembered me. I wished I could speak English. How wonderful it would be to tell them in their tongue that I'd remember them as long as I lived or that they'd see me in America some day. I also wanted to thank them for giving us hope when we had nothing to hope for and for being our Santa Claus every Christmas. I wanted to tell them also that we appreciated the chocolate bars or chewing gum they had given us whenever we bowed to them. We had given them something to remember too, by showering them with songs and dances when we visited them in a hospital downtown.

I kept waving and smiling to the soldiers until the last truck passed and the music stopped. As people scattered, I began walking toward home.

This is how war ends, I thought, feeling empty. They came when we desperately needed them but now the war ended and they were returning to their families in America. Although they would have painful memories of the war, I wanted them to remember something about our country, like the taste of *Bulgoghi,* Korean barbecue, just off the grill, or intricate designs on porcelain jars and vases or a breathtaking view of the countryside in autumn where red persimmons ripened under the cobalt sky.

The Americans hardly knew anything about us when they first arrived in Korea three years earlier: some didn't even know Korea existed on the other side of the globe. But three long years, billions of American dollars, and two million lost lives later, we were no strangers to the world, certainly not to Americans. The world map had shrunk while the fighting went on and the six continents moved closer to one another. And perhaps they would never stop moving and shifting until the end of the world.

I was getting closer to home, but I didn't want to stop walking. I let my feet carry me. I passed the entrance of our middle school, crossed the narrow brook where several women did their laundry, and headed toward the Buddhist temple where our elementary school had been two summers earlier. I was dying to see the temple again. Were the smiling Buddhist gods still there? Were the cows, pigs, and chickens there, too? I missed my old friends. I still saw some of them almost every day at school, but many of them, like Mia and Jinsook, had moved away.

Much had changed since. I was in Kyong-Nam middle school now, the best girls' middle school in town. I wasn't a helpless child anymore: I was a teenager who had a secret dream.

When the narrow trail ended, I saw the temple rising before me, as majestic as it always had been, and I took a deep breath. I could almost hear kids chattering and laughing around me, just as before. At the seashore faraway, American ships floated, their horns blaring. It saddened me to remind myself that I might not see them very long. The war brought those ships to our harbors, making us wonder about America and the big wide world beyond the horizon, enriching the view of our town, and now, with the war ending, they would go away, leaving the shore empty. But my dream wouldn't go away: it would live with me until it would blossom into a reality. I couldn't wait until the day I'd stand on American soil.

A long line of miniature army trucks, probably the same ones I had waved at earlier, was snaking through the town in the direction of the shore, each dragging clouds of dust behind them. They were leaving us for good.

Cupping my hands, I shouted as loud as I could, "See you in Americaaaaa…."
"See youuuu!" a ship honked.

0-595-30876-7